SPECI

THE ULVERSCROFT FOU
(registered UK charity num ... 73)

was established in 1972 to provide funds for research, diagnosis and treatment of eye diseases. Examples of major projects funded by the Ulverscroft Foundation are:

hildren's Eye Unit at Moorfields Eye
pital, London
lverscroft Children's Eye Unit at Great
ond Street Hospital for Sick Children
ding research into eye diseases and treatment
e Department of Ophthalmology, University
Leicester
e Ulverscroft Vision Research Group, Institute
ild Health
n operating theatres at the Western Ophthalmic
ital, London
hair of Ophthalmology at the Royal
alian College of Ophthalmologists

W

n can help further the work of the Foundation
making a donation or leaving a legacy. Every
ribution is gratefully received. If you would like
elp support the Foundation or require further
information, please contact:

THE ULVERSCROFT FOUNDATION
The Green, Bradgate Road, Anstey
Leicester LE7 7FU, England
Tel: (0116) 236 4325

website: www.ulverscroft-foundation.org.uk

THE GIRL AT CHANGE ALLEY

Sheffield, 1867. It's the height of a long-running and violent campaign known as the Outrages, where murderous acts are carried out on behalf of a rogue union leader.

Louisa Leigh, a former maid-of-all-work, is trapped into prostitution and desperate for money to escape. She befriends Ginny Hinchcliffe, a young widow who will do whatever it takes to break free from a life of servitude to her in-laws. The two women become entangled with Joe Crookes, henchman to the man responsible for the Outrages. Joe is looking for a way out even if that means betraying those closest to him.

With a single act, Louisa's freedom would be paid for. But it's not just her life on the line, and she'll need to decide if she can live with the choices she's about to make . . .

JOANNE CLAGUE

THE GIRL AT CHANGE ALLEY

Complete and Unabridged

MAGNA
Leicester

First published in Great Britain in 2022

First Ulverscroft Edition
published 2023
by arrangement with
Kate Nash Literary Agency

This book is a work of fiction. Names, characters, businesses, organizations, places and events are either the product of the author's imagination or are used fictitiously. Any resemblance to actual persons, living or dead, events or locales is entirely coincidental.

A catalogue record for this book is available from the British Library.

ISBN 978–0–7505–5037–6

For Janet, my lovely mum

Part One

1

June 1st 1867

She had walked past the façade of St Peter's and St Paul's countless times, in daylight and in darkness, and never spared a thought for the parish church built when the high street was a dirt track in a meadow, the seed of the town that had grown around it.

But, tonight, its familiar bulk oppressed her. The spire was an accusing black finger against the moon-brightened smoke of factory chimneys. She slowed, falling behind the two men she was with, men she only now realised she didn't really know at all. She couldn't breathe. She stopped and put her hand to her chest. Her lungs were pieces of damp cloth, squeezed through a mangle, and a merciless fist gripped her heart.

Later, she would tell herself this was the moment when she might have turned and fled home, or pretended to faint. She'd have risked a slap, either way.

'What tha playin' at?'

Her gut lurched with a fresh wave of the nausea that had swilled in her stomach since the two men had knocked on her front door and told her to come, come quick. It was time. She tasted bile in her throat.

'Gonna stand 'ere all night?' Joe Crookes was challenging her, getting in her face, his furrowed brows like wide smudges of soot beneath a mop of dark curls. As usual, he was bare-headed, overly vain of that thick head of hair, strutting like a peacock even though his only audience was his brother, and her.

'What's up? Are tha gettin' cold?' she said, thankful that her voice didn't waver.

The shorter man behind Joe sighed and took off his cap to run a hand over his balding scalp. Seth Crookes was the older brother but always deferred to Joe and she could not count on Seth to stick up for her.

'Come on,' Seth said. 'Let's get the job done.'

She wondered if her face was set like theirs in grim and bitter lines. *Butter wouldn't melt,* her mother used to say, whenever she concealed whatever wrongdoing she had just committed behind wide eyes and a dimpled smile. The trouble was, she'd never done anything like this before, not even at her lowest ebb.

Needs must.

'What were that?' said Joe and she realised she'd spoken her mantra aloud.

'Nowt.'

'Get movin',' he said. 'Tha the one that volunteered thee services.'

She didn't respond to this but fell into step between the two men, like the accused being led to the scaffold. Now St Peter's and St Paul's was behind them and they were on the downhill. She stepped gingerly over the uneven slabs that paved the bottom of the high street where it widened into the marketplace. An irrational part of her mind told her that the laces of her boots had loosened and would trip her at any moment, even though she had tightly knotted them around her ankles. *Watch your step, love.* It was advice she'd only recently given out, but whoever took their own advice? Nobody, that's who.

Her boot-heels and the feet of the men marching

her along made hollow sounds on the stones at the edge of the square. In a matter of hours this would be the site of noise and colour, packed with carts and vendors offering the best prices on herrings and eggs, oysters and cockles. There would be rabbits strung in lines waiting to be purchased and skinned, and piglets squealing in pens. But in the dark it was an open throat ready to swallow her up.

She yelped when Joe took her by the elbow and swung her against his body to steer her across the road.

'Shush theesen,' he said, shaking her arm, but not too hard. She had something up her sleeve he needed.

She realised Seth had gone ahead and was now standing outside Turnell's wine and spirit merchants on the corner where the high street met Change Alley. The cobbled road behind him rose on a slight incline and was narrow, made to seem narrower still by the three-and four-storey buildings that loomed like tombstones from the flagstone pavements. A horse whinnied, a nervous sound that made her flinch. Change Alley was one of the town's staging posts, with stabling round the back of the King's Head Hotel. She flattened her palm against the advertisement board on the wall of Turnell's that hid the shop's contents — *The Finest Jamaican Rum, French Brandy, London Gin* — and looked up Change Alley, which curved gently out of sight. She glanced at Seth, who was now rubbing his hands together anxiously.

Joe looked up and down the deserted high street before moving towards her, pressing her back into the wall, until all she could see was the upturned collar of his thick wool coat. His breath smelled of stale ale, and his clothes of dried sweat and pipe tobacco. She raised her eyes and her lashes brushed against the stubble under his chin, he was that close to her.

'Gi' us it,' he said.

She bent her head and shrugged her shawl from her shoulders.

'Hurry up.'

'I am. Calm down.'

'Tha's the one breathin' like a pair of chuffin' bellows,' Joe hissed.

She snorted with laughter, shocking herself. Or was it a sob? Finally, the ribbon she was fiddling with, that she'd tied around the cuff of the sleeve of her dress, came undone and the hard iron bar she'd been concealing slipped into the palm of her hand.

'Here.'

She was glad to be delivered of it. She rubbed her arm to erase the memory of the roughly sawn edge of the pipe that had pricked the soft skin of her underarm all the way here. It had been a necessary precaution, having her carry it. She was less likely to be searched or locked in a cell if they'd encountered a watchman and aroused his suspicions. Joe moved a step back, tapping the hateful thing in his palm. Its hollow interior was packed with gunpowder and a fuse stuck out of one end like a child's spiteful tongue. She looked away.

Fifteen sovereigns for an easy night's work, to be split three ways.

Joe took her by the elbow again, manoeuvring her as if she was a doll to be manipulated this way and that, this time setting her roughly against the cold bricks of the chandlery store next to the King's Head, right on the junction. She wanted to tell him to keep his hands off her but she knew him well enough to see he was on his last nerve, jumpy as a scalded cat, and she bit back the retort.

'Tha to stand 'ere and keep thee eyes peeled.'

He bent to search her face, to be sure she had heard, and she turned her face away and nodded.

'Reight then, this is it,' said Seth.

Seth walked away, quickly, up Change Alley, soon disappearing into the shadows.

'Don't budge,' said Joe, and loped after his brother.

No going back. Strangely, the realisation calmed her. Events were already set in motion and out of her hands. She could walk away but there was the princely sum of five pounds to consider, and Joe's fists. She was grateful that the print-works was around the bend in Change Alley, safely out of sight. Seth would have reached the other end now, posting lookout on the Norfolk Street junction while she kept vigil on the high street side. She'd hear the explosion; she was braced for that. Joe would be back with her before it went off, unless he got caught up in it somehow, hit by flying debris, a shard of glass slicing through his muscular neck, his eyes bulging like a cow's at the moment of slaughter. Her heart skidded, trying to escape these images that flew at her viciously. It was no use closing her eyes. That made it worse.

Instead, she looked up at the façade of the King's Head. Lamplight from within lent a sickly glow to a couple of windows but there were no silhouetted figures peering down. Only a minute had passed. The urge to get away, to scurry home, was like a rope tugging at her gut. She glanced over at the marketplace. Beyond it, columns of smoke rose from the stacks in the distance, where the steelworks were congregated, a part of the town that never slept nor slowed.

Movement caught her eye, a flicker of black, and she whipped her head around to look back up the high street.

A moan escaped her lips and she willed the cloaked figure near the church — the man who was following the same path she and the brothers had taken — to do what she could not. *Walk away. Please.*

Instead, he crossed the road towards the grand façade of Cutlers Hall that faced St Peter's and St Paul's. A watchman. It'd be the noose if someone got killed. Or she might spend the rest of her days in jail if the judge felt kindly towards a female led astray by wicked men. But she'd heard what happened to young women in those places. Better to die than live in hell. She'd be going to hell anyway, with blood on her hands. She was shaking as if she had the ague that had carried her mother off, and tried to remember what Joe had told her. *'It's a warnin' only, a bit of advice, really. They should stop printin' their anti-union crap. I promise thee nob'dy will suffer so much as a scratch. Shop's shut up, an' the money lender from above goes 'ome to his family every night, as does the watchmaker above 'im. See, I've done me research.'*

Even so. She was an accomplice in the setting off of a bomb. The watchman was still walking towards her. Soon, she'd be able to make out the features of his face and, worse, he would see her face and the guilt written all over it. He was still coming. Now she could see he was young and bearded. Oh lord, now she could hear him, whistling a tune she didn't recognise. It might be the Queen's anthem for all she knew. The swooping notes made no sense to her panicked mind. She pressed cold fingers into the cracks of the masonry behind her. She had rehearsed her excuse for pausing here, in the vicinity of a fancy hotel full of fancy gentlemen. She'd flash an ankle, smile. He would tell her to move along and she would walk as naturally as she could up Change Alley, to warn Joe, to stop him.

It was probably already too late. She braced herself for the encounter, trying to twitch her lips into a smile. But then the watchman abruptly turned down a side street — he hadn't seen her, or had, and decided to leave her be, turn a blind eye, *we all have to earn a living, don't we* — and her shoulders sagged in relief.

Her respite was short-lived. She knew every street and passageway in the town. What if he now turned left and left again? Her heart pounded, every beat a warning of catastrophe, and her throat constricted. If that was the route his patrol took him on, he'd soon be at the other end of Change Alley. She strained to hear the tinkle of falling glass that meant the pane beside the door to the print-works had been broken and the pipe, now primed, tossed inside. Something must have gone wrong. Or the brothers were playing a trick on her and had both scarpered, laughing at her gullibility.

A vice clamped her shoulder and she shrieked. Then calloused skin that smelled of rust and muck covered her mouth and Joe was behind her, mouthing in her ear, his breath damp and hot. 'Jesus wept! Tha'll wake the dead.' His arm tightened around her waist. 'Has tha pissed thee pants, an' all?'

She pulled away, turning on him so he would see the fury on her face. 'Tha dun't get to manhandle *me*, Joe.'

He'd opened his mouth to reply when the air was filled by a thunderous, rattling clap, like a giant force had simultaneously slammed shut every door in the town. It was over so quickly she hadn't time to react but Joe had cringed into a crouching position, arms over his head. He straightened and laughed self-consciously. 'Aye, that'll be it, then. Din't think it'd make me startle so. What?'

'Didn't tha hear it?'

'What's wrong wi' thee? A' course I 'eard it.'

'Not that.' She knew she hadn't imagined the scream that had been wrapped inside the sound of the explosion. A single high-pitched scream. 'I 'eard summat. Somebody screamin' out.'

'No, tha din't.' But now he looked uncertain.

They stared at each other for a moment then a terrible idea occurred to her and she clutched his arm. 'Seth.'

'Nah, he were lookin' out at the other end and I told 'im to leg it once he 'eard the bang. He'll be long gone.' He shook her off and gave her a sly look. 'Go and 'ave a gander.'

'What?'

'Go and see, go on, see if summat's happened that shunt 'ave.' He took her by the shoulders and turned her to face Change Alley. 'Tha can use tha story, about why tha's out on't street.'

She planted her feet on the pavement. 'No, I'll not. Get off me, Joe.'

He pushed her roughly in the small of her back. 'Get on up that road an' see what's what or tha'll have the gaffer to answer to, an' me an' all.'

She took a couple of steps, finally more afraid of him than angered by him, then stopped and looked back. Joe had gone, dissolved into the darkness. He might be waiting, though, in the shadows, testing her. His gaffer would be giving Joe the money to dole out between the three of them. She needed her share and she might not get it if he decided to spite her.

Her heart lurched when a small door beside the steps to the entrance to the King's Head swung open and a uniformed porter emerged, holding a lamp fearfully before him. He looked straight at her.

'Miss?'

She opened her mouth to speak but the words would not come. She was caught.

'Did you hear that?' he said.

Relief washed through her and she found her voice. 'Aye, I did,' she said through numb lips. 'I were walkin' by.'

The porter looked her up and down, head bobbing like a bantam on his scrawny neck. She looked back at him helplessly. 'Wait here,' he said. 'Don't move.'

He walked away hesitantly, holding his lantern high. After a few moments, she followed him, unable to remain standing between the twin evils of Joe and whatever had made that hellish sound. An animal had made it. A fox. A dog. The whisper of rising sash windows above her sent a shudder running through her body. Faces poked out from upper storey windows like cuckoos out of a clock, calling across to each other. *What were that? Can you see anything?*

Around the corner, where the street levelled out, a black blot had spread like ink on the pavement just beyond the print-works. The porter's torch illuminated the blasted doorframe of the premises, a jagged hole that confirmed the job had been done. A heavy weight settled in her mind. She was part of it now, the campaign that it pleased the newspapers to call the Outrages. No going back. Figures were moving beyond the print-works, people approaching from the opposite end of the street. Somebody called out. She couldn't make out the words. Later, she'd remember thinking — in that instant between heartbeats, before the porter shone his light on the black blot on the pavement — that at least it was over, that she would take her share of the pay-out and put the whole episode out of her mind. She was already thinking of crawling back into her bed, so that when she saw what lay on the pavement she could not at first believe the truth her eyes were showing her.

The young watchman sat on the pavement, slumped like a drunk, his black cloak settled around him and his hat askew. His cloak was the blot she had seen on the pavement. What had brought the man down was now picked out by lamplight in terrible detail. He was staring, almost comically, at his chest, at the fat spear of dark wood that stuck out of his body. Dreamlike, she moved past the porter, who seemed frozen to the spot, obeying an instinct she did not question, to grasp the man's outstretched hand. His other hand rested almost tenderly on the obscene stake protruding from his body. He looked at her, his eyes widening first in fear and then in heartrending defeat. She could not meet his gaze and looked down. When his grip on her hand loosened, she groaned at the effort required to raise her eyes back to his face. His eyes were fixed and blank, and his mouth, so recently pursed in whistling a tune she didn't recognise, hinged open, drooling liquid.

She closed her eyes and in the moment before a suffocating blackness blotted out the world, saw another face — a woman's pretty, heart-shaped face with knowing eyes and the thin smile of a cat that had got the cream.

2

Three months earlier

There were a couple of inches of gin in the glass that sat on the stone mantelpiece above the hearth. It was spotless, that hearth. It should be. Louisa Leigh had collected a pail of water from the street pump and swept and scrubbed it clean by the time the sun rose. She'd been a maid-of-all-work in a past life and old habits stuck. The upstairs room of her small cottage was a different story but the men allowed up there weren't fussed about a bit of dirt, not that kind anyway.

She pulled her heaviest shawl from its hook on the inside of the door that led up to the bedroom and wrapped it about herself. It smelled of winter, of coalsmoke and spice. She'd be putting it away soon, now that the snowdrops and daffodils were poking through the ground, and fetching down the blue worsted jacket that had been her mother's for church on Sundays. Louisa had no use for Sunday service. She sat in the rocker, scratching her neck where the rough wool tickled her skin, and gazed at the empty grate. She couldn't decide whether to build a fire and warm the oatcakes she'd bought from the bakehouse yesterday or eat them straight from the paper bag, washed down with a tot of mother's ruin.

The jiggle of the front door latch had her leaping to her feet, acting on an impulse to hide the gin.

She could guess who was about to step inside. Jemima Greaves was the only visitor who never knocked. Another reason to keep downstairs spick and span. Sloppy, though, not drinking the gin when she'd poured it. Some silly idea about not taking it on an empty belly. She'd tip it down the sink, quick as you like. Except gin was expensive, and not to be wasted, and these dregs were the end of the bottle.

She'd got the glass in her hand and was turning away from the hearth when the older woman peered inside, her round face rosy with cold. Louisa shivered.

'Ey up, love,' Jemima said. She began to tug at the ribbon of her black bonnet then seemed to change her mind about taking it off. Instead, she held up for inspection the wicker basket she was carrying. 'See here? Busy hens. Eggs to spare. It's brass monkeys, Lou. You need to get that fire lit.'

Louisa nodded. 'Aye, I will.'

'What you got there?' Jemima nodded at Louisa's hand.

Louisa tightened her grip on the gin glass. 'This?' *Mother's ruin.* 'Oh, nowt. Water.'

'I'll put these in here.'

Louisa moved quickly aside to allow Jemima into the lean-to and watched as she retrieved a bowl from the cupboard above the sink and transferred the eggs from the basket into the bowl. She had brought a dozen. It was hypnotic, watching her perform a simple and uncomplicated task, so she was startled when Jemima spoke.

'How's thee?'

She was grateful Jemima's back was turned. 'Grand.'

'Working today?'

'No, no, I went in last night, worked all night.' She

felt the heat rise in her cheeks and the uncoiling of the nausea that slept in her gut. 'It were a rush job for a weddin' gown, so I'm given today off.'

'Well.' Jemima turned to face her. 'I don't know what sort of employer gives time off like this. Who d'you work for again? I thought I knew every tailor in town.'

'He's new,' said Louisa. 'Anyhow, shall I get that fire goin'? Fancy a brew?'

'I do. Am parched. Been running all o'er the place since the crack o' dawn, trying to find Albert bleedin' Rowbotham.'

Louisa grimaced sympathetically. Albert Rowbotham was one of six drivers Jemima employed in her hackney cab, hearse and mourning coach business and when in his cups, which was often, would doss down with his fancy woman rather than return home to his long-suffering wife.

'You know, the other week his poor wife was left with what she stood up in,' said Jemima. 'He pawned her best dress as soon as her back was turned. It's the booze that's his real mistress. I should get rid before *he* turns a coach over, an' all. Trouble is, he's my best driver and the customers love him.'

Jemima's husband had been killed the previous winter driving a party of gentlemen to Bakewell village, overturning the coach on a slippery bend in the road. Louisa recalled Jemima's stony face at his wake, watching the mourners eat and drink. *Six mouths to feed and now a business to run.* Louisa wished she had half the older woman's strength.

Jemima gave Louisa a shrewd look when she accepted a cup of tea from her. 'An' when will we get thee married off? A girl like you should have a string of young men wanting to court her. Although I must say you're lookin' a bit green about the gills this morning.'

'Thanks a lot,' said Louisa, smiling to take the edge off her gruff response. She suddenly felt an urge to confess everything and clamped her lips over her traitorous tongue. The disappointment of this kindly widow, her late mother's friend who had taken it upon herself to treat Louisa as she would her own daughter, would be too much to bear.

She'd left the glass of gin on the table. Aware of Jemima's eyes on her, Louisa picked it up and drank the gin down.

The liquid moved like a living thing in her gut and she spluttered, she couldn't help herself, and for a terrifying second thought the whole lot was coming back up. She met Jemima's gaze through tear-filled eyes.

Jemima gently took the glass from Louisa's hand and guided her to the rocker. Louisa surrendered to these ministrations. The palm of the woman's hand was cool against Louisa's forehead.

'I'll get the fire going, shall I? And while I do that, you can tell me what's up.' She looked into the empty glass. 'Though I think I can guess, love.'

Her back to Louisa, Jemima crouched before the grill, poking the coals with the fire iron, goading flickering shoots from the kindling. The words were out, ejected abruptly, before she had time to consider whether she should tell Jemima, share the crippling burden, or ask her to leave with her suspicions unconfirmed.

'Am with child.'

The older woman's back stiffened. Jemima didn't

turn. She didn't speak. Just continued to poke the fire.

'It's early enough,' said Louisa, 'to do summat about it.'

It was easier, talking to the lace edges of the black shawl Jemima wore over her shoulders, the rounded back that reminded her of her mother, who had prized good sense over sentimentality.

'I can't have it.' Her voice wobbled and she took a deep breath to calm herself. 'Tha knows I can't.'

'Aye.' Jemima sat back on her heels but kept her gaze on the fire. 'I can understand that.' She finally turned and gave Louisa a frank look. 'There's risks though. Are you set on it? I'm wonderin' what your dear mother would have to say. She'd have helped thee to raise a child. She'd have wanted to.'

'She's not here.' Louisa said. She knew what the next question would be.

'What about the father?'

'No.'

Jemima peered over her shoulder at Louisa. She shook her head. 'No. Av thought about it. Av thought o' nowt else for the past few weeks.' She stood up and paced the small room. 'I can't, Jemima. Not in my . . . situation. I'll do it wi'out any 'elp. I were just hopin' for a kind ear.' Her voice dropped to a whisper. 'That were all, really it were.'

Jemima got to her feet and Louisa was afraid she would leave but she came close and took Louisa in her arms. Louisa buried her face in the older woman's shoulder.

'Tha can count on me, love. I'll help however I can, a'course I will.'

* * *

At dinner time, Louisa left her cottage and set off for the short walk to the town market, turning her back on the forest of chimney stacks of the large factory works that crowded the bottom of the valley. She lived in the centre of town, on the edge of Barker Pool in a cottage that was part of an old and ramshackle terrace built to house the workers of a long-since plundered coal mine. The terrace squatted behind and was dwarfed by the Cutlers Hall, the commercial heart of the town where grand concerts, dinners and balls were held. The rich folk who attended those weren't relying on shanks' pony so could live a bit further out, away from the muck that rose from the factories, but Louisa liked the convenience of having everything she needed right on the doorstep, not that she had any choice in the matter. The town had its wealthy residents too, who lived in grander houses than hers, admittedly, and people like Jemima, who ran their own business and needed to always be on the spot.

Tansy. Jemima had suggested Louisa try that as a first resort. A strong draught of tansy would dislodge it, especially if it was early days. And if the herb didn't work Jemima knew a doctor and would lend Louisa the money. Louisa had baulked at that. She would pay for it herself, if it came down to that. Which it wouldn't, she was certain it wouldn't.

A watery late February sun cast shafts of light between the buildings. Louisa stepped from shadow to light and back again, knowing the feeling of a weight lifted following her confession to Jemima would be short-lived and enjoying it the more for that.

She passed the side of a butcher's shop, lifting her skirts over a gutter that ran pink with diluted blood from the speared meat hanging in the window. The wind blew the scent of the tannery across the street towards her, a chemical smell underlaid with rot. It stung her nostrils. There was no advantage in having a sharpened sense of smell, not in this town. She hurried quickly across a junction, earning a rebuke from the driver of a passing wagon — *Has tha got eyes in thee head, tha daft cow?*

On the other side, she sat on a low brick wall, resting in the sunlight alongside a patch of rough ground buttered with dandelions, daisies and nettles. A gang of barefoot children were scratching in the dirt alongside a partially demolished cottage. Across the road, down the dark brick tunnel of a tenement passageway, a girl threw a white sheet over a rope line. Louisa wondered who she was, and whether she was content with her life. She tore her gaze away to watch customers come and go from Cooke's fish and game shop. An image of metal hooks through cold flesh made her stomach turn. She would buy vegetables from the market and make a stew that might last a few days. She'd been given a box of marzipan fruits last night by one of her regular gentlemen and the memory of eating them made her mouth water, and then she shuddered, thinking of what else had been shared last night.

Louisa got to her feet. She needed new boots, had to scrape the pennies together to pay her weekly rent, and yet ate expensive marzipan like she was the Queen of England. Here she went, sharing the pavement with poor folk, beggars who were a stumble away from the workhouse, and youths on one errand or another, darting this way and that like silverfish. She could pretend to be a lady, taking the air. She had put on her striped summer dress, blue to match her eyes; her smartest outfit, to hide her shame.

An approaching gentleman tipped his hat and she nodded and smiled. He slowed, fastening his gaze on her and raising an eyebrow. She realised with a sinking heart that she knew him. She could see recognition dawning in his eyes. She shook her head, minutely, pursing her lips, and he stepped aside to allow her to walk past him. Neither spoke, but the message was conveyed. *It's me day off.*

In Haymarket square, she sat on the stone rim of the ornamental fountain, shielding her eyes against the glitter of the sun-struck water. She had to get rid, one way or another. Women died trying to rid themselves of unwanted children but women died in childbirth too. She wished she could take another drink, muffle her senses against the clatter of carriages and wagons on the cobbles, the smell of horseshit and the proximity of the townspeople hurrying by. Their tailcoats and bustles and straw baskets full of bread and fruit were at eye level, hemming her in.

She looked up, gulping into a throat that felt hollow, and saw the red-haired woman a moment before her old friend's eyes widened in recognition. A wave of elation was quickly replaced by dismay, and fear. No time to march away, no time even to get up before Harriet Hinchcliffe was standing before her, smiling down. She should have stayed inside today. Jemima would have brought her something to eat, if she'd asked.

'Louisa! Is it really you?'

She rose and allowed Harriet to embrace her, patting the other woman's back gently when she realised Harriet wasn't ready to relinquish her. This should be a joyful reunion but Harriet was the last person she wanted to see, the state she was in. Finally, Harriet released her, holding her at arm's length so she could study her face.

'Where have you been, Louisa? We've not seen you for . . . I don't even know how long.' Harriet hugged her tight again, then stepped back. 'Let me look at you!'

Louisa couldn't meet Harriet's concerned gaze. She didn't want her to see the black shadows under her eyes, or the spots around her mouth, and she stepped back, covering her mouth with her hand and casting her eyes down. It pained her to deceive an old friend. Louisa had been the maid-of-all-work in the household Harriet presided over and the two women regularly put the world to rights over a pot of tea. The great flood of 1864 had swept all that away.

'Are you well?' said Harriet.

'Been a bit poorly,' she said, and shrugged. 'I'll be reight.'

She swallowed again, the same empty fathomless gulp.

'Well,' said Harriet. She sat down and patted the stone. Louisa obediently sat beside her. 'You do look a little tired. Are you still working as a seamstress?'

'All the hours God sends,' said Louisa. She put her hand to her mouth as if she could rub the lie away, sickened by herself. Three years ago, she'd thought herself lucky to be caught up in the great flood and survive when more than two hundred others had perished. But the filthy water had permanently weakened her lungs. She could no longer carry out the physically demanding work required of a maid and couldn't survive on the pitiful earnings of a seamstress. Harriet would be disgusted if she knew how Louisa earned a crust. It would be better to be cool with her, to keep her at arm's length, even if that wounded Harriet.

Louisa looked away, pretending to follow the progress of a child wheeling a hoop with a stick through the square and getting under everybody's feet.

Harriet leaned forward to catch her eye, frowning. 'Is everything quite alright?'

'Aye.' She could barely get the word out.

'You seem unhappy to see me.'

I miss tha companionship, Harriet. It's a terrible thing to sit beside thee and not tell thee the truth.

She met Harriet's eye and stretched her mouth into a wide smile. 'Don't be daft. It's grand to see thee.'

Seemingly satisfied, Harriet squeezed her arm. 'Louisa Leigh. It's been so long. I have so much to tell you.'

She should tell Harriet about her circumstances; she would. The two of them had been through so much together and Harriet was a good soul. Silas, too. *You haven't seen me because of my shame, Harriet. I've fallen on hard times.* She breathed in, her heart hammering — tell her, now. Tell her — then released the breath and patted Harriet's knee.

'So what's tha been up to then?' Louisa said.

'Well, we've been busy, getting the business going. Silas has taken on half a dozen grinders and we have a clerk now to do the books. Daniel Housley. Lovely boy. Wouldn't say boo to a goose but he's a capable lad.' She paused and Louisa dropped her eyes from her friend's enquiring gaze. 'Lou? Are you sure you're alright?'

Louisa pressed her fingers to her lips and shook her head. 'It's just that I'm reight proud o' thee,' she said, when she could trust herself to speak.

Harriet beamed. 'What do you mean?'

'Givin' up that life of comfort to throw tha lot in wi' Silas. He said reight from day one he was goin' into steel an' now look at the pair o' thee. Well on tha way.' She nudged Harriet's arm. 'I can see it now. The Hinchcliffe name o'er factory gates as big as Atlas Works.'

'Silas should like to hear you say that,' said Harriet. 'Won't you come and see us soon? We're in Neepsend. Where are you living these days?'

'Up by Barker Pool.' Louisa paused. 'I 'av a cottage.'

'A house to yourself!'

'Nowt fancy.'

'Oh!' Harriet jumped to her feet, startling Louisa, and raised her arm above her head. 'Over here!'

Louisa suppressed a sigh. She was already exhausted by this encounter and further wearied by the idea of having to converse with Silas too.

But it wasn't Silas hurrying towards them. A woman with a small boy hanging from her hand like an extra limb was marching their way. She was young and bareheaded, her loose dark hair framing a peaches and cream complexion. She had clever green eyes, like a fox. The boy was sobbing and being resolutely ignored.

Louisa burped and tasted gin. She covered her mouth, afraid she would be sick.

'Are you sure you're quite alright?' said Harriet, again.

Louisa shook her head impatiently and the nausea subsided. 'I were just thinkin' she looks like she should be drivin' a herd o' cows.'

Harriet laughed. 'That sounds more like the you I know. And here she is! I thought I'd lost you in the crowd.' She scooped the boy into her arms. 'Isaac. What's all the fuss about?'

The boy buried his face in her neck.

'He ran off, didn't he, the little varmint,' said the woman, glancing at Louisa then back to Harriet. 'You shouldn't indulge him, sister.'

Louisa raised her eyebrows enquiringly.

'This is Ginny, wife of Silas's brother who passed away,' said Harriet, putting her hand on Ginny's arm. 'She's come for a holiday, haven't you Ginny? And this lovely little man is her son, Isaac. How old are you, Isaac?' The boy gazed at her. 'You're four, aren't you? A big boy . . .'

'. . . who should learn to stop whining,' said Ginny.

Harriet shifted the boy onto her hip and he stuck his thumb in his mouth and regarded Louisa gravely.

Harriet said, 'This is Louisa. She's a dear friend of ours who we haven't seen for such a long time. Can you believe we just bumped into her like this? Let's go to market together, we three, and Isaac of course, who will get some sweeties if he's good.'

The boy's face lit up. 'Can I have a gobstopper?'

'I wish something would stop that gob up,' said Ginny.

'Now, now,' said Harriet. 'Ginny's been looking after Peter's parents, who have a farm, so you were right about the cows, Louisa.'

'What cows?' said Ginny. 'We farm sheep. Or they do. I can't stand the woolly little buggers myself.'

She caught Louisa's eye and grinned, and Louisa was surprised to find herself grinning back, the first genuine smile she'd been able to muster in months.

3

Ginny Hinchcliffe left the boy with her saintly sister-in-law and took the omnibus to Louisa's address in town, thrilled to be abroad alone and trying not to show it.

Silas had embarrassed her when he put her on the carriage at the Neepsend stop. He made a fuss of the horses and tipped his cap to the driver, asking him to give Ginny the nod when it was time for her to disembark, telling this man and the world at large that she was new to town. She'd clambered inside, partly mollified by the appreciative looks she was getting from the male passengers hanging from the sides of the omnibus and peering down from the roof.

'Where's your bonnet?' Silas called after her as the bus clattered away. Ginny ignored him, lifting her chin to look through the window at the road ahead.

She had brought a bonnet, a new one, handmade by Peter's mother for her holiday *to the big town*. She'd left the dowdy thing on the train, ramming it down the side of the cushioned seat. It was wasteful, but she was glad she had, as it would have only embarrassed her. Sunbonnets were for working in the fields. Harriet and Louisa wore head scarves or proper hats and she intended to do the same. If she could find a job, if Isaac continued to charm his aunt so that she wouldn't want to see them leave, if she found a local beau who would give her reason to remain, then she need never return to the farm and her life as a drudge to Peter's folks. So many ifs.

She didn't blame Silas for refusing to return to run the farm when his brother died. Her brother-in-law had, in three short years, established his own factory further down the riverbank from the big works with their high walls and rows of looming stacks. The couple lived in a simple redbrick house on the corner of a large yard containing a grinding hull, a blacksmith's forge, two-storey melting house and clerk's office. The Hinchcliffe home had a vegetable garden that stretched to the riverbank, chickens and a pig that Isaac frequently released into the garden so that he could chase it. In turn, Silas would throw open a window and pretend to be angry with the boy. 'We're tryin' to fatten that bleedin' thing up for winter, not make it the fastest pig in town!'

Silas had not got where he was without help. Harriet was of a higher station, Ginny had been able to tell straightaway. She had put her inheritance into the business. There was nothing wrong with getting a leg-up in life. Ginny hoped to take advantage too.

'Here's yer stop, love,' the driver called, and Ginny allowed a young man who was balanced on the runner to take her hand and guide her down to the pavement. He winked at her and she felt bold enough to raise her hand and wave farewell as the coach rumbled away. She stood on a flag-stoned pavement wide enough for three people to walk comfortably abreast. It was busy with pedestrians, while carriages and buggies and men on horseback clattered up and down the cobbled road. The town smelled of dung and burning coals, not unfamiliar smells in the countryside but dirtier here, blended with the alien smells of industry. She could see the pots of what must be a giant chimney in the distance, belching dense clouds of black smoke, and imagined she could taste the gritty particles. A light breeze carried other smells that tickled her nostrils, the eggy smell of fish on the turn, the sweat and pomade of the people pushing past her. It was exhilarating.

A skinny man bent over a barrow laden with sheepskins came towards her, elbows akimbo and at some clop on the gentle descent, his eyes on the barrow wheel that wobbled on the kerb edge, clearly relying on pedestrians to clear out of his way. Ginny flattened herself against the base of a tall column, one of several that flanked the entrance to the forbidding building behind her. She thought it must be a grand house for the town's lord or mayor, or perhaps the seat of power, the place where the aldermen who ran the town gathered. She craned her neck to read the words carved in stone across the length of the building. *The Sheffield and Hallamshire Bank for Savings.*

She was startled when the door swung open and a top-hatted gentleman pattered down the steps to the street, pausing when he saw Ginny standing on the pavement. She was acutely aware of her country wool and bare head.

'You look lost, miss,' the man said in a kindly tone. 'This isn't a place to loiter.'

The space between his high collar and his hat was filled by the bushiest pair of sideburns Ginny had ever seen. Grey and abundantly curly, they seemed to be trying their hardest to get as far away as possible from his florid face. The middle of his chin and his upper lip were cleanshaven, giving him a curiously vulnerable look. Peter had never worn a beard. A threshing machine and a face full of hair were not natural companions. Although as it turned out he might as well have had a beard to his knees. The machine took his arm clean off and even as the farm-hands carried him into the house, and his mother screamed for the doctor to be called, Ginny knew he was a lost cause. In the days that followed, she had scrubbed and scrubbed at the kitchen table until her hands were raw. Eventually, it had been burned and a new table purchased.

'Miss?'

Ginny raised her chin. 'Perhaps I have business at the bank.' She cursed the blush that rose in her cheeks.

The gentleman laughed. 'Far be it from me to presume otherwise.'

She was glad her scuffed boots were hidden under her skirt. It was clear as day that the likes of her would not have any business in this fine building but she wasn't aware of any law that forbade her from being *near* it. Then she heard her name being called and spun around to see Louisa, her new-found friend and present saviour, striding towards her. The man nodded abruptly and turned on his heel.

'Who were that?' said Louisa, breathlessly. 'Sorry. I were late an' I've run the last bit.'

'An admirer,' said Ginny. 'He won't stop following me about.'

Louisa had on the same dress she had been wearing when Ginny had first met her two weeks earlier. It matched the pale blue of her eyes and emphasised her figure; the top button of the blouse was daringly unfastened. She wore a dark blue shawl and her blonde hair was swept into a loose bun so that tendrils fell around her face. She would be beautiful, Ginny considered, if she didn't look so exhausted.

Louisa tucked her arm into Ginny's. 'So tell us how many blokes on that bus tried to kiss thee. Young girls shouldn't be gadding about alone in this town.'

'I'm twenty,' said Ginny, 'and can look after myself.'

Louisa laughed. 'I believe thee.'

'How old are you, then?'

'As old as me tongue and a little bit older than me teeth. Come on, then.'

The town was a chaotic wonder that delighted Ginny. The streets were a jumble of shops, trades and housing, with tumble-down cottages nestling alongside buildings nearly as grand as *The Sheffield and Hallamshire Bank for Savings.* It was as if the whole lot had been swept up into a net and dumped unceremoniously across an area smaller than one of the fields Peter had tended, and then strewn abundantly with people, horses, pigs and dogs. Louisa cut through the crowded pavements with ease, flapping a dismissive hand at a man with two fistfuls of russet apples.

'Wind-blown, I'll bet,' she said to Ginny. 'They'll be sour as owt.'

They had been walking for only a few minutes when Louisa led Ginny down an alleyway that opened onto a square where the cobbles ended and a fish market stood on the packed earth. A barefoot boy of seven or eight squatted on a three-legged stool beside one of the stalls, gobbling down a saucer of cockles.

'I love cockles,' said Louisa.

'Let's have a saucer each,' said Ginny.

'I've no coins on me.'

'I do! Silas gave me some money. By the way, he's wondering when you'll pay a visit. They both speak well of you.' Ginny paused. 'Did you have a falling out?'

‘No,’ said Louisa.

‘Then what?’

‘Then nowt.’

‘Harriet can be a bit . . . sanctimonious.’ She examined Louisa’s stony face. ‘She’s no better than she ought to be, really.’

‘She’d agree wi’ thee. There’s no airs an’ graces wi’ Harriet. They’re both good people.’

Louisa gestured to the fishmonger and Ginny took out her purse. So Louisa felt kindly towards Harriet, after all. Perhaps Ginny could engineer a reunion, get herself in both women’s good books.

‘They’ve moved a clerk in,’ she said.

‘Oh aye? Harriet mentioned that when I first met thee. What’s ’e like?’

‘He’s nothing to look at.’

‘Does that mean he din’t look at thee?’

Ginny laughed. She picked up her dish of cockles. ‘Can you believe I’ve never tried these?’

She copied Louisa, splashing liberal amounts of vinegar on her pile of cockles and spearing several at once onto a toothpick.

‘Lovely, aren’t they?’ said Louisa.

‘Mmhm.’ She gulped down a slimy pearl. It was fishy, but sweeter than she’d been expecting. The vinegar made her cough.

Ginny hoped a taste for cockles was one she’d be able to acquire at her leisure. Always, the threat of being called home hung over her. Peter’s father would not want to be long without his unpaid skivvy. She pushed the thought away and stabbed at another cockle.

‘Harriet said I should go to the covered market,’ she said. ‘I have money to buy Isaac a jacket.’

'I'll take thee,' said Louisa.

'She said I should buy myself an apron,' said Ginny.

Louisa eyed her. 'What's the mardy face for?'

'I'd rather buy a new bonnet.'

At the market, they found a stall selling new and second-hand clothes for men and boys, the sort of garments that couldn't be made at home using a needle and thread — heavy fustian trousers and jackets, slick waterproofs, boots and clogs. Ginny picked out a jacket for Isaac.

'That'll fit 'im now,' said Louisa. There was a critical tone in her voice.

'That's good? I'll get it.'

'No, I mean, get this 'un.' Louisa held up a jacket two or three sizes bigger. 'For growin' room.'

'That would fit me!' said Ginny, but the jacket went in her basket, along with a pair of knitted stockings. She didn't like any of the aprons that were displayed for sale.

'But an apron's an apron,' said Louisa.

'I'm bored of clothes shopping.'

'Want to visit wi' me for a bit?'

Louisa's cottage was the smallest in the middle of a terrace of eight mismatched houses, sandwiched between a taller house on one side and a wider one on the other. All eight slumped tiredly towards two wooden buttresses that propped up the gable end. There was at least one missing tile on every roof.

'Still 'ere,' said Louisa, and Ginny realised her face had given her away. 'Safe as, well, houses. For now. Cheap rent, as tha can prob'ly guess. Come in, I'll gi' thee the grand tour.'

Ginny had been envious of Louisa's status as the mistress of her own home so was disappointed to find the cottage was small and mean; one room downstairs with an opening leading to a small lean-to kitchen and beyond that a yard and the shared privies. Ginny used the privy closest to Louisa's back door, hopping over the channel of filth that ran down the middle of the yard. She returned inside to find Louisa brewing tea and buttering breadcakes. A door in the corner of the main room stood ajar, three bare treads visible before the staircase wound up and out of view. 'Boudoir,' said Louisa.

'Can I see?' said Ginny.

'Me bedroom?'

'I've never had a bedroom of my own, let alone a house.'

'It's nowt exciting,' said Louisa, already turning away to climb the stairs. 'It's a mess.'

The contrast to the downstairs room, which was neat as a pin, was startling. Bottles and jars were strewn across the dusty surface of a dressing table, reflected in a three-sided mirror that was so greasy as to be almost opaque. She almost trod on a piece of paste jewellery, a garish brooch featuring a red and green parrot, and picked it up but then couldn't decide where to put it.

'Horrible, int'it?' said Louisa. 'Summat I got given. Tha can have it, if tha wants.'

'I'll say no thanks.' Ginny placed it next to the pink silk stockings that had been thrown over the surface of a low chest of drawers. All of Ginny's stockings were cotton or wool. These silk stockings were the same colour as a faded satin gown that hung on the wardrobe door. Her eye was caught by a red garter on the floor by the bed. She picked it up and stretched it in her hands.

'Av bin lookin' for that,' said Louisa, taking the garter from her and shoving it in a drawer. She picked up a glass bottle from the dressing table and sniffed the contents.

'What d'you think?' she said, passing the bottle to Ginny.

The perfume was heavy and sickly and reminded Ginny of funeral lilies. She wrinkled her nose.

'Aye,' said Louisa. 'That's what I thought an' all.'

'Where did you get it?'

Louisa raised one eyebrow and a smile played on her lips. 'An admirer.'

'I'm looking for one of those.'

They drank their tea downstairs in front of the fire, and Louisa told her that she would like to visit her part of the world, one day.

'Well, I'm mystified as to why,' said Ginny. 'Cow shit and hay and more cow shit and sheep. And church. Oh, god save me from those endless services. I've got Peter's father on one side of me, snoring his head off, his mother on the other side with a dewdrop dangling off the end of her nose and Isaac shuffling his bony bum about on my lap.'

Louisa snorted. 'But all that fresh air!' she said. 'An' the quiet. I'd like that, I reckon. I'd get a little cottage, an alehouse downstairs wi' a maid to help, an' upstairs it'd be just me by meesen.'

Ginny threw up her hands. 'I'll swap with you.' She took a deep breath. 'I am intending to stay in town, you know. If there's any jobs goin' at your tailor's shop . . . I'm doing a bit of housework for Harriet but I'd like a proper job. Can you put in a good word for me? I'm a good sewer.' She sighed. 'I can't go back, Lou. Silas got away, and look what he's achieved.'

Louisa got up and put the fireguard in place. She looked uncomfortable and Ginny wondered if she had said too much. But here was an opportunity to find work, and a job would strengthen her case to stay in town. She took a breath.

'If you were to promote me to your employer, I'd not let you down.'

'Aye, I know,' said Louisa. 'Silas'll be expectin' thee back.'

Ginny was taken aback. 'He gave me the whole day to myself.'

'I'll walk thee back to Holly Street.'

'Can we meet tomorrow? Why don't you come to see me, and Silas and Harriet?'

'P'raps.'

Ginny pursed her lips. 'Have I said something I shouldn't?'

'No.' Louisa rubbed her forehead. 'No, am sorry.'

'Well, thanks for sparing the time.'

'An' I thank thee for the cockles,' replied Louisa, and her smile was so warm and genuine that Ginny could not stay cross. She had made a friend, an ally, and should try to be patient.

* * *

When they emerged onto the street, two men were standing outside Louisa's cottage, deep in conversation. Ginny guessed they must be in their thirties. One tall, one short, they were dressed like working men, in collarless shirts, waistcoats, thick jackets and trousers, and stout brown boots, although there was none of the factory grime or dust on them. They stopped talking abruptly when they saw the women.

'Ey up, Lou,' said one of the men. He gave Ginny an appraising look. 'We're headin' to the Saw Makers if tha fancies a pint.'

'Me?' said Ginny.

'Both on yer,' he said, not taking his eyes off Ginny. They were brown and narrow and sparkled with humour.

Ginny lifted her chin and gave him what she hoped was a haughty look.

Louisa shook her head. 'It's barely half two. Tha'll drink the day away.'

'Not like thee to be so puritan,' the man said, at the same time as the second man reached out his hand to shake Ginny's.

'I'm Seth,' he said, 'and this rude bugger is Joe. I'm Lou's neighbour,' he gestured towards the end house, the one being propped up to stop them all from falling like a deck of cards, 'and Joe's come round to pester me.' He laughed. 'He'll pester you an' all, love, given half a chance.'

Ginny turned to Louisa, trying and failing to keep the excitement from her voice. 'Can we, Louisa? Lou? I'm on my holiday, so why not? You took the day off work.'

'I thought our Lou were allus on the job,' said Joe.

'Shurrup,' said Seth.

Louisa frowned at Joe before turning to Ginny. 'I don't know that Silas would want you going to a . . .'

'Please,' said Ginny. She didn't add that she had never set foot inside a tavern.

'I'll be accused o' leading thee astray,' said Louisa. 'Oh.' She threw up her hands. 'One drink won't hurt, will it? I could use one.'

The women walked arm in arm back through the

square, a few paces ahead of the men. A delicious sense of anticipation rose in Ginny's chest. She was acutely aware of the swing of her hips, and the sure knowledge that Joe's eyes would be on her. She released her hair from its braid so it tumbled down her back, and caught Louisa's knowing smile.

'What?'

'Looks like tha's caught the eye o' bachelor Joe.'

Ginny flicked her hair and looked over her shoulder.

'Just look at 'im,' said Louisa. 'His mouth's hangin' open like a tramp's pocket.'

Ginny thought this was unfair. He had a lovely mouth, his lips as red as a girl's. He wore a moustache but was otherwise cleanshaven, like a soldier. He dressed well enough, too, in bright fabrics, whereas Seth was all in various shades of brown and grey. Joe looked to be in his mid-thirties, Seth a bit older.

'What do they do, this pair?'

'They were both apprenticed to a brass caster, a while back though,' said Louisa. 'They're allus together now. They keep strange hours. Not at work even now, eh? Must pay well, though. A good brass caster can get upwards o' five pound a week. It's not to be sniffed at.'

'A week?'

'Joe's lookin' more attractive by the second, eh?'

The four of them found a space at the end of the bar in the Saw Makers, and Ginny tried not to stare about her. She had seen these public houses on just about every street corner in the town, some with crowds of men outside them, and wondered what went on inside. This was a larger tavern than many. Louisa told her it had rooms for rent above, and Joe had waggled his tongue lewdly at Louisa.

All the furniture — the long bar, tables and chairs — was made of darkened wood, as were the floorboards. The walls were stained yellow. The place was busy, despite the hour of the day, and Louisa and Ginny were the only women present. An elderly man shuffled past and snarled at them. 'Puddin' burners,' he said.

'What does that mean?' said Ginny, directing her question at Joe.

He grinned. 'Tha should be in the kitchen, love. But if tha were my wife I'd want to show thee off at every opportunity.'

'Hark at it,' said Louisa, shaking her head.

'Look who's in,' said Seth, so quietly that Ginny almost didn't catch the words.

Joe turned his head and Ginny followed his gaze to a man who stood a few feet away. He had sleek striped whiskers that reminded her of a badger's pelt and was pressing his pronounced belly against the counter, whispering in the ear of the man who stood behind it.

'Who is it?' she said, using the opportunity to put her lips close to Joe's ear.

He kept his eyes on the man. 'That's William Broadhead, an important gentleman about town an' an acquaintance o' mine.'

Ginny saw Seth shoot Joe a warning look. Then the man rapped his knuckles on the counter. His voice was deep and pompous and reverberated around the room. Every head turned his way.

'I've been permitted, as secretary of the saw-makers' union, to make an announcement here today,' he declared. 'You will all be aware of the latest outrage committed against a humble working man, a grinder blown up at his own wheel.'

Ginny looked around but it seemed from the nods and whispers that she was the only one in the room who didn't know what this man was talking about.

'He was not a member of our union but I wish to make it known that . . . a moment please . . .' He took out of his pocket a piece of paper and flourished it. 'I have written to the *Sheffield Telegraph* as I wish to make it known that our union decries the fearful catalogue of events that disgraces the fair fame of this prosperous town.' He paused for effect. 'These insane and wicked practices cannot be allowed to continue.'

Ginny leaned into Joe, shocked by her own audacity and thrilled by the touch of her arm against his body. 'What's he on about?'

It was Louisa who answered. 'He's in charge o' one o' the unions that many reckon are responsible for these outrages, including this latest one that maimed a grinder. He's tryin' to clear 'is name, as far as I can make out.'

'Tha the expert then?' said Joe.

'Folk aren't as blind as tha thinks,' said Louisa.

'What outrages?' said Ginny.

A man swung his head round to hiss at her. 'Shush theesen.'

'Take care, fella,' said Joe, a warning note in his voice, and a fresh thrill coursed through Ginny's body.

The badger was still talking. 'In my letter to the *Sheffield Telegraph* newspaper I have declared my intention of offering a five-pound reward, money that will come out of my own pocket, to anybody who can provide information on the perpetrators of this most heinous crime.'

He gestured to the man standing behind the bar

who took an empty tankard from the shelf and handed it over. The badger slammed it on the counter and flipped a sovereign into it.

'I'm offering a reward and you fine gentlemen can do your bit too. I appeal to you today, to all you honest union men, to fill this to the brim so we may offer some small succour to Albert Batty, his wife and his five children.'

As a ragged cheer rose, Seth muttered something Ginny didn't catch. But she heard Joe's reply. 'Shut thee trap, brother.'

The badger had had his say and now stood by, nodding approvingly, as a steady stream of coins were dropped into the tankard.

'What was that all about?' said Ginny.

Louisa shrugged. 'The papers call them the Outrages wi' a capital O. They're nowt to do wi' me.'

'What *are* they though?'

'She's persistent, this one,' said Joe. He put his hand on her waist, only briefly, but she continued to feel the heat of his palm as if he'd branded her. 'Accordin' to the news-sheets, William Broadhead's got men goin' around blowin' up and shootin' them that don't agree wi' the unions.'

'But why?' said Ginny. She widened her eyes appealingly.

Joe grinned at her. 'I wun't worry tha pretty 'ead, love.'

'Tell 'er,' said Louisa. 'She might change 'er mind about wantin' to stay 'ere.'

'I'd like 'er to stay,' said Joe, 'so best not.'

Ginny tapped him playfully on the arm and he clutched her hand. His fingers were warm and strong. 'Vicious wench! Am mortally wounded. Time for more beer. Brother?'

Joe caught the coin Seth flicked into the air and went to the counter. Ginny watched him go then wrenched her gaze back to Seth, who was explaining the outrages to her.

'. . . but the unions are not recognised in law, so they use . . . other methods to try an' encourage workers to join, and employers to allow 'em. They're a good thing, the unions, they're just desperate. It's a means to an end, is all.'

Louisa snorted. 'Even when men are gettin' killed?'

Joe returned from the bar. 'Aye,' he said. He handed out cups full to the brim with brown liquid. 'Keeps people out o' the workhouse. No ale to be had in that place, that's what I 'ear. Cheers.'

Ginny made a show of hesitating. She'd drunk ale before, of course. And she'd tasted the strong home-brewed stuff too. She blamed that heady intoxication for the roll in the hay with Peter, who'd been forced to put a ring on her finger once her belly started to swell. Let this lot think her an innocent. It did no harm.

She put her lips against the rim of the cup and allowed Joe, who had a crafty grin on his face, to tilt her cup up with one finger so the liquid ran into her mouth. She swallowed.

'It's not the watered-down stuff, this,' said Joe. 'It's an acquired taste, tha knows.'

Ginny cut her eyes at him. 'I could get used to it.'

4

The gaffer had a list of premises he wished to visit, in the company of Joe Crookes, to pay his most humble respects.

Joe waited on the busy junction of Sycamore Street and Flat Street, nodding to the passers-by he was acquainted with. When the gaffer's gig pulled up, he climbed on board and took his seat, his presence acknowledged by a thin smile. He eyed the man wielding the reins as the gig travelled west towards Neepsend. The gaffer appeared unruffled by the encounter they'd had yesterday at Wilkins' works, where the master had spat on the ground at their feet and told them both they could rot in hell. The man had gone further than Joe had anticipated, warning the gaffer he was about to get his comeuppance, that the code of honour was broken, and men were talking to the authorities about atrocities they'd had a part in. Joe had moved to stand between the two men, making fists of his hands, and the master had glared at him before looking away and making the wise decision to stalk off, leaving the gaffer shaking his head in disappointment. 'Some additional encouragement may be required,' he'd said to Joe, which generally meant gunpowder in a grinder's trough, or the hamstringing of the master's horse. If the gaffer was feeling generous, a threatening letter would be delivered, usually addressed to the wife, warning of the penalties that might be incurred for defying the union.

The factory they were riding towards had, it was said, agreed to rent grinding troughs to no fewer than four men the gaffer had identified as obnoxious to the union. 'We have here a young upstart,' the gaffer said, 'who requires some schooling in the ways of our industry.'

Anticipating nothing more than a routine visit, Joe's jaw dropped when he walked into the factory yard alongside the gaffer. A young and pretty dark-haired woman was standing near the blacksmith's forge, chatting in an animated fashion to a tall youth who was inclining his head towards her politely but looking over her shoulder at the gaffer and Joe as they approached, an anxious frown on his narrow face. His clothes were of a finer cut than Joe's and his shoes looked fresh out of the box. Joe's boots still had the previous night's muck from the riverbank all over them. He shivered at the recollection but quickly recovered himself, and winked at the girl.

'Ey up, Ginny.'

He had to admit it was gratifying to see her face light up. 'Joe! What are you doing here?'

He glanced at the gaffer. 'I might ask the same o' thee.'

'Oh, this is where I'm staying, with my brother-in-law and his wife.' She gestured around the yard. 'Silas runs this place.'

'Then it's Silas I'd like to speak with,' said the gaffer.

The youth had a slight stammer but the gaffer waited patiently. 'Who shall I say is calling?'

'You can say Mr Broadhead, secretary of the saw-makers' union.'

The youth's eyes widened slightly. He nodded quickly and walked away, towards the hull. The gaffer set off after him, jerking his head to indicate Joe should follow.

Ginny put her hand on Joe's sleeve. 'That's Daniel. He's come to clerk for Silas while he learns accounting.' She smiled at Joe. 'He's got good prospects, you know. He'll probably end up a banker, one day.'

'Tha sounds keen on 'im,' said Joe.

'Are you jealous?'

'O' that? Don't make me laugh, love.' He rolled his shoulders back. 'Gotta go.'

'The man you're with, that's the union boss, from the alehouse? The one offering the reward for that outrage? Harriet has been telling me all about the union campaign.' Her eyes were shining. 'Silas calls it a reign of terror.'

Joe shrugged. 'Am lookin' forward to seein' thee at Louisa's on Friday. Dinner time, yeah?'

He trotted away without waiting for her reply. This Daniel fellow wasn't the only one with prospects, it seemed. He'd thought to string Ginny along, for he couldn't be expected to take seriously a girl who hung around with a harlot. He could already tell he'd soon get what he wanted from her. But now it seemed there was a bit of respectability about the girl. She had relatives with a few bob, that was for sure. Worth taking seriously, at least for now.

The gaffer was being led towards a thatched cottage on the edge of the yard. Another man, broad and strong, about Joe's height but some years younger, emerged from the hull and followed the other two into the cottage, closing the door behind him. Joe opened the door to find all three men standing in the middle of the room. It was sparsely furnished, dominated by a desk and chair, a fireplace and, mounted on the whitewashed wall, shelving divided into pigeon holes, some containing flat brown paper envelopes — wage packets.

'Who's this?' said the man who Joe assumed was the upstart factory owner.

The gaffer confirmed it. 'This is a colleague of mine named Joseph Crookes. Joe, this is Mr Silas Hinchcliffe and his wages clerk, Daniel Housley.'

'How do,' said Joe. He pulled out the chair and sat in it, lifting a booted foot and using a lucifer to dislodge dirt from the sole, allowing it to patter onto the thinly carpeted floor. The gaffer was soon in full flow, telling the unfortunate tale of a grinder named Harry Baxter who had refused to join the union but found a master willing to take him on, and he'd worked for less — far less — than the scale of prices regulated by the union. Could Mr Hinchcliffe see the problem here?

Joe caught a whiff of the riverbank and lowered his boot back to the ground. He'd stolen a boat and rowed himself and Seth onto the Don the previous night. Running brown and sluggish in the daylight, at night the river was as black as ink, a fathomless channel between the factories that lined the banks. The windows of these factories were ablaze with light but this had not concerned him, as they'd glided silently along. Steelworkers didn't have the leisure to contemplate the river. He'd rammed the vessel aground and gone with Seth, slipping and sliding in the rotten morass, to locate the outfall pipe of Wheatman's works and stuff a bomb inside it.

'A warning was issued,' the gaffer was saying, 'but crude methods sometimes result in dire consequences. Don't they, Joe?'

Joe nodded. He'd tried not to think, as they scrambled about on the riverbank, of the rats teeming underfoot, making their meal of the town's leftovers, their blind offspring squirming in a multitude of nests.

'And sadly,' said the gaffer, 'Mr Baxter was targeted by the unruly element and has lost his sight, and is unable to support his family. I wish I could help him in a meaningful way, but because he has never paid union subs . . .' He spread his hands. 'And now here we are. I'm sure your clerk here can confirm that there are certain men in your hull who are at the same disadvantage as our poor Mr Baxter.' He took a wages packet from a pigeon hole, shook it and replaced it. 'I should hate for any misfortune to befall them, or indeed your fine establishment here.'

Joe sat up straight. The gaffer was finally getting to the point.

'Are tha threatenin' me?' said Silas Hinchcliffe. The man was Ginny's brother-in-law. Joe hoped he would not have to put him straight.

'I'm offering a remedy,' said the gaffer. He chuckled. 'I can replace these men with good solid union workers, men who pay their natty brass so that others who can't work for whatever reason are well looked after.'

'Tha sounds like me wife,' said Silas. His tone was cheerful but the eyes he fixed on the gaffer were angry. Joe tensed, ready to intervene if necessary. 'Dun't he, Dan?'

The clerk nodded thoughtfully. 'We appreciate the information, Mr Broadhead.'

'I am able to replace those men this very day,' said the gaffer. 'Just say the word.'

'I've a job to get back to,' said Silas. 'Dan here will

show thee off the premises.' He opened the cottage door. 'Good mornin', gentlemen.'

Outside, the yard was deserted.

'Please thank Mr Hinchcliffe for his time,' said the gaffer.

They left the clerk twisting his hands together and walked back to the street where the gig waited.

'Did we deliver our message, Joe?' said the gaffer.

'Oh aye, I reckon so.'

Joe didn't care about the message. Joe's interest was purely pecuniary. The gaffer had used this expression, and he liked to repeat it. He enjoyed getting his mouth around the educated sound of it. Seth was a believer in the cause, more fool him. Don't get too invested, in causes or women. That was Joe's motto and it had always served him well.

* * *

The brothers reached the end of the row of cottages that stood on the edge of Barker Pool like a mouthful of blackened teeth. Seth fished in his pocket for his key while Joe watched a man step into the street from Louisa's cottage, looking away from the brothers as the front door gently closed behind him. In the still of the night, Joe could hear the lock turn. He could imagine he might even hear Louisa climbing her stairs back to bed.

The man turned his head to find Joe's grinning face looming over him. 'Ey up,' Joe said. 'I'm Horatio Radley Rowbotham. What's tha name?' The man's eyes widened and he spun around and set off in the opposite direction.

'No manners, some folk.'

‘Shurrup, Joe,’ said Seth. ‘Leave it be.’

Inside, Joe collapsed onto his brother’s lumpy settee. They’d been on the ale all night and now he finally told Seth the story of meeting Ginny a week earlier at a factory premises the gaffer was keeping an eye on.

‘Bit close to home,’ said Seth. ‘Has she guessed what tha does?’

‘Am bein’ careful, don’t worry theesen.’ He burped. ‘Speakin’ o’ home, can tha put me up toneet?’

‘Landlady after the rent, is she?’

‘Am paid up! But it’s true I could use a bit o’ brass,’ he said casually. Seth would probably refuse his request for another loan, especially as he’d not paid back the last one. That had gone on beer and inside Mrs Addy’s brothel. He’d lied about paying the rent, confident he could charm his landlady for a while longer before doing another midnight flit.

‘Ginny wantin’ a trinket, is she?’ Seth laughed. ‘She’s got thee in her sights, lad.’

‘She’s a game lass.’

Ginny had already let his fingers wander to the top of her stockings when they’d had a minute to themselves round at Louisa’s house. He’d got his hand near her quim when she squeezed her thighs together and pushed him away. He’d told her then that he wanted to court her. It did no harm, buttering them up a bit.

‘So can tha lend us a few bob? I’ve not got a threp’ny bit to me name.’

Seth laughed. ‘What does tha do wi’ it all? We got fifteen sovereigns for doin’ Baxter. Has tha spent it already?’

‘What’s it for, if not for spendin’,’ said Joe, ‘though I wonder ’ow much I’d ’ave if I saved most o’ what the gaffer’s given us.’

'Three hundred sovereigns,' said Seth.

Joe spluttered. 'What?'

'Aye.' Seth rested his head back and closed his eyes. 'That's how much I've got, so far. Am thinkin' I might emigrate wi' it, to America or maybe Canada.'

'Wait on.' Joe shook him. 'Wake up. This is the first I've 'eard of it. Tha windin' me up?'

'Nope.'

'Then, why din't tha tell me?'

Seth opened his eyes and looked at Joe. 'Am tellin' thee now.'

'So where's tha stashed these savin's?'

'Am not tellin' thee that.' Seth elbowed him in the ribs. 'What's the mardy face for?'

'Nowt. Am just . . . dunno. I thought tha' were settled 'ere.'

'In this town? Why'd I want to stay 'ere?'

We're a team, Joe wanted to say, *you're my brother and all the family I've got*. But it would sound soft.

Seth got to his feet and picked up the lamp, his shadow leaping onto the wall behind him. The wall was unadorned save for a mahogany clock that hung a foot above head height. It was an ugly, boxy thing, especially sitting so high, like the face of a decapitated grandfather clock.

Joe took off his jacket, folded it to use as a pillow, and stretched out on the settee.

''ome from 'ome,' he said. 'Hang on, Seth. Before tha teks theesen to bed, if tha's got a sovereign to tide me over 'til we get a payout . . .'

'Aye,' Seth said as he left the room, taking the lamp with him. 'If tha can just wait 'til the mornin'.'

Joe rubbed his arms. Moonlight filtered in, showing him the pile of unswept ashes that sat in the grate.

The mantelpiece was bare and he already knew that all he'd find in the sideboard were candle ends and a bible. He should have asked Seth for a blanket but he couldn't be bothered to get up again. If there'd been a woman in the house she would have gladly fetched Joe a blanket and brewed him a cup of tea, if he'd asked for one. Seth had been on his own for too long; it was clear he no longer concerned himself with the niceties.

Joe wondered where his brother kept his fortune; stashed in a hole in his mattress, maybe, or hidden behind what little food there was in Seth's kitchen cupboard. Joe's eyelids drooped. There was the risk of rats chewing up the notes. Then he remembered that he and Seth were paid in coin, every time. He could hear it now, the chink of coin on coin as the gaffer counted it out. The cupboard or the mattress or inside one of Seth's books, if he could bring himself to make a hole in one of them — the bible, perhaps — would do the job nicely.

The clock ticked on, a comforting sound that would soon carry him off to the land of Nod. The glass covering the clock face reflected the blank light of the moon. He couldn't see the hands and wondered idly what time it was. The small bit of fancywork, a thin three-sided trellis of intertwined leaves that hid the flat top of the clock from view, couldn't redeem the overall ugliness of the thing.

He heard Seth thump downstairs, his footsteps fading away towards the back of the house. He'd be going to use the privy. Joe tucked his hands into his armpits and turned on his side. He could use a piss, and a blanket, but he couldn't be bothered to get up, and he had something to ponder on. He'd just realised where a purse full of coin could be stashed in plain sight. Joe closed his eyes, and his lips twitched into a smile.

5

Reclining on her elbows on the picnic rug, Louisa watched Ginny's son as he repeatedly threw a stick in the river for Shandy to retrieve. She could tell from the sidelong glances the boy threw her way that he was desperate to follow the dog into the water.

'Isaac, I've got me beady eye on thee,' she said. 'Don't step foot off o' that bank.'

Ginny and Harriet were busy erecting climbing fences and sowing seeds and bulbs in Harriet's garden — radishes, peas, cabbage, beetroot, all manner of vegetables. Louisa had offered to help but Harriet had commented on her pallor, insisted she rest and plied her with tea and buns. *These won't cure what I've got,* Louisa had thought, and been ashamed of her sourness. The truth was, she was thankful to forget her troubles for a short while, and grateful to Ginny for persuading her to reconnect with her old friends.

She sighed and fiddled with the fringe of her shawl. Isaac had become bored of his game with Shandy and was tramping on the ferns that proliferated on the riverbank. In a couple of months, these plants would produce pretty round flowers like yellow buttons. Tansy.

Louisa tipped back her head to gaze up at the milky disc of the sun in a sky hazed from the smoke of a thousand chimneys. Harriet and Ginny were talking in low murmurs; she couldn't make out their conversation. No doubt Ginny was advancing her campaign to be allowed to remain in town. She would be aware the decision lay with Silas and that he would walk over hot coals if Harriet requested it. Ginny was whispering in the right ear.

Louisa got to her feet and walked down the garden to crouch beside Isaac. The dog sniffed at her boots.

'Shandy, gerraway, tha soakin' wet.' She set about ripping the leaves from the stems, gathering them in a pile on the ground.

'What you doin'?' said Isaac.

'Some weedin' for Auntie Harriet. Go an' ask her for a paper bag.'

'Why?'

'Me neighbour makes herbal concoctions from these, tha can tell thee auntie that, if she asks.'

'Alright.' He ran off, pumping his skinny arms and legs as if he had a mile to run rather than a few yards. She envied him his energy.

Louisa put the tea tray on grass that still held the chill of winter. She rolled up the picnic rug.

'Are you getting cold?' Harriet walked over, Isaac hanging on her skirt. She brushed dirt from her apron and peeled off her gardening gloves. 'I'm going to the yard then I'll get you a bag for the leaves. Do you want to go inside?'

'No,' said Louisa. 'I'll come wi' thee. Silas were wantin' to show me round.'

'I'll come too,' said Ginny.

'What about Isaac?' said Harriet. 'We don't want him running about when the factory's going full tilt.'

'Alright.' Ginny gestured for Isaac to come to her. 'But can you have him later, if I go back with Lou? She's asked me to accompany her home, while she's feeling under the weather.' This was news to Louisa but she held her tongue. 'I'll be straight there and back.'

'That's kind of you,' said Harriet.

'I don't mind one bit.'

'If tha sure,' said Louisa. She gave Ginny a crafty smile. 'We can go via the Saw Makers if tha wants, see who's about.'

'The Saw Makers?' Harriet laughed. 'I hope you're not leading my sister astray.'

'Other way about,' said Louisa.

Ginny looked uncomfortable. She tugged Isaac's arm. 'Get off your auntie's skirt. Come on.'

Louisa and Harriet watched Ginny pull Isaac into the house.

'There goes a handful,' said Louisa.

'Oh no, he's a lovely little lad.'

'I were talkin' about her.'

'Ha. Yes.' Harriet touched Louisa's arm. 'We wondered, after your mother died, where you went, why you stopped coming to see us.'

'Harriet, I . . .' A lump rose in her throat and she couldn't go on. Instead, she hugged Harriet to her, then stepped back and laughed self-consciously.

'If you're in any trouble, Lou, please do . . .'

'No, no,' she interrupted, 'am not. Am glad to be 'ere.'

'Well, we missed you.'

'An' I missed thee, both o' thee and Shandy an' all.'

Let's leave it at that was left unsaid, but she could see that Harriet, although still curious, understood and Louisa could have cried with gratitude for that. For now, there would be no more awkward questions.

She took Harriet's hand. 'Let's go an' find that husband o' thine.'

The two women followed the path at the side of the house. It opened up into a large and noisy manufactory, the buildings arranged in an L-shape around a cobbled yard. A smithy faced the wide entrance from the street. Silas walked out of this and strode past the smelting house, grinding wheel and forge, stopping outside the cottage near the entrance. The man who emerged from the cottage had to bend almost double to avoid the lintel. Silas spotted the two women and waved to them, gesturing to the wheel. 'Got a new fella startin' in the hull,' he called.

Louisa felt suddenly at a disadvantage, seeing the boy she had met on his first day in town now commanding his own business. How far she had fallen in those few intervening years and how far Silas had risen.

He pulled her into a rough embrace. 'Ey up, lass.'

'Gettin' soft in thee old age,' she said. She smiled at the young man beside him, a skinny sapling of a fellow with a mousy mop of hair, cleanshaven above his high collar. 'How do.'

His cheeks flamed as quickly as if he'd opened a furnace gate into his face. 'How do you do.'

'This 'ere's our new clerk,' said Silas.

Harriet had wandered away and was peering into the lamplit interior of the hull. Louisa and the men joined her. The hull was a long low-ceilinged room filled with men crouched over their troughs like jockeys urging their horse over the finish line. The collective sound of blades being sharpened against stone reached Louisa's ears like a field full of crickets, or ice skaters on a frozen pond, magnified a thousand-fold. The man nearest the entrance sat upright to cough, a dry explosion that made her flinch. Lung disease and an early death was an occupational hazard for these men.

Harriet turned to Daniel Housley. 'The new man . . .'

Silas held up his hands. 'I know what tha goin' to say. Is he in a union? Is he payin' his subs?'

Harriet pursed her lips. 'They are valid questions. We know what happens to those who oppose the unions, and we've already had a visit. I don't want it happening here, Silas, that's all.'

'It won't,' said Silas.

'What about the saw grinder who had his horse hamstrung? The poor beast had to be put down. And I read in the newspaper about the man who just happened to see the glitter of gunpowder in his trough, else he'd have been blown sky-high.'

'Tha reads too much, love. The papers exaggerate, don't they, Dan?'

Daniel Housley folded his arms, then unfolded them to clasp his hands together, his forehead creased in consternation. 'No, sir. I would say not.'

'Pah. This sort o' thing's allus gone on,' said Silas. 'I don't take a side.'

Harriet shook her head. 'It's not as simple as that. What *would* you say, Daniel?'

The clerk glanced worriedly at Silas. 'Hal Rogers' machines were done over again, and that's only down the road from us. The saw-makers' bands were missing for five days.' He nodded when Silas frowned. 'Yes, that's five days of non-production. In the end, Hal appealed directly to the union boss — he went to see him at the pub he has — and Broadhead told him where the bands had been hidden. But the chief handle maker is still refusing to join and now Hal's had a letter.'

'What does the letter say?' said Harriet.

At the same time, Silas said: 'Who's it from?'

'It's anonymous. Signed *A Grinder,*' said Daniel Housley. 'I haven't seen it myself so I wouldn't wish to comment on the contents.'

Silas snorted. 'Come on, Dan. Tha can tell us what tha knows.'

The clerk looked uncomfortable. 'I believe it says this handle maker is making of himself . . .' he glanced first at Harriet and then at Louisa '. . . a busy tool that shall end up costing Hal dear if he keeps him in his employ. That's the gist of it.'

'Threatenin' letters, blow-ups an' rattenings.' Silas shook his head. 'What's the police doin' about it? Nowt, as far as I can see.'

'But what protection is there against unscrupulous employers?' said Harriet.

Silas looked hurt.

'Husband, I'm not talking about you.'

'It should be a choice, though,' said Silas, 'joinin' a union, an' them that don't shouldn't be punished. What's tha think, Lou?'

Louisa laughed and glanced at Daniel Housley, slightly disconcerted to find he'd already been gazing at her. 'Ask Dan here. I know nowt about it.'

He coughed and made a strangled sound, his Adam's apple working up and down his long throat. 'I'm sure I'm not the expert,' he said, finally.

'Well said.' Silas clapped him on the back. 'None o' us are. But I think tha's the clever clogs o' this little group, Dan.'

He ducked behind Harriet and wrapped his arms around her waist, looking over her head at Louisa.

'Dan's takin' the burden o' the accounts off this one. She's got more important stuff to be getting' on wi'.'

Harriet cast her eyes heavenwards. 'Stop it, Silas.' She laughed. 'Louisa, don't look at me like that. I'm not expecting. Not yet.'

Louisa caught Daniel Housley's eye and grinned at him and the blush that had been subsiding from his cheeks bloomed again.

* * *

The man's neck was crumbed with dirt. She turned her head to the side but that put her nose near the muggy pit of the arm he was using to brace himself against the bedhead. A thick feeling in her throat told her she would vomit if he didn't hurry it up. She thrust her hips a couple of times, dug her fingernails into his scrawny buttocks and whispered his name. That should do the trick. They were all the same between the sheets. This one was a working man she had a loose acquaintanceship with; she would never have let him over the threshold otherwise. He lived in the next street, a furnaceman with half a dozen kids who handed his weekly wage over to his wife, and had decided after a rare win on the horses to try for a drunken to-do with Louisa Leigh.

The grime on him, though. She wouldn't be surprised if seed potatoes were sprouting behind his ears.

He grunted, finally done, and she moved across the bed before he could drop his weight on her. He stopped her from rising by putting his hand on her breast. His fingers were cold and she shuddered and batted him away.

'Yer a proper pretty lass,' he said.

Louisa laughed. 'How much did tha win?'

He reached for her again. 'I can see tha's thinkin' the same as me . . .'

She removed his hand gently, sat up and reached for her nightgown, afraid for the few seconds it took to drop the garment over her head that he would grab her and wrestle her back down. It had happened before, with a gentleman who'd had her a second time, for free, treating her roughly while telling her she should be grateful for his kind attention. She supposed she should consider herself lucky to be able to count the assaults against her on the fingers of one hand.

This one, the furnaceman, just lay on the bed, scratching his belly and smiling at her.

He left the way they all did, with a furtive look up and down the street. Before stepping out, he took hold of her wrist — squeezing it, telling her without words that he could touch her whenever he liked — and pressed a shilling into her palm.

'Down payment, rest on me next win. Wish me luck, dearie.'

Louisa forced a weak smile. 'I'll keep me fingers crossed for thee.'

She rested the hard bone of her forehead against the equally unyielding cold wood of the door after she had closed it behind him, taking shallow breaths, trying to stem the tide of nausea rising from her gut. She would do it now; there was no reason to wait any longer. Get it over and done with and forgotten about. The mother's ruin hadn't worked.

The tansy would.

She lit a lamp and put the kettle on to boil. The leaves were in the pocket of the apron she'd left slung over the back of a chair. They were yellowed now, and lighter than feathers in the palm of her hand. She raised her hand to her nose and, after a moment's hesitation, sniffed the leaves.

They had no discernible scent, carrying only the faintly mouldy aroma of every shoot grown in the earth. Mother Nature provided tansy in abundance and Jemima Greaves had told her it had been taken for centuries to expel ill humours and purify the system. There was no danger. It wasn't as if Louisa had procured arsenic or mercury or prussic acid from a druggist. These innocent leaves came from Harriet's garden.

Poor Harriet. She had confided in Louisa that starting a family was her dearest wish. She would never understand.

What if the tansy failed? Louisa squeezed the leaves in her fist. *A natural remedy,* Jemima had told her, *and nowt to be afraid of.* Louisa strained to hear another voice, her mother's voice, but could not. She was alone in this. Better to stop whittling and get on with it.

She dropped the leaves into the bottom of the white china pot that had been her mother's, gifted to her by her employers when she had left her housekeeping post to nurse Louisa through pneumonia. The teapot was prettily painted with a scattering of mauve petals and had come with four delicate porcelain cups. Louisa had agreed with her mother on their beauty and did not voice the thought that a financial payoff would have been more useful. Theirs had not been a household that practised the modern ceremony of afternoon tea. Louisa had long since pawned the cups — her mother had never used them, for fear of breaking one — but had kept the teapot so that she could think of her mother whenever she got it down.

She lifted the kettle from the fireplace and poured hot water over the leaves. She put the lid on the teapot and set it down on the low table by her rocker before returning to the lean-to to fetch a cup.

Reclining in her rocker, she shuffled her stockinged feet over the knots of fabric in the pegged rug. She would go back to bed after she'd drunk the tea. Jemima had told her it would taste bitter but she should drink it down. Louisa wondered whether she ought to finish the pot.

Eventually, she took a deep breath and got to her feet, lifting the net in the window to peer out. There was a light in an upstairs window across the deserted street, illuminating the cobbles with a soft gleam. Returning to her rocker, she hunched forward and jiggled the teapot by the handle. She rose again, and heard her mother's voice, gently remonstrating — *Child, you're up and down more times than a fiddle player's elbow.* The memory raised a tremulous smile to her lips as she lifted the lid of the pot and stirred a teaspoon in the leaves, the warmth rising damply to cover her hand like a glove. Then she replaced the lid and sat, unmoving. There was a sudden yell from the street, the sound of heavy boots on the cobbles, growing louder and then receding, followed by a night watchman's piercing whistle. Louisa clutched the arms of the rocker, heart pounding. *Get a grip, Lou.* These were street sounds she was accustomed to and yet here she was, acting like a lady about to sink into her crinoline. Fainting fits were for the rich madams who had a man to catch them. She would only end up on the floor.

That thought brought a grim smile to her face. She lifted the teapot and half-filled the cup. She wrapped her hands around it, savouring the warmth. The liquid looked black in the candlelight. She lifted it tentatively and sniffed it as she had the leaves. No earthy scent remained. It didn't smell of much at all.

Herbal tea. That's all it was. A natural remedy for a female complaint as old as time.

But nature bites and time is cruel. Louisa hesitated, the rim of the cup against her lips. 'Alright,' she whispered, 'I consider meesen warned.'

6

Ginny could feel every trickle of sweat that ran down her sides in the loose blouse she wore with a plain cotton skirt to carry out the domestic duties allocated to her by Harriet. She resented being inside on such a beautiful spring morning, listening to Isaac's high-pitched chatter and the lower, patient tone of Harriet's voice being carried in from the garden on a light breeze. Isaac was Harriet's shadow, trailing after her wherever she went, and had been thrilled to be offered a lesson in training the tall shoots of the pea plants up the garden trellises. It was not this that Ginny resented; she was counting on the boy's Aunt Harriet falling in love with him as he had with her. Even now, her sister-in-law was telling Isaac he would be allowed to pick and eat some of the peas straight from the pod when they were ready, which meant Harriet was envisaging Ginny still being around in the early summer.

No, what she resented was being treated like a maid-of-all-work, even though she knew she was being unfair. How could she complain when she was earning her keep as well as accepting the wage Harriet insisted she be paid? Ginny had never had money of her own and thought herself very generous to have spent some of it on small gifts for Louisa — a beribboned pomade, a chocolate orange stick, a bag of cherries — to keep her close, a useful ally, but also because it pleased her to make Louisa smile.

Her friend was carrying a weight on her shoulders and Ginny knew she was hiding a secret from the guarded way she spoke to Harriet and Silas, although it was clear she was delighted to be reunited with them. That had been Ginny's doing, too.

A fat black spider ran across the floor and scurried up the wall to a web Ginny's duster had missed in the corner of the ceiling. Let her keep her web. Let her enlarge it and catch all the flies. Ginny leaned on her brush and gazed listlessly at the rug on the kitchen floor. Harriet had asked her to take it outside and beat the dirt from it but Ginny decided this could wait for another day.

'Good morning, Mrs Hinchcliffe.'

'Oh!' Ginny spun around, losing her hold on the brush, which clattered to the ground.

Daniel Housley was standing in the doorway that led back into the house. He stepped forward and picked up the brush, handing it to her. Ginny wiped her hand across her forehead, aware her skin was slick with perspiration and that she must stink to high heaven. It was interesting that this man felt able to let himself into the house, almost like one of the family. She thought it a bit impertinent.

'Good morning, Dan,' she said boldly. 'You've caught me hard at work.' She blew a strand of hair off her face and grinned at him. 'I'm usually a bit more presentable than this.'

Daniel Housley smiled nervously. Ginny sized him up. He had none of Joe's dangerous appeal but he was a clerk with a steady job in an up-and-coming manufactory, young and unmarried. He might just fit the bill. She leaned the brush against the wall and swept her long thick braid over one shoulder. 'Can I offer you a cup of tea?'

'Ah, thank you, but no.'

'Then what can I do for you?' She tilted her head and bestowed on him her most flirtatious smile.

'I was after Mrs Hinchcliffe.' He cleared his throat. 'The other Mrs Hinchcliffe.'

'Oh.'

'I'm sorry to disturb.'

'Always a pleasure to see you, Dan. Why don't you come back later, when you've finished being so busy?' She coiled a strand of hair around her finger. 'I do love a strong cup of tea. Keeping this house clean is thirsty work.'

'Hmm.' He looked around the room and ran his finger around the edge of his collar. 'I am accustomed to always finding dust in my office. Every time the door opens it swirls in from the yard.' He raised his hand and rotated his wrist, then scratched his head. Ginny suppressed a laugh. 'Women's work is never done.' He seemed to feel even more was required. 'I'm impressed by your labours.'

'Perhaps you've found the correct member of the Hinchcliffe family after all,' said Ginny.

He looked terrified. 'Ah! I think I hear voices in the garden.' Ginny stepped aside as he hurried to the back door. 'Ah, there she is, with your little lad. Excuse me.'

As soon as he'd closed the back door behind him, Ginny threw the brush into the pantry and ran upstairs to the room she shared with Isaac. She poured fresh water into the basin and used a flannel to clean the dust from her face and hands, relishing the damp against her skin. She brushed her hair, pinned it into a loose bun and changed into a fresh blouse, a pretty cast-off of Harriet's that was embroidered with green sprigs around the cuffs and neckline.

In the garden, Isaac was chasing the collie in circles, trying to grab hold of the dog's tail. Daniel Housley and Harriet sat at a small wrought iron table on the flagged path, poring over paperwork. Ginny called to Isaac and he abandoned his chase and ran towards her. She lifted him into her arms. 'Mam,' he said, patting her cheek.

She put him down. 'Don't cover me in dirt.' She put one hand on Harriet's shoulder and the other on Daniel Housley's, which stiffened. He moved slightly, almost imperceptibly, away and she let her hand fall.

'So, how's business?' she said.

Harriet looked up. 'Are you going out?'

'Yes.' Ginny pulled out a chair and sat down, teasing a ringlet of hair from behind her ear and winding it around her finger. 'I'd forgotten I promised Louisa I would call on her this afternoon.'

Daniel Housley looked up, pushing back his fringe with ink-stained fingers. She gave him her most brilliant smile.

'How is Miss Leigh?' he said, stumbling slightly over his words.

'Miss Leigh is very well, thank you.'

'Will you pass on my kind regards?'

Ginny sighed and stood up again. He was hopeless. 'I'll be sure to.'

'You're going now?' said Harriet.

'Yes.'

She hoped Joe would be there, feet up on the table as if he owned the place. Joe wouldn't hesitate to tell Ginny how lovely she looked, and would probably try to kiss her again. Joe had asked Ginny if he could court her and she was yet to give him an answer. She decided now that her answer would be yes, and she would let him kiss her all he wanted.

'Can I come?' said Isaac.

'No, but I'll be back to tuck you in, love.'

* * *

She was now accustomed to riding on the omnibus, no longer intimidated by the men who perched on it or the matrons who sat inside. Her feet rested alongside theirs on damp rushes that clung to her skirt hems. She had borrowed a bonnet and jacket from Harriet and could pass for one of them, an ordinary townswoman going about her business. She no longer peered up, open-mouthed, at the pillars, cornices and stone and marble carvings of the tall buildings in the centre of town, affecting instead the same world-weariness as the rest of the population, while remaining secretly thrilled by it all.

There was no reply when she knocked on the door of Louisa's cottage and the grey net in the window concealed the room within. The light rain that had begun to fall intensified on a gust of wind, the drops now a downpour. Two boys who were squatting in the gutter gathered up the marbles they had been playing with and scrambled to their feet. 'She's in,' said one. 'I saw her go in a bit ago.'

'An' she's not come back out since,' said the other.

They looked at her expectantly.

'Oh!' she said, and fumbled in her purse, handing the boys a farthing each. Hard-earned coins. A seamstress like Louisa would be on a higher wage than a maidservant and wasn't required to always be on her knees clearing out grates. Ginny had asked again whether there were any positions at the tailor's Louisa worked for. Louisa had been evasive, but Ginny would remind her friend today that she had promised to make enquiries.

The handle of the door to Louisa's cottage was slick in Ginny's palm. She grasped it and pushed down. Unlocked.

She opened the door into a cold and dim room. The nets were drawn and the lamps unlit. She jerked in surprise at sudden movement glimpsed from the corner of her eye. It was a mouse scuttering away into the lean-to kitchen. She considered whether it would be worth trying to catch it and throw it out. It wasn't worth the effort required. She would tell Louisa she ought to get a cat.

'Lou?'

The white painted door that concealed the staircase to the bedroom was closed.

Ginny opened it and called into the stairwell. 'Louisa?'

A floorboard creaked above her head. There was a sound like a dry cough, coming from upstairs.

Ginny put her foot on the first tread but was suddenly afraid to continue. Why hadn't Louisa responded to her call, if she was up there? 'Who's there?' she said. She thought about taking the poker from the fireside, or just leaving this cold place, returning to the warmth and safety of her brother-in-law's house. There could be thieves up there. What if Louisa was lying dead on her bed, stabbed or strangled to death? Ginny would be next. Reduced to a headline in the newspaper to be gossiped over. *MURDER HUNT.* She turned her head slowly to look into the gloomy room behind her. What if the killers were hiding in the lean-to the mouse had run into, waiting for her to trap herself in the upstairs room? There was a keyhole in the staircase door but it was empty. She examined the bare treads. No key to be seen. Another cough from above, and a moan.

'Come up, Ginny.'

She let out a shaky breath. 'Lou? Is that you?'

'Who else would it be?'

Louisa lay on top of her bed, fully dressed. The room was cold and she wore fingerless gloves over her trembling hands. Her eyes were dark and sunken, her face a whitely shining disc in the gloom.

Ginny hesitated in the doorway. 'Why have you got the curtains shut? Are you cold? Why didn't you light a fire?'

'I'm not too well, love. Can tha do it? Sorry to ask.'

'What have you got?' said Ginny. She paused half-way across the room. 'Can I catch it?'

Louisa laughed, which was a relief, but then pressed her hands against her stomach and winced. 'No, love. You can't catch this.'

Ginny sat gingerly on the edge of the bed and put her hand on Louisa's forehead. It was cold, clammy. 'Should I fetch a doctor?'

'What? Does tha think I can afford that sort o' money?' Louisa looked away, biting at her lip.

Ginny patted her leg, gingerly.

Louisa sighed. 'Sorry, love. Don't mean to snap at thee. If tha could just light the fire that would be grand. An' there's a rag on the clothes horse. Bring that. Then I'll 'av a little sleep. Sleep it off.' She closed her eyes and turned onto her side, facing away from Ginny. 'Aye,' she said faintly. 'I'll sleep it off.'

Ginny made up the fire and was halfway down the shadowy stairwell to fetch matches to light it when she heard the rattle of the front door latch. Heavy footsteps and men's voices floated up on an eddy of air that carried the now familiar smoky odour of the town.

'. . . not like 'er to leave the door unlocked . . .'

'Lou! Are tha up?' That sounded like Joe.

She froze when the door to the staircase was gently but firmly closed, leaving her in darkness.

'Sleepin' off a heavy 'un or sleepin' under one.' Joe again.

'Just keep tha voice down.' And that was Seth, she was certain of it.

Ginny moved down to the next tread, then hesitated. What did the brothers have to say that they didn't want Louisa to hear? She put her hand on the wall and tilted her head towards the sound of their voices.

'I told thee we should've been discussin' this at mine,' said Seth. 'Tha's like a dog on heat. Anyhow, Ginny's not 'ere.'

Ginny smiled in the dark but remained where she was. She'd surprise him in a minute or two. She longed to see the expression of delight on Joe's face when she revealed herself. Waiting would make it all the sweeter. It was the right choice, picking Joe over Daniel Housley, who anyway seemed impervious to her flirtations and was always asking after Louisa. Still, she knew even less about Joe than she did the diffident clerk. She recalled the advice she'd been given as a small child. *Be still and listen. You might learn something*.

'Are tha listenin' to me, Joe? Ginny's not 'ere.'

'Aye but she might be 'ere soon.' Joe's voice grew

fainter and she guessed he'd gone into the lean-to. 'Let's see what Lou's got in . . . there's breadcakes, an' cheese. Ey up, some cherries, an' all. She must be feelin' flush.'

'So what's the gaffer sayin' then?'

'Hang on.'

Seth was pacing the room. He was a quiet sort, serious. She believed he might be kinder than Joe. It would be a neat solution to have him court Louisa. Ginny decided on the spot she would try to engineer it.

So, she waited, listening to the ticking of the clock that sat on the mantelpiece over the fireplace. Now, plates were clattering on to the table and chairs pulled out. She could reveal herself while they were eating, startle them, have Joe chase her round the kitchen. She would let him catch her.

'Ta,' said Seth. 'So what's goin' on?'

'Gaffer an' a few o' his men 'av been called in for questionin'. Love cherries, I do.'

'Called in for questionin'?' Seth kept his voice low but she could hear the alarm in it. 'By the police?'

'Aye, ahead o' the inquiry. They're drawin' up a list o' witnesses to call. Anyhow, he were 'appy wi' the Wheatman's job, an' he's got summat else for us. Me an' thee and p'raps one other for a lookout. Two jobs, two good pay-outs then we're out o' it forever. Things, as they say, are comin' to a head.'

'Has he mentioned us, in these interviews he's 'ad wi' the bobbies?'

'I 'aven't a clue. He reckons this inquiry'll be good for the trade. Get the unions legalised, lay off on the strongarm stuff. 'Course, he's still denyin' he had any part in it.'

'Why risk two more jobs?'

'Grudges. Scores to settle. Then he'll have no more need o' us. So.'

Joe clapped his hands, making Ginny jump. She gasped and pressed her hands over her mouth to stifle it. There was silence from below, except for the ticking of the clock, and she closed her eyes tightly, all thoughts of surprising Joe chased away. Now she was afraid of being found. Then Seth said something about his share of a payment that Joe still owed him and she breathed out quietly through her fingers. Her mind was racing. She knew about the outrages committed on behalf of the trade unions; Harriet said it had been going on for years, that the brutalities were generally accepted as a means of enforcing union rules that had no power in law. Rough and ready justice meted out when, for example, an out-of-work man took union money to keep his family out of the workhouse but refused to pay subs once he'd found a job. Turn and turn-about. But the government wanted the unions crushed and this was why, according to Harriet, an inquiry was taking place, to encourage confessions of guilt with a promise of immunity from prosecution, and finally put an end to the whole thing. This didn't fit with what Joe had just said about the unions gaining recognition.

Joe had been in Silas's yard with the union boss, and Silas had gone about with a face like thunder afterwards.

'What did the gaffer say about Wheatman's then?' Seth again.

'Like I just said, 'e were 'appy. Nob'dy got hurt but there were enough damage to the works to gi' satisfaction. I'll gi' thee tha share later, alright?'

'It were some explosion.'

Joe laughed. 'I've never rowed off so fast in me life. An' then I thought it were gonna throw us off of Rutland bridge.'

'Tha's the one that wanted to watch.'

Ginny stroked her fingers over the bare plaster of the wall. Was Joe a thug, or was he fighting for the rights of the working man? A thrill raced up her spine. It was the latter. He was a hero.

Her brother-in-law would disagree. Ginny had overhead Silas and Harriet arguing about the grinders who weren't unionised. She was recalling Harriet's warning — *We'll receive a letter next, and then another visit, this time under cover of darkness, if you insist on being so pig-headed, Silas* — when Joe's words penetrated her ears.

'So this lad in Neepsend is tekkin' on men that are obnoxious to the trade. He's small fry, just needs tellin', tha knows? Teach the upstart from out o' town a lesson in 'ow we do things 'ere.'

'Tek the tools?'

'Aye. Ratten 'is troughs, maybe bash a few bits o' machinery up. Easy in an' out. Nowt too extreme. The bloke upset a bigwig friend o' the gaffer's a few years back, so he's doin' 'im a good turn, ahead o' the inquiry.'

'Linin' up his allies.'

'Aye, so no time to waste. Next new moon. We'll need gunpowder for the other job, an' all. Twice the amount. An' somebody to post lookout for us.' She heard the drumming of fingers on the table top. 'A woman o' the night would be the best bet.'

Seth snickered. 'Well, tha knows a fair few o' them ladies, Joe.'

Ginny decided to disregard this. Seth was joking, ribbing his brother. Joe had no need to pay a woman to go with him. Anyway, his past was irrelevant when she was his future.

'What about the harlot that lives in this very 'ouse?'

Ginny didn't hear Seth's reply. She stared, wide-eyed, up the stairwell, her heart hammering in her throat. She had been presented with the evidence but had not seen the truth. The red garter she had picked up from the floor, the garish brooch Louisa had tried to give away.

And when Ginny had asked who bought her the perfume she had answered *An admirer*. This was the secret Louisa was keeping from her friends. And from Ginny, too. It explained why she was so evasive about helping Ginny find work as a seamstress. There was no tailor's shop, only what her father-in-law would call a *knocking shop*.

Yet, somehow, Joe knew all about Louisa. Ginny tried not to think about why that might be but her body betrayed her with a stab of jealousy that weakened her knees. It was vital that she not be discovered. Slowly, she turned to ascend the stairs, one step then the next. She froze when a further realisation dawned.

She needed to find out when the next new moon was, and warn Silas.

7

He went to the home of Tom Garland, an engine tenter presently enjoying a period of penal servitude for blowing up a manufactory in Dore. Garland had been put away on the evidence of several witness, but remained loyal to the gaffer throughout his trial, refusing to admit to the offence or to name who he'd been working for — the newspapers labelled it a union outrage, regardless — and getting six years for his trouble. That's why Joe was here, to sort out his wife.

The sun was still an hour or more off rising but Polly Garland opened the door seconds after Joe knocked gently on it. She made a moue with her mouth and Joe kissed it quickly and pushed past her.

'I were about to come to thee,' she said. 'An' tha's weeks overdue wi' me payment. I'm down to me last farthin'.'

He patted his coat pocket. 'I've bought thee ticket.'

'Where's me money, though?'

Joe counted out ten shillings into the palm of her hand and folded her fingers over the coins, squeezing lightly. 'Sorry it's late but 'ere's three months' worth, with the gaffer's compliments for tha continued loyalty.' He bent to examine her face. Polly Garland was a lusty, voluptuous woman in the prime of her life. Joe hadn't been able to work out who first seduced who, but he wasn't complaining. Poor old cuckolded Tom Garland. 'Train leaves in two hours, so there's plenty o' time. Bet tha bed's lovely an' warm still.'

Afterwards, they dressed in silence. Joe was moody, not relishing the prospect of the day ahead. Tom Garland's wife no doubt felt the same way.

Derby jail was a notorious place, housing all manner of crooks, from petty thieves and debt defaulters to cutthroats waiting for the paperwork to be completed so they could be hanged. The buildings in the prison compound were enclosed by a thirty-foot-tall boundary wall topped by broken bricks and shards of glass. Joe and Polly queued with the other visitors to be allowed into the grounds. He glanced about as they walked towards the main building along a path surrounded by dew-soaked grass. On his right, sat a long, three-storey building pockmarked by rows of windows. There were cells behind those small square openings. Joe shivered and ran his hand through his hair. They'd shave it all off, his crowning glory, if he was ever brought here as an inmate. He wondered whether he'd stand the humiliation, or if that would be the least of his concerns by then.

He looked for a set of gallows but there was none. He supposed this was because public hangings were going out of fashion and those unfortunate enough to be sentenced to death were being executed behind closed doors. The main building, with its Doric-style columns and oak double doors that were as tall as two men, was designed to intimidate, and it did. A chill ran down Joe's spine. He had shot James Linley about the same time as Garland had blown up the factory, but he'd been lucky. He'd got away with it. Nevertheless, stepping into a jail felt like offering his neck for the noose. Surely, they'd see his crimes written all over his face and carry him, kicking and screaming, into the room where the rope was looped, ready to choke the life from him.

Waiting for Tom Garland to be brought up, he leaned over to whisper in Polly's ear, acutely aware of the guard at the door watching his every move.

'If anybody asks, I'm tha brother that's brought thee down to see 'im. Reight?'

She nodded.

He glanced at the guard. The man was still looking at him. Joe examined the toes of his boots that were resting on dirty oilcloth flooring. A smudge near his foot was the exact shape of an airgun. Perhaps only to his eyes. He hadn't killed Linley outright with the airgun, he hadn't been aiming to murder the man. But he'd delivered a fate worse than death, a tortuous decline as the bullet in Linley's head gradually penetrated his brain. The man had died in agony six months after the shooting. A handful of men, perhaps half a dozen including Seth and the gaffer, knew who'd pulled the trigger. It was half a dozen too many for Joe's liking, especially now, if men really were opening their traps and releasing damning information to the bobbies.

He rubbed his hands together to warm them. The grate in the waiting room was empty, a layer of grey ash in the tray beneath. It had been cold the night he'd finally done the deed. He'd been offered the use of a revolver a mate had purchased from a pawn shop for fifty shillings. He might have agreed to rent it but he'd already bought an airgun from Naylor's on Snig Hill, to shoot coneys and grouse, and then was given the Linley job and decided he'd use his own gun. He'd gone to Ecclesall Wood for target practice and spent weeks following Linley from public house to public house. *He's obnoxious to the trades. Make it so as he can't work*, the gaffer had said. Joe had done that all right.

After weeks of stalking, his unwitting victim had made it easy for Joe, visiting The Crown in Scotland Street and making himself at home in a back room, clearly visible from the alley in which Joe crouched. Linley even sat, conveniently, with his back to the window, on a wooden bench. The window was open to allow in the balmy air of the August night and Linley was chatting to somebody out of Joe's sight. There would not be a better time.

He remembered clearly the moment he fired the gun, aiming for Linley's shoulder. At that moment, Linley had thrown back his head in laughter. There was a split second when Joe thought he could adjust his aim but the gun had gone off, and he was scrambling away, exiting the alley and running hell for leather down Scotland Street, turning onto Furnace Hill where he slowed to a gentle jog and then a stroll. When he reached the newly made iron bridge that crossed the Don he stopped and threw the gun end over end into the water where it landed with a satisfying splash and sank into depths that no doubt concealed a multitude of sins. The gaffer had given him fifteen sovereigns and said he was glad the shooting had not been fatal, although he'd heard Linley was in a bad way.

The gaffer sent a man to demand Joe's attendance at the Royal George on the frosty February morning when Linley finally relinquished his grasp on life. *It's a murder inquiry now, Joe. You broke our contract but I won't hold it against you. It was bad luck. We'll consider the matter as dead and buried.* It had been a deliberate choice of words so that Joe would not miss the meaning. The nasty old sod.

Joe blinked when Polly nudged him. He had forgotten where he was. 'Come on,' she said. They were led into a room where a guard searched them. Polly put up with this indignity by staring at the ceiling throughout. It was something she'd clearly been through before. Joe allowed the guard to pat him down and rummage in his pockets, although a quiet fury built in him.

'Tha's treatin' us like we're the criminals,' he said eventually, when he could no longer hold his tongue.

'Shush.' Polly smiled at the guard. 'He's not been 'ere before.'

When Joe set eyes on Tom Garland he barely recognised the man. Garland was wearing the same prison uniform as the rest — a boxy felt hat, a faded shirt that might have once been black or blue or green or red but had been washed and worn so many times it had no discernible colour. The baggy trousers he wore were stained the colour of chimney pots. His face was grey too, his eyes sunken, and the short fringe under his hat was almost white. It was as though he was being rubbed slowly out of existence.

Joe tried and failed to suppress a shudder.

Garland's voice was rusty, as if it didn't get enough use. 'Comin' down wi' summat, Joe Crookes?'

Polly kept a distance from her husband and Joe guessed that if she had tried to touch him, to embrace him, they might have been separated by a guard. Or it might just be that she felt guilty, standing alongside the man with whom she'd cuckolded her husband. Maybe she was afraid Tom Garland would smell another man on her.

'Are tha lookin' after me missus?'

'Aye,' Polly said, before Joe could speak. 'Am gettin' the money tha were promised. It's enough to keep us goin', for now.'

Joe nodded his agreement tersely, still rattled by his recollection of the Linley shooting, and by the idea that he could be standing in this man's tattered boots. He wiped sweat from his brow.

Garland's eyes bored into him. 'Tha'd not get on 'ere, Joe. There's nob'dy tha'd be able to charm into doin' thee bidding. Well, there might be summat . . .' he trailed off, squinting out of the corner of his eye at one of the guards. 'Anyhow, I'll be out by the end o' this year, all bein' well.' He tapped the side of his nose with a bony finger. 'Keepin' me nose clean, Joe. Is tha? Or has tha come to get theesen locked up an' all?'

Joe coughed. He could barely stand to look at Garland, but what had he expected? They weren't chewing the fat in a Turkish spa. His mouth twisted into a smile at the thought and he regained his composure. He was here to deliver a message from the gaffer, that was all.

'Am as straight as a plumb,' Joe said, 'just wanted to accompany thee lovely wife, make sure tha's all reight, and tha's got thee head screwed on right for when tha gets released.'

Garland's eyes glittered. He went to spit on the ground but glanced at the guard and obviously thought better of it. 'What does tha' mean?'

'Keep thee gob shut an' thee eyes peeled. Am sure I don't need to tell thee why.'

'Av kept my side o' the bargain.'

'Aye. So far. Tha knows if tha speaks now, to any soul, that the gaffer's got a long reach. Tha'll end up transported to Australia.' Joe put his hand on Polly's arm to stop her speaking. She shook him off angrily, but held her tongue. 'An' when tha gets out, say owt and tha'll find thee head might get blown off thee shoulders.'

Garland sneered. 'Tell 'im that while Polly 'ere is involved, I'll be as good as gold, as reight as rain, and owt else tha thinks he needs to 'ear.' He turned his attention to his wife. 'Are they treatin' thee well?'

Her cheeks coloured. 'Aye. I'm not complainin'.'

Joe worried at a loose bit of skin on his lip with his teeth. 'I'll wait outside,' he said. 'Gi' thee a bit of husband an' wife time.' The truth was he felt as if the whitewashed walls were closing in on him.

He was glad to get outside, to be *free* to walk out and breathe fresh air whenever it pleased him. He watched a man in a guard's uniform hurry two boys — they looked no more than six or seven years old, but could be stunted youths — towards a horse and cart standing outside the entrance to a small building set apart from all the others. Joe guessed it must be some sort of stores, judging by the sacks the children were being directed to offload and carry inside. They buckled under the weight, stumbling, but made no complaint.

Were these boys prisoners?

Joe had been six years old when his parents were killed in a factory fire. If Seth hadn't taken him on he might have been one of these children, driven to desperation by poverty and locked up. Joe had been lucky. Seth had been sixteen when their parents died, already a working man, and had been able to keep paying the rent on the Barker Pool house by taking a second and then a third job. Joe had started work at eight, fetching and carrying water in a grinding hull, and was bringing in a wage of his own when Seth married, so that despite her protests, Seth's new wife couldn't afford to throw him out. She'd gone herself, running off with the neighbour a couple of years after they were wed. Seth never talked about her and he'd never, as far as Joe knew, been with a girl since. Instead, he told Joe stories their parents had told him, about them being descendants of the Vikings that settled at Crookes Moor, where the reservoirs were, how the family name had altered from Kruk to Crookes. So they were descendants of Viking warriors and the world was their oyster. As a child, Joe had loved hearing that story.

On the train back to town, he asked Polly whether she'd ever seen any child prisoners at Derby, but she wouldn't answer. She was off with him, for the way he had spoken to Tom, the threats, although she must know he was only passing on the gaffer's words. He clung onto the hope she'd ask him home for a bite to eat and another go at it, but they parted ways at the foot of the steps of Victoria station.

There was a way he could soon be back in her bed. 'I'll try an' get the payments to thee weekly from now on.'

'Aye,' she said. 'Do that, or I'll make mesen known to them that wants to bring tha boss down.' Her frightened eyes made a lie of the threat and she looked down. 'I'll see thee soon, I'm sure.'

Joe dragged his heels back to the room he rented on Mowbray Street, creeping up the stairs so as not to alert his landlady. He was unaccountably miserable. He knew it was time to get out of the game he was in. Two more jobs, the gaffer said, that was all. Joe would stop after that, find something else to do, something respectable he could impress Ginny with. He knew without asking that Seth would give it all up when he did.

8

Louisa stood at the window, looking down on the street below. Cold air penetrated the thin pane, fluttering the net curtain against her cheek. The curtain concealed her well enough so that she could gaze freely at her neighbours as they went about their business.

There was Mrs Hindle, emerging from her cottage across the way, locking the door behind her and setting off for her shift at Ward's filers in Kelham Island. Her ample hips swayed as she walked down the hill. Child-bearing hips. *Wide as Wicker Arches*, the late Mr Hindle liked to boast. Mrs Hindle had three surviving children but it could be worse. She'd borne eight, and if they'd all survived she'd have ended up in the workhouse. Louisa watched her until she had disappeared around the corner then switched her attention to a man, a farmer by the look of him, who had hopped down from the cart he was driving to piss in the gutter before moving on. A stooped man in baggy trousers that puddled around his feet stepped over the steaming pile of dung the farmer's horse had left behind.

This old fellow rarely ventured out of the shack he rented but got a free feed twice a week at St Martin's and would be heading there now to get a pie for his dinner. Louisa couldn't remember his name but they'd talked about his youth in what he proudly called *the metropolis of steel*. By the time he'd retired, in the summer of 1842, the town was already meeting half the world's steel needs. *Tha has to be caught young and trained up to it, he'd said, 'cos it's an art, not a science, an' a dangerous art at that. Has tha ever stood over a hole in the ground an' lifted a pot weighing as much as thee that's full to the brim wi' molten metal that'd strip the flesh off thee bones?* Louisa had to admit she hadn't.

A few days ago, he'd thrust at her the pamphlet that had been shoved through his letterbox. Louisa had taken it from him. 'What's this about?'

'It's gone all o'er the town, supportin' that Leng fella that runs the newspaper. He thinks he can put a stop to the unions.' He spat on the ground. 'Well, 'e's got another think comin'. It's offerin' a reward to capture whoever blew up Wheatman's t'other day.'

'I din't get one,' said Louisa, turning it over in her hands.

'Jus tek it, will tha? I don't want that muck in me house. I'll be a union man to me grave. Toffs like Leng don't 'ave a clue about the lives o' workin' men.'

She smiled at the memory, wondering what she had done with the pamphlet. Chucked it on the fire, probably.

Dark grey smoke, tinged with a hellish red, climbed into the sky from the lead mill behind the building at the foot of the road. A while back, when she'd had more energy, Louisa had complained to the smoke inspector about bringing in clothes from the line that were dirtier than when she'd hung them. He'd waxed lyrical about the wildness of the hills and peaks on the doorstep of the town, the pure air she could step into after only a short stroll, finally suggesting she dry her washing indoors, on a rack over the fire like normal folk, and sending her packing.

The sheets she'd just risen from needed washing. Louisa didn't know how long she'd lain in bed. Days, certainly. Ginny had been there, on and off, hovering over her, Jemima Greaves too, wiping her mouth with a cool cloth. And she'd heard the voices of the Crookes brothers, Seth and Joe, floating up from downstairs and also from the street. Seth's raised voice. Keeping the customers at bay. A knot of anxiety rose in her throat. They'd have talked, the four of them.

Finally, she turned away from the window and forced herself to look upon the distressing sight on the crumpled bed, the rags and sheets she had carefully positioned beneath her so that she wouldn't ruin the mattress. Clotted with blood, soaked in gore, fit to throw on the fire. Except that they weren't. They were sweat-soaked but otherwise obscenely clean.

Louisa dropped to her knees and pulled the potty from under the bed, supporting herself on her arms, hair hanging. When the urge to vomit had passed, she sat back on her heels, gradually becoming aware of a sensation in her lower belly she had never felt before, like butterfly wings against glass. She'd been poisoned but had the tansy stopped the life growing in her? She knew, instinctively, what these tiny movements deep in her womb signified. Now she'd need to find the money to pay those people who helped women in her circumstances, who used curling irons and knitting needles to scrape wombs clean.

There was fresh water in the basin on top of the chest of drawers that had been tidied and dusted, no doubt by Jemima, and a clean flannel folded neatly alongside. Louisa splashed water over her face — the chill of it made her gasp — then dried herself with the flannel and sat at her dressing table. Jemima had replaced the lids on her cosmetic pots and lined up her perfume bottles. She could give herself a little colour in her cheeks before facing the world. It might cheer her. But a face clarted in powder and paste was not a clean face and it attracted the worst sort of attention. Louisa kept off the streets but she'd heard of a girl who had been arrested for lingering outside Hillsborough barracks, her red-painted mouth setting the seal on the watchman's suspicions, and hauled away to be checked for the clap. Louisa had heard on the grapevine of girls being tied down like animals if they refused to submit to the doctor's ministrations. Anyway, she had no need of her paint, not today.

She dressed herself and shoved her feet into a pair of slippers she'd received as a gift from one of her gentlemen. Second-hand, for certain, but warm and cosy. Beggars can't be choosers.

Downstairs, in Louisa's little sitting room, Joe sat in the rocker, Ginny on his lap. They were talking in low voices, Joe's hands kneading and bunching the material of Ginny's dress hungrily.

'Ahem,' said Louisa.

Ginny's head whipped round. Her hair had come loose and framed her face like a dark cloud. She smiled archly — 'Look who's up.' — and Louisa guessed immediately that Ginny was under no illusions about her line of work. There'd be no more requests for help in finding work as a seamstress. But there was something else in Ginny's smile, something Louisa couldn't identify. Well, she could mind her own business. Louisa wasn't beholden to her or to anybody else.

'Ey up,' said Jemima, coming in from the lean-to. She was drying her hands on a dishrag. 'I've made thee some soup and there's bread bakin' . . .'

'It smells wonderful, Mrs Greaves,' said Ginny.

'. . . so I'll get off. Make sure me drivers are where

they ought to be. Get the hearse ready for tomorra. It never ends. Fancy a breath o' air, Lou?'

'I . . .'

'Just walk us to the end o' the street, love.'

It was clear she wasn't going to take no for an answer. Louisa looked at Ginny and Joe but they were back in their private little world, Joe murmuring in Ginny's ear, Ginny laughing quietly, her hand over her mouth, all coquettish. Louisa smiled inwardly and took down her jacket. She couldn't decide whether Joe had met his match or Ginny had met hers; either way, they were a match made in heaven, or maybe hell.

She and Jemima walked a few yards in silence. 'That wind's sharp,' she said, eventually. Jemima didn't reply but she took Louisa's hand when they reached the corner.

'Wait a minute, love,' she said.

Louisa kept her eyes on the pavement where potato peelings and other leftovers, scraps blown out of a pigsty or tossed out of a window, circled lazily on an eddy of wind.

'Louisa.' Jemima squeezed her hand and she finally met her gaze. 'Listen, I've not told 'em what's the matter wi' thee, alright?' She waited for Louisa's nod. 'But it's come to light, love . . . how tha's makin' tha livin'. I'll hold my peace, except to say I'm lookin' for help and I can offer thee a job, a respectable job,' she paused, 'if tha'll take it. Get away from this lark.'

A lump rose in Louisa's throat. She looked down again so that Jemima wouldn't see the tears in her eyes and gently extracted her hand. 'I thank thee, but if it's a maid tha's after me lungs aren't . . .'

'No, no. It's not physical work. Help wi' the business, is what I mean. God knows, I could use a reliable hand. I'll teach thee the ropes. That other one, the one lettin' Joe Crookes put his hands all over 'er . . .'

'Ginny.'

'Aye, her. She asked me if I've got a job goin' for 'er. She's not backwards at comin' for'ard is she?'

Louisa laughed. 'She's not.'

'Anyhow, it set me thinkin'.' She patted Louisa's arm. 'I'll say no more for now. Think on it.'

'Aye, I will.' She didn't have room to think about anything except the predicament she was in. And it wouldn't do to get her hopes up, about anything, let alone a job she knew she'd be useless at. 'Bye, love.'

'Bye, Lou. I mean it. Just think on it.'

Louisa watched her walk briskly away then turned back to her cottage.

Joe emerged onto the street and set off in the opposite direction. Louisa hurried to catch up with him.

'Oy! Joe!'

He turned and held up his hands in surrender. 'I never told Ginny about thee. She worked it out for hersen.'

'Tha dropped enough hints,' said Louisa, but her heart wasn't in a scolding. Joe wasn't to blame for this. 'Where tha off to?'

'Am goin' down Owlerton, to the gaffer's place. He's 'aving a meetin'. Compulsory attendance for all union men an' supporters. Why don't the pair o' thee meet us after, me an' Seth?'

'The Royal George? It's the other end o' town.'

'Up to thee.' He shrugged. 'Ginny's keen. In fact, it were 'er idea.'

Inside, Ginny was fastening the ribbon of her bonnet. Louisa saw she'd been into her bedroom and dipped into her pots of cosmetics; she'd coloured her cheeks and lips and there were specks of pale pink powder in her hairline.

'Tha can't go out lookin' like a china doll,' said Louisa. 'Rub it in a bit, at least.'

Ginny lifted her chin. She reminded Louisa of a petulant child. 'Why didn't you tell me?'

Louisa shook her head. 'Why would I? It's none of tha business.' She sighed. 'Look, I've not the patience for this. Go home to your boy, Ginny, an' leave me be. Av got stuff to think about.'

Ginny's expression softened. 'I'm sorry. I feel foolish about it, that's all. I'm too innocent for these townie ways.'

Louisa raised an eyebrow. 'There's nowt innocent about thee.'

Ginny laughed. 'Come on, let's go and meet Seth and Joe.' She rubbed the heels of her hands against her cheeks. 'I'm only wearing this to show Joe I can be a help to him, instead of you.'

'Help wi' what?' Louisa frowned. 'What's tha got theesen into? An' how am I involved in . . . whatever tha's on about?'

Ginny's eyes flashed with a mixture of mirth and excitement. 'Joe's a soldier for the union cause. So's Seth, though you wouldn't think it would you? He's such a mouse. But they're on the right side, Lou, on the side of the common man against the masters.'

'Joe's been pourin' honey in thee ears, I see.'

'Don't look at me like that. I'm not judging you, but I could, couldn't I? What would Harriet and Silas have to say about this?' Ginny gestured towards the stairs. 'They won't hear it from me.' Then she took Louisa's hand, as Jemima had only minutes earlier, and gave her a pleading look. 'I'm going to prove my loyalty to Joe, but I have a loyalty to Silas, too. He's Peter's brother, after all. Isaac's uncle.'

Louisa shook her head. 'What does Silas 'av to do wi' it?'

'He's getting rattened. I've already warned him about it.' Ginny bit her lip. 'In four days. On the new moon.'

Louisa pulled her hand free and stepped back, away from Ginny, as if she could distance herself from her own rising sense of foreboding. 'What's tha on about now?'

'Silas doesn't know it's Joe. I've not told him that. I've just said I overhead it, in a public inn. It's true I did overhear it, from Joe. Wait, wait. Listen. He was here with Seth while you were poorly in bed, and I listened in. I hid on the stairs.'

'Tha's told Silas tha were in an ale house?'

'Yes.' Ginny coloured. 'He's forbidden me from going in one again. But what he doesn't know can't hurt him, can it?'

'Aye, but I'll be the one havin' to answer to Silas for that.' Louisa shook her head. She'd allowed Ginny to distract her. 'Hang on. Joe is doin' Silas's factory?'

'Don't fret, Lou. I've told Silas to keep the lamps burning, tie the dog up outside the hull, make some noise, and Joe'll stay clear. He won't risk it. Will he?'

Louisa ignored Ginny's question. 'Does Joe know you know?'

Ginny smiled craftily. 'No. You see, I can keep a secret, even from Joe.'

'Tha doesn't get it.' Louisa paced the room. She felt the ever-present nausea slosh in her gut and clenched her teeth. 'It won't be like that.'

'What do you mean?'

'I know Silas better than thee. He'll want to catch 'em in the act.'

9

William Broadhead, secretary of the Saw Grinders' Union, treasurer of the United Kingdom of Great Britain and Ireland's Alliance of Organised Trades, and proprietor of the Royal George public house, stood framed in the early evening light coming through the window behind him and declared that the commission of inquiry into the outrages — outrages he had no part in, but a good deal of sympathy for — would, ultimately, advance the union cause.

Joe and Seth had slipped into the room and taken up positions on either side of the door, their only view the backs of the men who stood facing their union leader. Joe could hear the gaffer clear enough; the man's gravelly voice always raised a tickle in Joe's throat. He coughed and earned a glare from the man standing in front of him. Joe shrugged with a smile and the man turned back to face the front of the room.

The gaffer's arm extended above the heads of the men. He was waving a sheet of paper.

'We struggle against the enmity stirred up by pamphlets such as these,' William Broadhead said, 'that talk about the unhappiness of living under a system of terror. Yes, there is disgust, regret, consternation and alarm over the acts that have been perpetrated in our name, but our cause . . .'

Joe stopped listening to him. He'd heard it all before, anyhow. He could hear the occasional raised voice from downstairs — the bar was directly beneath this room. Most of these men would adjourn for an ale or two before sloping off home; all money in the gaffer's pocket.

After the meeting, Joe remained in place as the men filed past. Seth made a drinking motion with his hand as he left the room and Joe nodded. He wondered fleetingly whether Ginny had persuaded Louisa to make the trek through town.

The gaffer was deep in conversation with a man Joe didn't recognise so he hung back and waited his turn. The gaffer finally indicated that Joe should come forward, patting the other man's arm to signify he was now dismissed. The man ducked his head at Joe and left the room.

'Mr Broadhead,' said Joe.

'What's doing, Joe?' The gaffer rubbed his hands together. 'Do you know that gentleman I was just speaking with?'

'No.' Joe shrugged.

'He's a police-detective who has been most supportive,' said the gaffer. 'Most supportive.'

Joe pasted a suitably impressed look on his face. The gaffer strode across the bare floorboards to a bureau in the corner — it was the only piece of furniture in the room — and unlocked a drawer. He drew out a gun. 'Dispose of this afterwards, if you would. Are we all set?'

'Aye.' Joe took the gun, checked it, and stuffed it in his pocket. 'Grinder in three nights, print-works night after. Seth's got the powder, an' we've got a lookout for the Change Alley job.'

'I hope he'll exercise discretion, as you brothers have always done, Joe.'

'It's a lass,' said Joe, 'a good lass I can count on.'

The gaffer nodded quickly and walked Joe to the door. 'Well, the less I know about the detail the better, eh?'

* * *

Downstairs, the drinking lounge was gloomy, the wall and table lamps yet to be lit by the staff who were busy serving thirsty customers. Joe spotted Seth at the counter and was satisfied to see Ginny and Louisa already with his brother.

He joined them, taking a gulp from the ale Seth handed to him.

'Christ, I were thirsty enough but what's the gaffer puttin' in this?'

'Still safer to drink than the watta,' said Seth.

Ginny leaned into Joe and he put his arm around her waist. She rested her head on his shoulder. He raised his eyebrows when Louisa gave him a withering look.

'Don't play the innocent,' Louisa said, and turned to Seth. 'I thought thee at least would have more sense. Ginny's told me. I know the sort o' business the pair o' thee are involved in. It's nowt to do wi' me but don't involve Ginny in it.' She stopped and put her hand to her mouth, her eyes watering, and Joe thought for a moment she was going to be sick all over herself. Silly woman. Two silly women.

He peeled Ginny away and glared at her. 'It were for me to ask Lou to 'elp out, not thee. I told thee to keep thee gob . . . wait a minute, what's tha got on thee face? Tha's painted up like a harlot.'

'Keep it down,' said Seth. He walked a few steps away. 'Snug's empty. Come on.'

Joe took hold of Ginny's chin. 'I don't want thee endin' up like 'er so there'll be no more o' this. It's for tarts and toffs. Tha makin' a fool o' theesen an' I hope tha's got a good reason for it.'

He marched into the snug, confident they would follow.

Once they were all seated, Ginny made a show of wiping her eyes on the handkerchief Louisa handed her. Seth whistled tunelessly through his teeth and examined the frosted glass panel in the mahogany partition that prevented the other customers from seeing who was inside. Joe tapped his foot on the floor impatiently.

Ginny finally looked at him through tear-filled eyes.

'Don't turn on the waterworks,' he said.

'I just wanted to show you I could do the job as good as Louisa,' she said. 'We're courting, Joe. I'm your woman, not her.'

Louisa laughed. 'There's never been owt between Joe an' me. Is that what's rattled thee? Anyhow, don't include me in tha schemes, Joe Crookes. I've enough on me plate. An' tha'll 'av Silas Hinchcliffe after thee . . .' Joe saw Ginny's eyes widen in fright '. . . if owt happens to this one.' She gestured to Ginny.

Joe started to protest but was cut off by Seth: 'Alright, alright. Calm down and listen. We've been workin' for one o' the unions, Lou. But it's done now, two more jobs an' we're finished. There's to be an inquiry . . .'

'Aye,' said Louisa. 'I've heard o' it, startin' any minute. What'll come out, eh? Who were it, Joe, who shot Linley and made 'im suffer for six months before 'e died? What about that old woman blown up in 'er own bed? Old Bert Williams up in Dore findin' his horse hamstrung in a field?'

Her voice had risen during this tirade. Joe gave her a look he hoped was threatening enough.

It was. Louisa looked away and lowered her voice. 'Never thought tha'd be involved in owt like this, Seth.'

Joe curled his lip. She obviously didn't have the same high opinion of him. 'Findin' thee morals a bit late, love. At least the unions are 'elping men to keep earnin', men that then use their coin to 'elp themselves to thee.'

'Cool it, Joe,' said Seth.

'Don't gi' me that,' said Louisa. 'Ginny, don't get theesen involved, love. I'm tellin' thee for tha own good. Joe's in it for the coin, nowt else.'

Joe laughed and downed his ale. 'She's got me there, Seth. Fetch us another round o' drinks?' He patted Ginny's knee, aware she was simmering quietly away. He didn't want her on the Change Alley job. He needed somebody streetwise, a woman with a steady head on her shoulders, like Louisa. Although this Ginny lass had gumption, he'd grant her that. And, it now occurred to him, if he allowed her in, he'd keep her share of the payout too; they were courting now and whatever she earned belonged to him. A three-way split between Joe, Seth and Ginny meant he'd get the lion's share of the money.

'I'll come wi' thee,' Louisa said, and for a second Joe thought she meant on the job. Ginny dug her fingernails into his thigh. But all Louisa did was get up to follow Seth.

When they'd closed the snug door behind them, Joe leaned forward and nuzzled Ginny's neck. 'I'd 'av thee now if I could.'

She spoke softly, rubbing and squeezing his bicep.

'Joe, what's the other job?'

'Can't tell thee, love.'

'But I could come on that one, too. I could help you.'

'Shush.' He kissed her. 'That's doin' enough. Am glad tha came to me after tha little spyin' session. No secrets between us pair, eh?'

When the others returned, Joe fished in his trouser pocket and produced a sovereign that he spun on the table. He took Ginny's hand, put the coin in her palm and folded her fingers over it.

'Summat for thee,' he said. 'Buy some soap and wash that muck off thee face. Lou can lend thee some more of it, for when a painted harlot's needed.'

'What am I to do?' Ginny asked. Her eyes were shining. Joe caught the look of triumph she gave Louisa.

Louisa sighed. 'Ginny, listen. Does tha want to swing in the air alongside this pair? Just because tha's a woman don't think they won't string a rope around thee neck —'

Joe's patience had run out. He slammed his hand on the table, making them all jump.

'Alright,' he said, straightening his back, 'now I 'av your attention, let's 'av less o' the hysterics. I'll tell thee what's planned for Change Alley an' how we'll be treadin' careful so nob'dy gets hurt an' 'ow this little lady,' he hugged Ginny close to him, 'will do 'er bit for the rightful cause.'

10

The deed was done and Ginny hoped it would be enough to secure her new life in the town.

Joe buttoned up his trousers and told her they would walk to the alehouse in Alma Street. Ginny had no idea where that was in the rabbit warren of narrow streets in the basin of the town. Joe could abandon her and she would not know which way to turn. He never would, though, not now. She hoped she had made sure of that.

They had spent the morning at Seth's, making the best of the lumpy settee while Seth slept upstairs. The brothers had had a late night on the pop, said Joe. 'Seth got a bit too merry and dragged me along to a house o' ill fame in Love Street.' He mock-cowered from her glare. 'I din't do owt, am courtin' thee! Anyhow, don't worry theesen. We've only just got back an' he won't be down for a bit, an' even if he is, he'll soon scarper.'

Joe's breath was stale and his eyes reddened with fatigue but Ginny decided she'd just have to grit her teeth and make the best of it. Harriet had agreed to take Isaac and Ginny didn't know when the next opportunity to spend a whole day in town would come. Today would be the day she would bind Joe to her, and her alone. She was still smarting from the knowledge he'd rather have Louisa on the Change Alley job, and couldn't rid herself of the niggling idea that Joe and Louisa had been closer than either were admitting. It had been a mistake to paint her face like Louisa. Joe had taken her for a common tart, and he could have one of those whenever he wanted. *Had he had Louisa?* Ginny was different. She would make Joe see that. It was time to cement their courtship as solidly as an engagement. In the community she had come from, the act they had just committed was a formal engagement, even if Joe didn't appreciate it.

She'd sat astride his lap on the settee, facing the door behind it, her skirts spread about her. 'As lady-like as owt,' Joe had said. He had bitten and sucked on her neck, just above her collarbone, and she had made a mental note to wear the high-collared blouse for a few days. *Did a Love Street tart have Joe's mark on her body this morning?* He had told her she was the reason he had not yet skipped town. 'Things are hottin' up, love,' he said, fiddling with her stays so he could release her breasts. 'In lots o' different ways.' And when she'd lifted herself up so he could penetrate her, he'd gasped and told her she was his woman now. 'I've bin wantin' this since the first time I clapped eyes on thee.' She had put her arms around him so his head was buried against her and, when the door opened and Seth appeared, flashed her eyes at him to leave. He did.

Now, Joe wanted that drink.

'There's no ale in jail,' he said, and laughed at her horror-stricken face. 'Am jestin'. Stick wi' me, love, an' tha'll go far. I promise thee.'

In the Alma Street alehouse, he sat her in a corner with a gin and orange. 'Back in a bit.'

'I promised Harriet I'd get the omnibus before tea-time,' she said.

'I'll walk thee to the stop,' said Joe, 'don't worry theesen.'

He said that a lot. Ginny sipped the gin. The taste of it reminded her of the ether she'd been given by the doctor when Isaac wouldn't come, a chemical compound her tongue tried to refuse. Joe had gone to another corner of the alehouse where he was talking quietly to two shorter men. Most men were shorter than Joe. It was one of the things she liked about him. Joe was head and shoulders above the rest.

The clerk, Daniel Housley, was tall, too, but in a different way. There was an awkwardness about the clerk that Joe didn't have. Joe had confidence. He was a more dangerous prospect, but Ginny knew she'd never become bored with Joe. Daniel was already boring. She imagined telling Daniel the truth about Louisa. She never would, of course.

But she had not been able to resist, the day before, popping in to the clerk's office to sow a little mischief. Daniel Housley was sitting at his desk, writing names and figures on wage packets. He'd nodded and smiled nervously when Ginny poked her head around the door. 'Lovely morning,' she'd said, and gone on to tell him about her new friends. 'Joe's very handsome. We've begun courting,' she'd said, and then almost as an afterthought, 'and I must say Louisa seems very taken by Seth. He's older of course, more experienced. Ladies like that.' She'd watched Daniel's face fall.

Ginny sipped her gin. It was a bit of fun, that was all. Nothing malicious.

Joe brought her a second drink.

'You look brighter than you did,' she said.

'Aye, I just needed some hair o' the dog that bit me.'

'What were you talking about, to those men? Was

it the job I'm helping you with? Or the other job?' She clasped his hand. 'I wish you'd tell me. We should have no secrets now, you said that yourself. There's nothing I wouldn't do for you, Joe.'

Joe laughed. 'Calm theesen down, love. It's nowt to worry tha pretty head over.' He frowned. 'I could use a word wi' Seth though. Drink up, lass. Let's get back to 'is place.'

'I'd like to see where you live,' said Ginny. She put the gin down, half-finished.

Joe laughed. 'Trust me, tha wouldn't. Come on.'

They encountered Seth as they rounded the corner into Barker Pool. He had his head down and almost collided with the two of them.

'Where's tha goin'?' said Joe. He didn't wait for a reply. 'Listen, av been chattin' to George and Walter an' they say the inquiry'll be startin' soon, like, in a few weeks only.' He looked up and down the street but as far as Ginny could tell none of the passers-by were paying him any attention. 'Our names 'av come up as associates of,' he glanced at Ginny, then continued, 'the gaffer. We might get called up to gi' evidence.'

'I'm aware o' it,' said Seth, mildly.

'They'll get nowt out o' me,' said Joe. 'Or thee. Reight, brother?'

'Aye.' Seth looked past them, towards the bustling market where Ginny had her first taste of cockles. 'Anyhow, av got to dash. See thi later.'

Ginny watched him walk quickly away, soon lost in the throng. 'Where's he going in such a rush?'

Joe shrugged. 'Maybe he's givin' us lovebirds a bit o' room. He's good like that, is our Seth.' He took her by the hand and pulled her towards Seth's cottage. 'While the cat's away . . .'

Inside, he ushered her upstairs ahead of him, reaching past her to push open one of two doors on the landing. There was an armchair piled with clothes and a double bed in disarray. Joe pulled the counterpane that was puddled at the foot of the bed over the crumpled sheets and blankets.

'Is this Seth's?' said Ginny. She wrinkled her nose.

'Well, it's this or the settee again,' said Joe. 'This is the only bed in the 'ouse an' av got me second wind from that ale. Don't look like that, Gin. We've got time before tha needs to go back to tha keepers.' He kissed her throat. 'Who knows when I'll see thi again?'

'Why? What's happening? Joe, tell me what you're up to. I'm worried.'

'Am jokin'.' He laughed. 'Stop naggin' and get o'er here.'

Afterwards, Ginny rested her head on his chest, listening to his heartbeat slow. Her skirts were bunched uncomfortably around her waist and a musky smell rose from the sheets. Joe's breathing slowed and after a few moments he snorted. He'd fallen asleep.

Ginny rose, fastened her blouse and rearranged her dress. Neither of them, she realised, had taken off their boots, such had been their haste. Joe's haste. He lay on the bed, mouth open, snoring away, his manhood exposed. Ginny shook him by the shoulder, afraid Seth would return and find them in his bedroom. Joe grunted and turned away, pulling the quilt with him.

'Joe!'

'Mnh.'

'Joe! We need to get out of here. Come on, get up.'

'Alright, alright.' He sat up on one elbow and pushed his fingers through his hair, yawning widely then blowing her a kiss. He was a handsome brute and he knew it. 'Is tha gonna be one of them wives that nags all't time?'

So he could see them married. Ginny hid her satisfied smile.

They strolled arm in arm to the high street, like any courting couple in love. Joe broke away to speak to a man sitting on the box of an omnibus.

He returned to Ginny and kissed her on the cheek, a courtly gesture that made her smile archly, thinking about the day they had spent together. 'This is goin' to Neepsend. Come tomorra, if tha can.'

'I'll try my best.'

Joe left her with the other passengers waiting to board the carriage. She watched him walk away, turn, and give her a salute before disappearing in the crowd. Ginny smiled at the woman alongside her and gestured to allow her on board first. They were engaged now, she and Joe. She might even be carrying the seed of his child. She'd wrested control of her life from Silas by delivering herself into Joe's hands.

Let her brother-in-law try to stop her now.

11

He needed to piss again.

'It's nerves,' said Seth.

'Shush theesen,' said Joe. 'Nerves o' steel, me.'

It was the night of the new moon. When Joe looked westward, the black sky was filled with pinpricks of light like spilled salt. But in the east, the heavens were obscured by the thick smoke pumping from the Cyclop Works in Savile Street, a metal and brick monster belching out flames and crawling all over with men. The vast manufactory's rolling mills, tilts and forges made up a town within the town and employed many of its inhabitants. Joe had shovelled coal there, one of a bunch of scrawny apprentices trying to keep from under the feet of the smoke-blackened and muscular furnacemen. This was before the gaffer had taken him under his wing. Seth had taken more persuading. He eventually relented on his return to Cammell's after a four-day recuperation from a scalding to find his job had been given away. That was when Seth had come around to the idea that the crimes being committed on behalf of the unions were a necessary evil. Still, Joe retained the suspicion his brother had agreed to partner up only to keep an eye on Joe.

The tenements and factories of Neepsend sat on the north bank of the Don. Neepsend was fast becoming one of the most densely populated parts of the town but two men abroad in the hours before dawn might still be stopped by a suspicious watchman.

Joe was carrying the gun that had been supplied by the gaffer in the right-hand pocket of the oversized wool jacket he wore. Joe was a tall fellow and wondered, when he'd first picked up the coat from the Norfolk Street pawn shop, what sort of giant had been its original owner. Not somebody he'd want to encounter on a dark night like this one.

He could feel the gun's weight against his thigh as they strode over a junction and entered a lane that led back towards the river and the forge on its banks that was their destination. He recalled the last time he had pointed a gun at a man and squeezed the trigger. He dreamed about it still, and wondered if it would ever leave him alone; Linley throwing his head back in laughter at the exact moment the gun went off, the bullet already on its fatal trajectory. But in Joe's dream, he didn't run away — although his mind screamed at him to *move* — instead remaining at the window, rooted to the spot. It was always the same, Joe stuck, unable to move or look away, and the back of Linley's head, a writhing mess of hair and gore, becoming a nest of snakes rushing towards him, blotting out everything else, leaving only the black, the nothingness, of death. Sometimes when he woke from this he'd find himself on his feet, shivering at the side of the bed, his heart hammering.

Joe shook his head. It was a dream only and couldn't hurt him. He needed to focus on the job in hand, that could.

'Tha alright?' said Seth.

'Aye. Got the tools?'

'A'course.'

They slowed their pace as they approached the entrance to the forge. There were no gates. The packed dirt of the road gave directly onto the cobbles of the yard. The brothers strolled past the entrance, casting a glance into the yard to confirm the one- and two-storey buildings that bordered it were in darkness. Joe made a conscious effort to unclench his jaw.

'All the bands,' he said.

'Aye.'

'An' a warnin' shot if we're challenged, just a warnin' then we scarper. I'll fire into the ground or summat.'

A head, thrown back in laughter. A bullet speeding into the back of a skull, then crawling into a brain, the first journey too fast, and the second too slow, for the eye to see.

'Aye,' said Seth.

'Reight. Let's get on wi' it.'

The two men about-turned and walked briskly into the yard, Seth leading the way to the grinding hull he'd scoped out in daylight hours. He gestured for Joe to follow him around to the back of the building. They kept as close to the wall as possible, their breathing harsh and loud to Joe's ears against the velvety silence of the yard. Their boots made no sound on the packed earth at the rear of the building but it was pitch black and, looking down and seeing nothing, Joe experienced a moment of disorientation. He froze when a dog barked, once, twice, sharp reports, like rifle shots. Seth put his hand on the back door to the hull and turned back to Joe, his eyes glittering in his skull.

'Alright, get on wi' it,' Joe said. He came up close behind his brother who had turned his attention to breaking the bolt on the door. It was a rusty apparatus, half falling apart, and blunt force would easily do the job, Seth had reckoned. Seth took off his coat and used it to muffle the sound of metal on metal. Joe winced when the broken hinge hit a stone in the dirt with a dull ring. He glanced back into the deserted yard and the empty road beyond, braced for the blackness to be suddenly pricked by lamplight, for calls of alarm and a dog lunging out of the dark to attach its teeth to his backside. But all was still.

Joe stamped his feet and cupped his hands to blow warm air onto his face. 'Hurry it up.'

His brother was shoving his arms back into his coat. 'We're in.'

Seth pulled a candle from his pocket and struck a lucifer on the sole of his boot to light it. He entered the hull first, holding the candle high. Flickering shadows moved over the deserted troughs. It was as if the hull had come to life. Joe closed the door behind them quickly, anxious no light should escape, and took up position beside Seth, taking the candle from him and holding it aloft.

'What's that?' he said, gesturing to the far end of the room where a faint orange light glowed.

Seth bent over the trough nearest the door. He looked up. 'Nowt. Just embers. Coal stove's at that end, by the front entrance. We're at the back, aren't we? Let me get on wi' it, Joe.'

Seth always carried out the rattenings, disabling the troughs of grinders who had stepped out of line, while it was Joe's job to keep an eye out for trouble, and to act if trouble appeared. With a single punch, he'd broken the jaw of one master who had come to check his wheel late one night, laid the man out flat and given himself and Seth time to escape without being identified. They'd been told to disable only one machine on that occasion. Tonight, however, the gaffer had ordered all the troughs put out. Providing candlelight where it was needed, Joe followed Seth as he worked methodically down the length of the hull, removing from each trough the broad leather strap that connected it to the drum in the back of the room. Once disconnected from the drum, the stone could not turn. It was a simple thing to remove the band without damaging it or the machinery, and put a grinder out of work until he'd negotiated the return of his equipment.

Seth draped the bands around his neck, tucking them into his coat and pulling up his collar.

'Done,' he said. 'Are we tekkin' owt else?'

'No,' said Joe. 'He said just bands. Has tha got them all?'

'Aye. Like I just said.'

'Reight then.' Joe rubbed his hands together. 'Reight then.' He blew out the candle. 'Let's get goin'.'

He'd begun to open the door they'd broken in through when a dog, perhaps the same dog he'd heard earlier, unleashed a volley of barks, muffled, as though the animal had been put inside a building, perhaps to provide a guard. Not this building, fortunately. Joe closed the door and backed into the hull, almost colliding with Seth.

'Watch theesen.'

'Bleedin' animal,' Joe said.

'Did tha see it?'

'Nah. Shush.'

They waited, unmoving, in the dark hull. He considered telling Seth to dump the bands but it would make no difference now, if they were caught. The deed was done and here they stood, a pair of fools. After a few moments, he reached into his pocket and removed the gun, the metal cold and slick in his fingers. The renewed silence was deep, and troubling. He pictured a man, or several men, on the other side of the door, also waiting, also plucking up the courage to move. Would there be men at the door on the opposite side of the hull, the one that opened into the yard?

Or was it just a dog, tied up nearby — or far away; sound travelled peculiarly in the dead of night — and nothing more than that.

If the animal was somewhere in the yard, if it belonged here, then he ought to shut it up. He'd shot enough coneys in his time. A dog wouldn't present any difficulties. Joe cracked the door open, bracing himself for glaring lamplight, angry voices. At the same time, he raised the gun while his other hand found and closed around the sleeve of Seth's coat in the dark. If there were men out there he would fire a warning shot into the sky and they would leg it. His hands were shaking, making the gun tap against the wooden doorframe, as if someone was gently knocking on the door, and he heard Seth gasp, felt his arm jerk, but there was no time to explain it was him knocking on the door, and what would he say anyway? Admit to being so afraid his hands were not obeying him and he could barely draw breath?

The yard was empty. Joe opened the door wider, creating just enough space for the two of them to slip out. The urge to run was overwhelming but he kept hold of Seth's arm and pulled them both against the wall of the hull, staring into the dark. Nothing moved and all he could hear was his own blood pounding in his ears.

'Joe?'

'Aye.' He didn't know why he was unable to propel

himself away from the solid brick at his back, why he felt in greater peril than ever.

'Come on, Joe.'

All they had to do was walk back around the building, across the yard and they'd be out, on the street. Joe imagined himself strolling away, free and clear. 'Alright,' he said. 'I'll follow thee. Tek it steady.' The last thing they needed, so close to making their escape, was to take a tumble over a piece of machinery they'd earlier somehow managed to avoid. 'An' be quiet.'

He drew the night air into his lungs and got moving.

⋆ ⋆ ⋆

Ginny let out a shaky breath.

Her brother-in-law had acted exactly as Louisa had predicted by alerting the police with the idea of catching the ratteners in the act. Now, Silas paced up and down the kitchen floor. She wanted to tell him he'd wear a groove in it shortly but decided it would be wiser to hold her tongue. She should focus on hiding her jubilation, a temporary jubilation, but nevertheless. The police weren't coming.

'They say they're not actin' on a rumour,' said Silas, 'on summat overheard in a beer house, by a girl. They'd come if I paid 'em but why should I, eh?'

Harriet sat tight-lipped in one of two chairs that were placed either side of the hearth. The only illumination in the room came from the dying fire. Daniel Housley was sitting in the other chair. He had made a nervous knot of himself, folded arms akimbo and legs crossed at the knee *and* ankle. Ginny had an urge to go across and untie him.

Silas pointed at her as he strode past her. 'If tha

weren't wi' Louisa when tha goes into town I'd think tha'd got in wi' bad company.' He stopped and cocked his head. 'Thought I 'eard Shandy. Where is she?'

'In with Isaac,' said Ginny. She had put the boy to bed hours ago, leaving Shandy lying alongside him, Isaac's fingers tangled in the dog's pelt.

'Aye,' said Silas, 'they might — might, only — send an investigator once the deed's done but they won't gi' me some manpower now. Sometimes I wonder whose pocket they're in, these people that are s'posed to protect us from thugs an' murderers. If I were one o' the town bigwigs they'd soon send somebody.'

Harriet stood up and put her hand on Silas's arm. 'Be still, Silas.'

He put his arms around her.

'Am sorry I've brought trouble to thee,' he said. 'I never thought these unions'd bother wi' me. Am small fry.'

'They're fighting for a cause,' said Ginny and immediately realised she'd said the wrong thing.

Silas threw up his hands. 'Hell's bells! It's not a cause, it's thuggery!'

Harriet raised her eyes to the ceiling. 'Ginny, you know I support the unions. You've heard me and Silas argue about it often enough. But what these rogues are doing, it ruins people's livelihoods.'

'It does more than that,' said Daniel Housley quietly from his seat by the fire. 'These people who do the dirty work for the union bosses have blood on their hands. I listen to the men when they come to collect their pay, the ones who can't get in the union for some imagined slight and the ones who have to go begging, cap in hand, to get an apprentice approved.'

Ginny glared at him. It was a shame his tongue

wasn't tied up in knots like the rest of him, but it wasn't, sadly, and he continued to speak. 'The net's closing in, though. They're investigating rattenings going back ten years.'

'Who is?' said Silas. He was sitting at the kitchen table now, putting on his boots. Ginny had preferred it when he was pacing the room. Her heart pounded in her chest. She ought never to have warned him. A few disabled grinding machines was a better prospect than violence. There was a dangerous glamour about Joe but Silas was broader in the shoulder and she knew Joe would come off worse if it came to a fist fight.

'The police,' said Daniel.

'Fat lot o' good the police are.'

Harriet took Silas's arm to prevent him fastening his boots. 'Silas, it's too dangerous. What if these ratteners have weapons?'

Had Joe mentioned a gun, when she'd been hiding on the stairs, listening in on his and Seth's conversation, or was that later, when she'd come clean to him and been allowed into his confidence? It had felt unreal, then, like a game they were playing. It didn't now.

Silas shook Harriet's hand off. 'So I'm to sit 'ere an' let 'em ruin the hull? I don't think so, love.'

'Do as Ginny suggests,' said Harriet. 'Get the lights blazing and take Shandy out with you. They'll think twice if they hear a guard dog.'

'Shandy's soft as shite,' said Silas.

'They don't know that,' said Ginny.

'No. Am decided. Dan, come on, let's teach these buggers a lesson. You pair, stay put. Lock this door behind us.'

Daniel Housley got to his feet — he looked afraid, Ginny thought, but determined — and Silas slapped him on the back, almost propelling him across the room.

'We'll catch 'em red-handed an' 'av 'em locked up in the constable's cottage before tha knows it.'

* * *

Joe followed Seth through the yard, his heart racing with a combination of triumph and trepidation. The grinders would turn up in a few hours to discover they'd been rattened. Some were union men, some weren't. Those who paid their subs would turn their anger on those who hadn't. Divide and conquer, and Joe had conquered, that was for sure. They weren't in the clear yet. What if they were set on as soon as they stepped foot into the street? What if there was an ambush? No, it couldn't happen. Only three people knew about this job. Two of them were doing the deed and the third was the gaffer.

Calm theesen down.

They crept past the two-storey brick residence that sat back from the entrance to the yard. He glanced at the building. Window panes that were as black as soot stared back. No lights flickered from within. He felt the heft of the gun in his hand and walked on, resisting an overwhelming urge to run but unable to resist casting another glance back at the dark shape of the hull.

* * *

'Silas wants to send you home,' said Harriet.

Ginny caught her breath. 'Why?'

'Because he thinks you've got yourself involved in something dangerous,' said Harriet. 'Do you really think he believes your little story?'

'Ask Louisa. She was with me, when we heard the union men talking about . . .'

Harriet interrupted her. 'And what were you doing in that place?'

'Louisa sometimes eats a meal in the Saw Makers. She's friendly with the landlady.'

'Oh? What's that lady's name?'

'I forget.' Ginny bit her lip. 'Sister, I have met somebody . . .' She held up her hand to forestall Harriet. '. . . and I've enquired about schooling for Isaac. I know you would hate to see Isaac go. Please speak to Silas on my behalf. I know he can be stubborn but he's such a kind man at heart.'

'He's only thinking of your welfare. Who's this man you've met?'

Ginny could no longer hide her exasperation. 'Silas Hinchcliffe came here from the same place I did. And he was a runaway, too. And he got in trouble before he set going with this place, I've heard all about *that*.'

Harriet's face was set.

Ginny took a deep breath. Harsh words wouldn't help her. She shook her head sadly. 'My worry is for Isaac. Why shouldn't he have a chance to make more of his life than chasing sheep about a hillside? He loves you so much, sister. He loves living in this house with you, in this town.'

Harriet sighed, and in that moment, a gunshot rang out.

They stared wide-eyed at each other. In one fluid motion Ginny turned and unlocked the door and ran outside, leaving Harriet stumbling in her wake.

* * *

It was a stupid mistake.

He'd got ahead of Seth as they exited the yard and gestured with his gun hand for his brother to follow his brisk jog. The sooner they put some distance between themselves and Hal Roger's hull the better. But somehow the gun had gone off as he'd brought it down to stuff it back in his pocket and for an awful moment Joe thought the bullet had struck Seth, and he had frozen, his mind blank with fear. Then Seth was on him, shoving him against the wall, cursing him with a quiet fury. Joe shook him off and they ran along the street.

After a few hundred yards they were brought up short by a figure that ran onto the pavement, blocking their way. Linley's ghost, was Joe's first wild thought. But as they got near he could see it was a woman, crying out incomprehensible words. Seth hopped into the gutter to run past her, not sparing her so much as a glance. The woman ignored him completely but reached out to clutch at Joe's arm. A mad woman, escaped from the asylum. He went to throw a punch, to get her off him, then saw it was Ginny.

'What the devil!' He dropped his arm then grabbed her shoulders, shaking her so hard her hair flew about her face.

'Stop,' she sobbed. Like a fish on a hook, she was struggling to free herself from his grasp. 'I'm sorry, I'm sorry.'

He became aware of pounding feet. Two men emerged from the gateway behind her, one sparing a glance at Seth as he ran around a corner — *at least he was away with the bands* — then running towards

Ginny, *towards him*. It was the lanky clerk, followed by the factory boss, Silas Hinchcliffe. Ginny's brother-in-law.

He cursed, pushing Ginny away and turning to run. But they were on him. He was yanked back by the collar of his coat and almost lost his footing. He roared in fury and swung his arm, his fist connecting satisfyingly with bone. Freed, his knuckles ringing in pain, he staggered forward, and ran.

12

'She got it wrong. It was Hal's place got rattened, but she'd said it would be mine.' Silas scratched his head. 'She reckoned she heard that it'd be me.'

'Aye, she did overhear summat,' said Louisa, carefully. 'She got the wrong end o' the stick, I suppose.'

'They got away wi' it, anyhow. One o' 'em had his hands on Ginny.' Silas laughed, a sudden bark. 'Our Dan got hold o' 'im, tackled 'im. Can tha believe that? The bloke got away from 'im and the poor lad's got a broken nose for his trouble. Brave, though.'

Louisa wondered whether it had been Joe or Seth almost brought down by the plucky wages clerk.

'An' now she reckons she's courtin'. Who's she courtin'? This same fella who had hold of 'er? It seemed they knew each other.' He didn't wait for a response. 'I've a mind to pack 'er off home, except Harriet'd miss Isaac. I'd never 'ear the end o' it.' Silas paused and took a deep breath. 'We've no babbies yet, you see.'

'I know, love. Gi' it time.'

Louisa realised she was pressing her palms down her skirt, over her lower belly, and took her hands away casually, her face burning. Silas was leaning tiredly against the wall by her hearth, examining his nails, and didn't notice. He had turned up early that morning, as soon as it was light, knocking at her door. Louisa had brushed off his apologies and dressed quickly while Silas thanked the neighbour who'd brought him in his cart. He'd got Louisa's address from Ginny, under duress no doubt, and the thought of him arriving at this ramshackle backstreet made her burn with shame. She wished she could unburden herself to Silas but that was impossible. She would be judged, and found wanting. Better to listen to Silas and offer what advice she could and, for now, put her own troubles to one side.

'She's sayin' she won't go back to the farm.' Silas fished in his coat pocket and brought out a crumpled piece of card. 'Don't tell Harriet, but I bought 'er a train ticket an' she won't 'av it.'

Louisa smiled. 'I remember thee arrivin' in town, Silas. Tha'd walked all the way from that same farm.'

'Aye, I know I did, it were my feet that were blistered. Am hardly goin' to forget that.'

'An' look at thee now.'

'It's not the same, Lou. She's a girl wi' no sense about 'er. Head in the clouds.'

'I'd rethink that if I were thee.'

'Come back wi' me this mornin'. Harriet'll be happy to see thee. She's shook up after what 'appened at Hal's place. Could 'av been us, easily could 'av been.' He let out a shuddering sigh. 'They had a gun, an' all. Could've been a lot worse than it were.'

The two friends hailed an omnibus on the busy main street. The air was relatively fresh, stirred by a warm late spring breeze, and as clear as could be for a town stuck all over with chimneys like pins in a cushion. Louisa inhaled deeply, turning her face towards the warmth of the sun. On the bus, she became aware of Silas observing her from the opposite bench.

'Aren't tha hot in that get-up?'

She was wearing the velvet cape Jemima Greaves

had made and gifted to her the previous winter, when snowstorms had laid a clean white coat over the town. She was glad she had not pawned it; the cape was long and, draped over her skirt and petticoats, adequately concealed the sin growing inside her.

'I've not been well,' she said, and suddenly there was a lump in her throat and she had to turn away from Silas's friendly gaze.

'An' I were thinkin' how bonny tha's lookin',' he said.

Louisa gulped and recovered herself. 'That another way o' sayin' I'm gettin' fat, Silas?'

When they arrived at the Hinchcliffe yard, Harriet was standing outside the hull, holding Isaac in her arms so he could feed bits of apple to the two horses hitched to a flatbed wagon. Jagged slabs of sandstone lay jumbled on the cart like rocks on a dry river bed.

Harriet's face lit up when she saw Louisa.

'I hoped Silas would persuade you,' she said, shifting Isaac to her other hip, 'and you'll have some dinner with us?'

'Aye, I will.' Louisa scratched the head of the nearest horse. 'Am famished.'

Isaac eyed her shyly and offered a piece of carrot.

'Thanking ye, but I think I'll wait,' said Louisa.

A door slammed and a few seconds later Ginny walked into the yard. She made a beeline for Louisa and embraced her.

'I'm glad to see you,' she said.

Louisa smiled uncertainly. She wasn't the saviour they all seemed to think she was. She wasn't sure what she was supposed to do.

Silas was chatting to the driver of the cart and two men who'd emerged from the hull.

Harriet put Isaac down and he ran at Silas, reaching up to tug at his belt.

'Ey up, tha'll 'av me britches down!'

Ginny ruffled Isaac's hair. 'He's been wanting to see a new wheel made,' she said, too brightly, 'haven't you, son?'

'This 'as just been delivered from Crookes' quarry,' Silas told Louisa.

'Crookes?' said Ginny.

'Aye.' Silas looked at her, frowning. 'The quarry, up yonder.' He lifted Isaac into his arms and patted one of the blocks of sandstone. 'Want to see a trough bein' made, little man? First, we 'ave to fix the stone. Does this look like a wheel to thee?'

Isaac shook his head.

'Well, just wait an' see. In an hour, two maybe, it'll be transformed.'

Louisa smiled. 'He loves showin' off, does Silas.'

'Oi! Less o' the lip,' said Silas.

Isaac giggled delightedly.

'As I were sayin' before that rude interruption, we drill a hole through the middle so we can get it mounted then we race it. Ever notice how a grinder allus has a wet shirt? That's because watta is kept in't trough that the wheel runs through, an' it splashes up. Trough's made o' metal like . . . a bit like the bath tha mother washes thee in.' He tickled Isaac's chest. 'Watta everywhere. But we don't use watta when we shape the stone — we do it dry — an' that makes more dust than tha's ever seen in thee life.'

'Can I be a grinder?' said Isaac.

'Aye, I'll gi' thee thirty shillin's a week, how's that?'

'Is that how much grinders earn?' said Ginny.

Silas nodded. 'I wun't recommend it.'

'I can hardly find employment as a grinder's apprentice.'

'I were thinkin' o' Isaac. It's not woman's work. It might pay well but it's tough. If lung disease doesn't get thee a shattered wheel might. Or gunpowder put in thee trough by a union man.'

On that parting shot, Silas walked away with Isaac in his arms.

'Don't clart him in dust,' said Ginny weakly.

'Get theesen inside,' Silas called back over his shoulder. 'Harriet, she's not to leave the 'ouse, not for owt.'

'Tha's under 'ouse arrest, then?' said Louisa.

Ginny grimaced. 'He can't lock me up forever.'

Harriet took Louisa's arm. 'Let's take a turn around the garden. There's a meat pudding in the oven. Ginny, can you go and check on it?'

Louisa caught the pleading look Ginny gave her before she returned to the house and only now remembered that the Crookes brothers were out again tonight, causing mischief. It would be better for Ginny if she was prevented from seeing Joe, tonight or ever again.

Shandy was zigzagging up and down the garden, nose glued to the ground.

'Hunting down a scent,' said Harriet.

The dog perked her ears and ran over, barking joyfully at Louisa. She crouched to fondle Shandy's ears. 'Who's a good lass then?'

'I know a lass who's not,' said Harriet, in an uncharacteristically gruff voice.

Louisa straightened. 'Ginny's a bit reckless but she's a good girl at heart. An' Silas might be narked wi' 'er but he'll come round. He knows 'ow much tha loves Isaac. I can't see 'im sendin' the pair o' them away.'

'That's kind, Lou, but I know he's bought their train ticket and he's not allowing her out, not even to see you. Oh, you should have heard her this morning after he'd left. He's forcing her back to a prison, to be a slave to his folks, then servant to whoever takes it on once they're dead and gone and it passes to Silas.' Harriet threw up her hands. 'Or Silas sells it — which he might well do, to make more investment in this place — and she's homeless and destitute, and knocking on our door anyway. So, she says, why not just let her stay?'

'She's as stubborn as 'er brother-in-law.'

'I'm exhausted.' Harriet gave her a sharp glance. 'Who's this man she reckons she's engaged to? What sort of a father would he be to poor Isaac?'

Louisa felt the weight of her shame resettle on her shoulders. The seed in her might have been started by a wealthy gentleman or a humble worker; she had no idea. Her child, like Isaac, would never meet their true father. Unlike Isaac, born to his father's widow, they'd never even know who it was and have the label of bastard attached to them. This was a train of thought she didn't want to pursue. The tansy hadn't worked but there were other methods.

'Louisa? Do you know him? This Joe? He sounds like a rogue.'

Louisa laughed. 'Ginny can look after hersen, tha knows. And who can resist a rogue, eh?'

'We can. Thank you for confirming that he is unsuitable.' Harriet folded her lips together. There would be no more discussion.

The kitchen was warm and smelled of cooked pastry. Ginny stood over the stove, stirring a pan of gravy. Harriet asked Louisa if she'd mind fetching Daniel

Housley over to have his dinner with them. 'Or ask him if he'd like something brought out to him. It's wages day and he may want to work on.'

Louisa crossed the yard and opened the door to the clerk's cottage to find Daniel Housley bent over his desk, his nose almost touching the sheet of paper on which he seemed to be totting up figures. He held up one finger without looking up and Louisa gently closed the door behind her, and waited. It was cosy in the cottage with a little fire blazing in the hearth, a world apart from the noise and pumping smoke of the factory next door.

Light from the desk lamp cast a warm glow on the clerk's face when he looked up enquiringly. His blackened eyes widened when he saw Louisa standing there and he jerked in surprise, knocking over a bottle of ink.

'Oh dear!' said Louisa. 'I din't mean to startle thee. Am sorry.'

'No, no, please, it's my fault, I'm so clumsy. A clumsy fool.' He knelt on the rug, righted the ink pot and patted ineffectually at the spreading black stain. 'Well.' He rolled up the rug and stood it on end against the wall. 'A chore for later.'

He ran a hand through his hair, leaving a streak of black ink on his forehead and succeeding in knocking off the spectacles that had been perched on his head.

Louisa caught them before they hit the stone floor. 'Here.' She laughed. 'Am sorry, I'm not laughin' at thee.' On an impulse, she laid her palm against the side of his face. 'Poor love. Silas told me what tha did. That were brave o' thee.'

He was staring at her and she dropped her hand, suddenly self-conscious. He touched his cheek where her hand had been.

Louisa broke the awkward silence. ‘Harriet said tha’d be busy. She asked to see whether tha’d be comin’ over for dinner or . . .’ she trailed off.

He seemed to come to himself and cleared his throat. ‘I’m very pleased to see you again, Miss Leigh. I hope you are well?’

‘I’m alright, Mr Housley.’ Harriet had said he was a bit intense, this fellow. He was still staring at her. She cast about for something to say. ‘That looks sore.’

‘It is, and I still have a terrible headache but I think my pride is hurt the most. I’m always brighter for seeing you, Miss Leigh.’

‘Aye, well, dinner’s gettin’ cold.’

‘Yes, yes, I’ll come with you. And please call me Daniel, Dan. Call me Dan.’

‘An’ tha can call me Miss Leigh,’ she said.

‘Oh. Indeed I shall.’

Louisa laughed. ‘I’m havin’ thee on. I’m Lou.’

‘Ah.’ He laughed, nervously. ‘Allow me.’ He reached beyond her to open the door and Louisa stepped outside, raising the hood of her cape. A light rain had begun to fall.

‘An early summer shower! How unexpected.’ He cleared his throat. ‘Well, I’ll just lock up. One moment.’

He disappeared inside, returning with an umbrella which he raised and handed to Louisa. She watched him fumble with the keys. Then he dropped them into his pocket, took the umbrella from Louisa and held out his arm for her to take.

‘I feel like am promenadin’ in the park,’ she said, ‘in me fancy cape.’

‘It’s a lovely cape.’ He cleared his throat again, a nervous tic. ‘You should always wear just that shade of blue.' He was stammering now. 'I'm sorry, I'm being presumptuous.'

'Presump away.'

He touched the bump on his nose and Louisa wondered whether he'd had that already or if it was a result of being punched.

'Tha should watch thee step, love,' she said. 'Don't go rushin' in where angels fear to tread.'

'I'm grateful for your concern.' He coughed again. 'Louisa, I should like to take you promenading, on a sunnier and warmer day than this.'

'Those days are comin',' said Louisa. She couldn't even contemplate the prospect of high summer. Contemplating the following day was difficult enough. 'Though to be honest wi' thee, Dan, av never really got the point o' walkin' unless tha's got somewhere to be.'

'Oh.' He laughed. 'Yes, I can see your point. Ginny tells me you work as a seamstress.'

Louisa had been enjoying ribbing Daniel Housley, and had briefly forgotten about her own problems, but now her heart plunged.

'Does she,' she said flatly.

They reached the steps leading to the front door.

'Ladies first,' said Daniel Housley, and Louisa forced a smile and climbed the steps on legs that were suddenly heavy as lead.

13

It was late afternoon by the time Louisa got back into town. She deliberately missed her stop, remaining in her seat as the omnibus swayed down Burgess Street towards Union Square. She was trying not to think about the errand ahead of her and instead focused on her encounter with Daniel Housley. She knew he was attracted to her, and could allow that she liked him back. If her circumstances were different . . . but it wasn't wise to wish for a different life. It was tricky enough getting through this one.

From Union Square, she faced an uphill slog of a walk home. She hoped this little excursion would be worth it.

She'd seen the advertisement in one of the newspapers Harriet took. Louisa could read but she was slow — having to reveal the full extent of her illiteracy was one of the many reasons she would not accept Jemima Greaves' job offer — but the illustration of a respectable but miserable-looking woman with both hands resting on her belly had told her everything she needed to know. 'Is this an address?' she'd asked Ginny, taking advantage of a moment when they were alone together in Harriet's kitchen. She'd run her finger along the elaborately penned text at the foot of the advertisement.

Ginny, as she'd guessed, was so wrapped up in her own misfortune she didn't question Louisa at all. 'Barber's Chemist,' she said, squinting at the text.

'Number nineteen, Union Street. Lou, what am I to do about tonight? I'm minded to sneak away once Isaac is asleep.'

'No,' Louisa had told her, 'just leave 'em to it.'

'But Joe needs me.'

'He'll just 'av to manage wi'out thee. Tha's in enough bother as it is.'

Then Harriet had returned from her trip to the grocer's, with Isaac in tow, cradling a jar of black-currant jam as if he'd found the treasure at the end of the rainbow, and Louisa had put her hand over the newspaper advertisement, ignoring the inquisitive glance Ginny gave her.

Barber's Chemist was inscribed above a glazed door that stood between two large plate glass windows. These were crammed with bottles of all shapes and sizes and containing potions and powders in every colour of the rainbow. Stoppered porcelain jars decorated in fancy calligraphy Louisa couldn't interpret fought for space on the shelves. She opened the door carefully, wincing when the bell jangled, afraid of bringing the whole fragile edifice down. The back wall of the shop was dominated by a walnut-coloured bureau of drawers. Open shelf space above the drawers featured more glass bottles full of potions and powders. To the right, chairs had been arranged around a small round table. To the left, a glass-fronted counter ran the length of the shop, a large brass weighing scale in the centre of it.

A cleanshaven man with neatly combed hair so dark that it must have been augmented with boot polish stood behind it.

'Can I help you, miss?' he said politely.

Louisa cleared her throat but before she could

speak the bell jangled again and a well-dressed woman entered. The man straightened his back. 'Mrs Needham. It's a pleasure to see you. Won't you take a seat?'

He came out from behind the counter and guided the woman, who looked more than capable of getting there herself, into one of the chairs. 'One moment, please, Mrs Needham. I shan't keep you waiting.'

He turned back to Louisa, raising his eyebrows.

'Av come about the advert,' she said, glancing at the woman, who was gazing out of the window. 'The one about women's predicaments.' She swallowed. The man was still giving her an enquiring look. 'Am in one.' She hadn't meant to snap at him but at least it got him moving.

He hurried out from behind the counter. 'Come with me,' he said.

He lifted aside a brown wool curtain she hadn't noticed in the corner of the room. There was a small landing behind it with a door on one side and a staircase leading down into darkness on the other. There wasn't much room once he'd dropped the curtain behind them and she was stifled by the man's proximity, his stertorous breath in her ear. He nodded at the door. Louisa twisted the knob and opened the door into a pleasant if sparsely furnished sitting room. She released a shaky breath. She wasn't sure what she'd expected, a butcher's slab perhaps, a tray of sharp instruments and a basket of rags for afterwards. In reality, there was a teal-coloured chaise longue in front of a colourfully tiled fireplace. A round pot filled with violets sat on the mantelpiece. The grate was empty, the room cold but richly carpeted.

'Take a seat,' he said, and left her there, closing the

door behind her.

Louisa went to the window instead. The shop was on street level but the ground fell away behind the building so that she found herself looking down on a spacious yard with a raised bed of vegetables beside the wooden shack that held the privies. She rested her hands on the window ledge and wondered whether she would be asked to taste any of the potions from the glass bottles, and how much it might cost her. She'd have to make sure to get the prices before agreeing on any treatment.

A knock on the door startled her. A woman Louisa thought must be about her own age entered. She wore an apron over her skirt and a high-necked blouse. Her mouth was stretched in a reassuring smile.

'Good afternoon, dear,' she said. 'I'm Milly Barber. Father tells me you're here because you read our advertisement in the newspaper?'

'Aye,' said Louisa. Her tongue felt thick in her throat and she couldn't continue. The young woman seemed to recognise this and guided her to sit on the chaise longue.

'How far along are you?'

'I don't know, a few months?'

'Have you quickened?'

'I don't know.' She wanted to wail at her own ignorance. 'I think I 'av. I've felt summat, just lately.' She shrugged. 'Somethin' movin'.'

'May I?' Milly sat beside Louisa. Her hand was reassuringly warm and firm in Louisa's. 'My mother can help you. Were you sent here?'

Louisa was puzzled by the question. She shook her head.

'You weren't directed to us?'

'Like I told thee, I saw tha advertisement.'

Louisa drew in her breath when Milly pressed her other hand against Louisa's belly. 'You're small, still. Does the father know?'

'No.'

'Please excuse me. I don't mean to offend. It's only that sometimes we experience . . . difficulties . . . and it helps to know a little of the circumstances.'

'Only a friend o' me mother knows.'

'Not your mother herself, then?'

'She's dead.'

'I'm sorry.' Milly squeezed her hand and Louisa bit her lip. She wouldn't cry, not in front of a stranger.

'How's it . . . what d'you do, to get rid?' she said.

'We'll get to that. It's very safe. My mother's done many of these. She even has married ladies who come back to see her.'

'More than once?'

'Oh, you'd be surprised. One lady has eleven children and can't manage any more. We've helped her twice.'

'Twice.'

'There's no cause to feel shame.'

Louisa let out a shuddering breath. 'Do you do it now?'

'No, no, you'll have to make an appointment. My mother is out today, anyway. Let's see, come back next Wednesday, around this same time? You'll need to allow yourself a few days afterwards, to recover.'

'Alright.'

'And you'll need to bring the full payment with you, and a bit extra for pain-killing medication.'

'Tha can prob'ly see I 'aven't much money.' Louisa looked away, her humiliation complete. 'If tha could see thee way to showin' me a kindness.'

Milly squeezed her hand again. 'It's not up to me. I'm sorry. It's a costly business, in all sorts of ways.'

''ow much?'

'Ten pounds, twelve if you need a course of medicine.'

Louisa detached her hand gently and stood up.

'I'll 'av to think on it.'

'Of course. You know where we are.'

Mr Barber was alone in the shop, standing with his back to her and grinding a pestle into a mortar on the bureau. He turned his head and nodded curtly to Louisa as she let herself out.

Little wonder tha can afford so much glass. She carefully closed the door behind her.

* * *

The walk home was every bit as draining as she'd expected. When she turned the corner onto her terrace, Joe was standing on her doorstep, scuffing his boots on the kerb edge.

'Where's tha been all day?' he said.

''Ow do to thee, an' all.'

He stood so close to her, while she found her keys and unlocked the door, that his breath whistled in her ear. He smelled of onions and beer. She shuddered, she couldn't help it, and he snickered. 'How much for a quick 'un?'

'Shut up, Joe.'

He followed her into the house.

'Where's Seth?' she said.

Joe shook his head impatiently. 'Makin' the pipe for tonight. We've both on us been up all night. I want to know, Lou, what went on. Has tha seen Ginny? I should tan that girl's hide for 'er.'

'I'll put the kettle on.'

Joe wouldn't stop following her around. He jogged her arm, trod on her skirt when she knelt to light the stove, elbowed her in the side when she got to her feet.

'Joe, tha gettin' in me way.' She was afraid to push him away, afraid of what he might do in his present wound-up state.

She flinched when he touched her hair, finding a blonde curl and pulling it. Keeping her voice steady, she finally asked, 'Joe, what's up?'

He spoke slowly, deliberately, into her face. 'I want to know — from thee — how it came about that she were on the street last night, lyin' in wait for me.'

Determined not to show her fear, she spoke in the lightly unconcerned voice she used for clients. 'Sit down, will tha? I'm sick o' bumpin' into thee. I'll tell thee, alright?'

When she'd finished, Joe sat back and rubbed his hands over his face.

'It's a sorry tale but it's the truth,' Louisa said. 'She were tryin' to protect her brother-in-law as well as thee an' she made a mess on it.'

'Wait 'til I get me 'ands on 'er. She on 'er way 'ere? She'd better be.'

'No, 'course not. Silas is keeping a beady eye on 'er now, so there'll be no . . .'

'What?' Joe leaned forward and grasped Louisa's wrist. 'I need 'er for tonight. This job . . .'

'Tha still doin' it?'

'Why not? We 'aven't got caught. It's the last job, an' all, for me an' Seth, an' I need this last payout. Gaffer's callin' it a day. He thinks all 'is birthdays are comin' at once wi' this inquiry.'

He turned her wrist, this way and that, so that her hand flopped over and back and over again on the table. 'Lou . . .'

'No.' His fingers were hard and cold. 'Let go.'

'There's five sovereigns in it for thee.' He finally relinquished her wrist. 'I know tha needs the coin.'

She looked at him sharply, wondering if he had guessed her predicament. But he was gesturing around the room. 'Times are hard, Lou. Tha can do a lot wi' five sovereigns. How many bottles o' gin will that buy thee?'

'Make it ten an' I'll consider it.'

Joe tipped back his head and laughed. 'All tha doin' is comin' for a walk before the sun rises. It'll tek an hour, at most. Ten sovereign for that? Don't joke wi' me.'

The abortionist wanted ten pounds. If she did as Joe asked, she'd have half the funds required and could go with her begging cap to Jemima Greaves for the rest, despite her earlier refusal of the other woman's help. Jemima would understand Louisa's change of heart. She needed to get it over and done with. She'd go down to the barracks where pickings were rich and work all hours, do anything that was required, despite the risks, until she had paid Jemima back. She got up, to buy some thinking time, and took the teapot into the lean-to, opening the back door to throw the dregs into the yard. If she had a garden like Harriet's she'd sprinkle the leaves on the soil to enrich it. As it was, they spattered onto the always-damp clay, wasted.

She heard Joe come into the little kitchen and turned around. 'Alright, then. I'll do it.'

His grin was wolf-like.

'Our lovely Lou. I knew tha wun't let me down. Just wrap theesen up warm and wait for the knock.' He rubbed his hands together. 'We'll tek a gentle stroll, me an' thee an' Seth, from 'ere to Change Alley and back.'

Part Two

14

June 1st 1867

Darkness. Scuffling noises and heavy breathing. Her arm clamped in a blacksmith's vice.

Louisa gasped and opened her eyes. She was being dragged along the pavement, her feet scuffing and bumping on the cobbles, between two men. Hugged close around the waist to the body of one of the men, her arm was raised uncomfortably, flung across his shoulders, her fingers crushed in his. The man on her other side was squeezing her upper arm so forcefully he was practically lifting her off the ground. It took all her strength to lift her chin, and she glimpsed smoke stacks against a lightening sky, but the action made her dizzy and she dropped her head again.

Two pairs of boots, marching her along, slinging her about as if she was an animal carcase. She tried to find her feet, but the men holding her were moving too quickly. She gave up scrabbling and went limp again. She'd killed a man, and had fainted, and been caught. She wished for the oblivion of unconsciousness again but her mind was clearing, a mental torture as vicious as the vice on her arm. She recalled the watchman's blood escaping from his crumpled body and her collapse into a blessed oblivion against the unyielding cold of a wall. If there was an afterlife, and she'd soon be finding *that* out thanks to the hangman's noose, he'd haunt her for the remainder of her short life, a black shadow filling her prison cell, and he'd watch while she swung. If only she could succumb to oblivion but the pain of being dragged along between these uncaring brutes was too much to bear.

Louisa tried again to find her feet.

'Ey up,' said one. 'We've got a live 'un.'

'Reight. Stop. I need a rest,' said the other.

She was lowered to the ground, her back propped against a wall. The back of her head hit the brick and she cried out.

'Shush theesen.'

Now there were footsteps approaching and a third, authoritative-sounding voice. Another man. 'What the devil is going on here?'

'Nowt much,' said the first voice she had heard. She recognised it now and was dizzied again by the conflicting emotions of relief and revulsion. 'It's me sister, wi' a bellyful o' ale in 'er.'

'But that's disgraceful! You should take better care of her.'

'Aye, well, tha can get theesen to buggery.'

The footsteps receded, quickly.

Louisa peered up at Joe and Seth, one brother glowering and the other with a concerned frown on his face. 'Gi' me a minute. I can walk.'

Joe, hands on hips, stared after the man now hurrying away from them. 'I 'ope he dun't put two an' two together. Get up, Lou. We've got no time for the faintin' female act.'

Seth held out his hand for Louisa to take and pulled her to her feet. He peered into her face. 'Joe's reight for once. Let's get goin'.'

Louisa secured her shawl more tightly around her head and it was then that she noticed it, a smell that reminded her of the taste of pennies. In the growing light, she could see black stains around her fingernails. The watchman's blood, from his hand and his beard, smeared on her. She stumbled forward and Seth caught her in his arms.

Joe rolled his eyes. 'Bleedin' ell. This is what 'appens when tha brings a lass along.' He spat on the pavement.

'Give over, Joe. It were tha idea in the first place,' said Seth. 'Come on, Lou. Let's get thee 'ome.'

'An' get our stories straight,' said Joe.

In Louisa's cottage, Seth brewed tea and Joe paced about, briefly sitting in the rocker before getting up to pace the small room again. Louisa climbed the stairs to wash her hands in the basin. The water she used to scrub the watchman's blood off was clap cold and her hands were red and raw afterwards, reminding her of when she was a maid and dry skin was her biggest bugbear. Harriet had purchased cream for her, once, from the chemist, to soothe her hands. She wondered if the cream had come from Barber's chemist shop.

Louisa sat on the edge of her bed, lost in contemplation of her life before and how the great flood of 1864 had changed its course. She'd been grateful, at first, to have survived a dam burst that killed hundreds along the Loxley valley, although it left her with weakened lungs, unable to work. That was when the downward slide had begun. Surely, now, she had reached the bottom. She put her hand on her belly, pressed her fingers against the hard rounding. She did have further to slide, right into the noose. She could plead pregnancy. This sin she was planning to erase might end up saving her. She smiled bitterly to herself. Once sentenced, she'd be permitted to go to term and have her baby, then she'd hang for her crime alongside Joe and Seth and maybe their gaffer too. Odious company. But now, she was no better.

Downstairs, Joe and Seth were sitting at the table, heads together over steaming cups of tea, conversing in urgent voices. The enormity of what had happened in Change Alley hit Louisa again. She could barely believe she'd thrown in her lot with this feckless pair.

'I should never 'av agreed to take Ginny's place,' she muttered.

Joe looked up. She was shocked to see how bloodless his face was, as if it was Joe who'd had the life drained out of him. 'It's done now,' he said. 'Gaffer needs to know what 'appened quick-sharp. He's got friends in 'igh places that'll see us fair if the bobbies catch up wi' us.'

'We could scarper,' said Seth. 'I'm sick to death o' this place anyhow.'

'Aye, so tha keeps on sayin'.' Joe leaned back in his chair. 'We sit tight. Nob'dy can connect us to it, if we all keep our gobs shut.' He pointed at Seth, then at Louisa. 'It's me, thee, thou an' Ginny.'

'An' the gaffer,' said Seth.

Joe shrugged. 'He's 'ardly goin' to say owt, is he?'

Louisa looked from one brother to the other. 'There's a man dead,' she said. 'Thanks to that pipe.' She shook her head. 'I saw him, comin' towards me an' then I were worried he'd turn an' turn again an' that's what he must've done, gone into Change Alley and been outside the shop right when it blew.' She stared into the fire and shuddered. 'I could've warned 'im.'

'An' said what?' said Joe. 'Ey up, love, I'd turn round an' leg it if I were thee. Joe Crookes is blowin' up a print-works just up yonder. Keep it to theesen, mind.'

'I saw 'im an' all,' Seth muttered. 'An' I said nowt. I hid in a doorway an' let 'im walk reight past me.'

'Don't thee grow a conscience an' all.' Joe pointed an accusing finger. 'Get a hold o' theesen, brother.'

'Think Ginny'd see thee as such a good prospect now, Joe?' said Louisa.

'Av done worse,' he said, turning her way, 'an got away wi' it. Ginny knows which side her bread's buttered.'

Louisa got up to poke the coals, shaking her head, disgusted with him and with herself. She didn't think she'd ever shift the dismay that squatted in the pit of her stomach, taking away her appetite. For the first time in months, she wasn't famished. She wondered whether the night watchman had a family, a wife and gaggle of kids expecting him home at dawn with no reason to fear he wouldn't be.

'What Joe's tryin' to say in 'is cack-handed way is that it's done an' all we can do now is protect oursens,' said Seth. 'We're safe enough.'

'What about that porter, the one I spoke to?' asked Louisa. ''e saw me.'

''e saw a harlot hangin' round his fancy hotel,' said Joe. 'That's all 'e saw.'

'There were folk standin' round the . . . round the body . . . and I were reight there wi' em . . .'

Joe interrupted her. 'Doin' what?'

'Tha sent me, don't forget.' Louisa gulped past the knot in her throat. 'I stayed wi' 'im for a bit.'

'Why would tha do that?' said Seth.

'I were holdin' his 'and.' She closed her eyes briefly but he was there, behind her closed lids, his hand wrapped around the stake in his chest.

Joe laughed loudly and humourlessly. 'I've 'eard it all now.'

Seth stood up. 'Reight, Joe. Over to mine. We say that's where we were all night. Keep it simple. Lou, tha were 'ere in thee bed all neet, an' alone. Tha can blame that dicky tummy o' thine.'

She nodded wearily.

'We'll convene 'ere at teatime,' said Joe, 'after I've bin to see the gaffer. Let's get our 'eads down. Get some shuteye. Lie low for a couple o' days.'

Louisa locked the door behind them and sat in her rocker under a blanket, too numb to feel the cold. She'd put some coal in the stove in a minute and make porridge. The coal scuttle on the hearth was full of the good stuff, not the coke she bought by the bag from the pit scavengers. Seth had filled it from his coal cellar and not asked for payment.

She thought about the bearded man, recalling how he'd been whistling a tune she didn't recognise, strolling through town on patrol, and, later, staring in disbelief at the stake protruding from his chest. He was young, for a watchman, so probably working two jobs, supporting a family. She didn't even know his name.

A life snuffed out, just like that, and here was she, wasting hers. A sense of deep shame overcame her. A gin would help, but she remembered the bottle was empty and she couldn't afford another until she'd had her five sovereigns from Joe, and even then the money was spoken for. Louisa shifted her weight in the chair and felt movement, a flutter, deep inside.

There was a way she could atone. No more gin; she could do that much. Experience the guilt with a clear head. It was no more than the night watchman was owed. She'd never touch a drop of alcohol again.

15

Two weeks had passed since the newspapers reported the murder of a night watchman in Change Alley and Ginny was as tightly wound as a steel spring.

She stabbed a needle into the seat of the small pair of trousers she was repairing. They were Isaac's first pair of proper breeches and he should count himself lucky; many boys didn't get into trousers until they were twice his age. The breeches were also the first item of brand-new clothing purchased for him, rather than being homemade. And what had he done on first wearing? Fallen out of a tree and ripped a hole in the seat on the way down.

Ginny pricked her finger with the needle and sucked the blood away, tears of frustration in her eyes.

'Young boys will always get into mischief,' said Harriet, who was sitting across from her in the parlour, also engaged in needlework.

Ginny wiped her eyes and clenched her teeth. She was afraid she would lose control of herself completely, start to sob and scream hysterically, and not even Harriet would believe it had anything to do with this silly pair of breeches.

The waiting was the worst.

Every time a wagon or carriage rattled onto the premises, or she heard voices raised in the yard, Ginny was at the door or window, breathless with hope. She had even succeeded in putting the dog into a state of permanent alarm; Shandy's alertness had become paranoia and Harriet frequently complained of her barking day and night. Ginny couldn't tell her the dog had simply caught on to her mood. Instead, she shouted at the collie. Shandy just barked right back at her.

'We haven't seen Louisa for a while,' said Harriet as if she had read Ginny's mind. 'I hadn't thought of it until just now. I suppose because we've been so busy here.' She tilted her head, enquiringly. 'I wonder why she hasn't called? Do you think something has happened?'

'No, no. I imagine she's been busy herself, sewing summer frocks for the fine ladies of the town.' Ginny bent to her needlework then looked up sharply as if the idea had just occurred to her. 'Why don't I call on her? I can take a posy of flowers from the garden, and we have peas to spare.'

'That's a lovely idea. I'll come with you.'

'Oh, that would be nice but I was going to ask you to watch Isaac.'

'Isaac can come too.'

Ginny wracked her brain. 'It's a long trip for a little one.'

'To Barker Pool? It's a couple of miles, and it's such a lovely day. If I can walk it, I'm sure Isaac can manage it.'

To hell with it. 'I really would rather go alone. I'm out of sorts and need to clear my head.'

Harriet pursed her lips. 'Ginny, I don't want you flying off the handle but . . .'

Ginny sprang to her feet. 'I'm not going to see him! He's probably forgotten me after all this time.'

Harriet looked up at her calmly. 'Two weeks? If this Joe can forget you after two weeks then he's not really worth the trouble, is he?'

'Why is he always *this* Joe? You'll never give him a chance, will you?' Ginny glared out of the window into the yard. Losing her temper would do her no good at all. She focused on the sound of metal on metal from the blacksmith's forge, on the rushing noise of water being fed round the wheel — it sounded like crackling fire in her ears. It was no good. Joe's voice was in her head, his narrow brown eyes and rakish smile all she could see. She needed to have him bestow that smile on her again, and more. She couldn't bear the thought that the night of the attack on the neighbour's factory might turn out to be their final encounter.

And Louisa. Louisa must hate her. That could be the only reason for her staying away so long.

She rubbed her temples.

'Silas has told me he intends to write to his parents,' said Harriet gently, 'and explain to them you wish to remain here, with us, and that we are willing to look after you and Isaac, but that they will be given the final say.'

Ginny snorted. 'I know what that will be. Oh, it's hopeless.' She threw Isaac's breeches onto the chair she'd been sitting in.

'Where are you going?'

'To see my son. Where else could I be going? Oh!'

Silas was leaning on the doorframe, grinning at the two women. His shirtsleeves were rolled up, the buttons on his shirt unfastened halfway down his chest and there was so much dust in his hair he looked old before his time.

'Silas, you look a fright,' said Harriet, laughing.

'I thought we were goin' over to see Dan, get the accounts sorted?' he said.

'Yes, I'd forgotten.' Harriet put down her needlework and rose to her feet, flicking her hands down the front of her dress. 'The dust gets everywhere and this room is the worst for it, and you're bringing in even more with you.'

Silas kissed her cheek.

'Don't make me dusty too!'

Their affection for each other only reinforced Ginny's belief that she was being unfairly prevented from pursuing her own love.

'What's up wi' thee?' said Silas. 'Today's a good day. We've taken on four new grinders an' two apprentices. Business is boomin'. An', madam, they're all union approved. So tha can tell tha new friends . . .'

'. . . I would if I could . . .'

'. . . we don't want any trouble 'ere. Especially after the latest ruckus.' He shook dust from his hair. 'Did tha overhear owt about Change Alley in that beer house tha frequents, love?'

'Don't tease,' said Harriet.

'Am deadly serious, love. Ginny, listen 'ere. Tha stays out o' town until we decide what's best. Tha won't see thee fancy man again and that's that. Tha's got that boy to raise,' he pointed upstairs, 'so think on that.'

Ginny took a deep breath. She could no longer contain the fury building in her. 'Silas Hinchcliffe, you're not the one being told how to live your life, are you? Write that letter, buy more of your stupid train tickets and be damned!'

She pounded up the stairs towards the room she shared with Isaac, terrified Silas would come after her. She'd lost her temper, after all, after endless days of holding her tongue. Her relatives would be keeping a closer eye on her than ever. Louisa had abandoned her. Joe had rejected her. She slammed the bedroom door behind her. She could imagine the scene below, Harriet trying to placate Silas, Silas determined to see Ginny off.

She squeezed her hands into fists, digging her nails in hard enough to break the skin. She wouldn't wait to be sent away like a cow to the slaughterhouse. The time had come to take matters into her own hands.

16

William Broadhead was holding court, as usual.

Joe sat in the tap room of Alvey's in Harvest Lane with five other men, all known to him, all of whom were to take the stand, and all of whom had committed violent acts on the gaffer's say-so. An extraordinary meeting of the committee of the saw-makers' union was due to take place later, over at Broadhead's pub in Owlerton. Most trade union secretaries kept a public house and hurriedly called meetings were being convened in pubs across the town by the unions that represented brick makers, fork grinders, ironworkers, scissor forgers and all the rest.

Heated verbal exchanges frequently spilled out onto the streets and Joe couldn't walk around a bend in the road without stumbling upon a fresh outbreak of fisticuffs.

'I don't presume to tell you what to say when you're called upon,' said the gaffer. 'Just remember rattening has always gone on in the trades, well before my time, and it will still go on, whatever the outcome of this inquiry. It's rough justice but it's justice nevertheless and everybody in the town knows it. I'm quite prepared to make a clean breast of it.' He paused. 'As to the more serious charges laid at our door, we can now admit them freely and escape any unfortunate consequences.'

The so-called Outrages were the talk of the town, and Joe was sick of it.

The gaffer had explained that more than two hundred acts of violence, a handful of confessions and a few convictions formed the basis for the special commission of inquiry that had commenced on the first Monday in June. Victims and the perpetrators of a decade's worth of crime were compelled to answer whatever questions were put to them, or be thrown in jail. To loosen tongues, a further and controversial rule was applied via an act of parliament — all witnesses would be given full immunity from prosecution, whatever atrocity they had committed.

'Aye,' said one of the men, interrupting the gaffer in full flow. 'If tha can believe a word that comes out o' the mouths o' politicians.'

Chairing the inquiry was the same man who had presided over compensation payments for victims of the great flood of 1864, William Overend, a Queen's Counsel and a local man.

Joe had gone along with the gaffer at eleven o'clock on that sunny Monday morning to see the QC welcomed into the crowded council chamber of the town hall to thunderous applause from masters and men alike. The wages clerk who had been on the receiving end of Joe's fist had been there, standing only a few feet away in the public gallery. This was the fool who had dared to manhandle Joe and got less than he deserved, which was a knife in the ribs. Joe had locked eyes with the clerk — who stared back, apparently unruffled — and it was Joe who was forced to turn away, to pay attention to something the gaffer was telling him. When he looked back, the clerk had gone.

He took a long swallow of his ale. If he ever came across that stringy streak of . . .

The gaffer nudged him. 'Joe here heard what was said, didn't you, Joe?'

'It's not a witch hunt,' Joe mumbled obediently.

'Indeed not. Although Mr Overend did call for the truth to be told candidly, however explosive it might be.'

William Broadhead paused here, then said: 'The first three witnesses to be called were two scissor grinders and a director of a steel works. They all duly lit the fuse.'

One of the names on that list of witnesses was Joe Crookes; he was mightily aggrieved that Seth's name was not.

Joe had committed his last outrage when he laid the bomb in Change Alley. He realised suddenly that this man was no longer his gaffer and he wasn't required to sit here, in a backstreet alehouse, and listen to him pontificate.

'I don't think I'll 'ang around to give evidence,' he said. 'Think I'll hoof it. Who fancies America, lads?'

William Broadhead looked at Joe but didn't speak. One of the other men said: 'Tha's on that list because somebody's dobbed thee in. If tha refuses to give evidence, they'll chase thee down and chuck thee inside, an' tha'll get tried for thee crimes. It's not tiddlywinks we're playin' 'ere.'

Another man added: 'Tha'll not reach America. Tha might end up crossin' an ocean, though. On a transport to Australia.'

Joe laughed. 'I'll stand thee a pint o' porter for tellin' that joke.'

The gaffer held up his hand. 'Every witness who incriminates themselves will be given a certificate that indemnifies them against prosecution.'

The man sitting beside Joe shook his head. 'Is it enough though? Putty Barton can't find work after admittin' he cut them bellows belonging to Joshua Dungworth, even though it were two year since.'

The gaffer stood up. 'I'm merely telling you what I intend to do. We've already been named. There's no shame, just remember that. Now, I must return home. I have a meeting to prepare for.'

Joe got to his feet. 'Can I 'ave a private word?'

The gaffer nodded and Joe followed him out. They walked down the road to where a curricle and horse stood waiting.

'What about that final job?' said Joe.

'What about it?'

'Can we admit to that, an' all, an' get away wi' another murder?'

'Shush, Joe.' William Broadhead looked up and down the street. 'We won't be questioned about that. It's not in the inquiry's remit. They'd need to build a case, find witnesses, as they have with the other . . . incidents.' He peered into Joe's face. 'Don't go blurting anything out, Joe. The consequences for you would be grave. Answer only the questions you're asked. But answer truthfully. Do you understand?'

'Aye,' said Joe. 'Me an' Seth an' the girl . . .'

'I don't want to hear about any girl. I told you, no details. It was your job.'

'Carried out for thee.'

'Well, I'm satisfied, if that helps. My contacts tell me the police have no leads. That poor young man was simply in the wrong place at the wrong time.' He put on his topper and got into the curricle. 'We shan't see each other again, Joe.'

He tipped his hat and started his horse. Joe stood in

the road, his arms hanging by his sides, and watched him ride away.

Seth wasn't at home. Joe knocked on the door, tried it again — unsurprisingly, still locked — and peered through the window into the gloomy interior. He walked along the terrace and pushed down on the handle of Louisa's door, which gratifyingly gave way. He strode in to find Seth, Louisa and another woman, her back to him, sitting round a table filled with empty plates. For an instant, he thought the second woman must be Ginny and was taken aback by his sense of elation. He'd thought he'd be furious after her betrayal of him but the truth was that he missed her. He couldn't prevent a foolish smile from spreading across his face.

But it wasn't Ginny. The smile dropped from his face. It was Jemima Greaves.

'Din't save me any tea?' he said.

'Just walk in like tha owns the place, why don't tha,' said Louisa.

Both his brother and Jemima Greaves wore grim expressions that Joe decided to ignore.

'I'll tell thee what, Seth,' he said, pulling out a chair and sitting down, legs splayed. 'I've just been wi' the gaffer an' it's good news for thee. Tha's not been named by any o' the witnesses, so far, but I 'av. I'm to admit to the lot. I'll 'ave a lynch mob after me!'

'Maybe tha's had tha day bein' cock o' the yard,' said Seth.

'Easy for thee to say. I can't understand why I've been called an' tha's not. We've allus done everythin' together, me an' thee.'

'What about me then?' said Louisa. 'The girl at Change Alley.'

Joe couldn't keep the startled expression off his face. He nodded towards Jemima Greaves.

'She knows,' said Louisa. 'I told her.'

Joe gaped.

Jemima broke the silence. 'I already knew. I was given some information an' I thought fair warnin' might be required. Louisa and Seth have been tellin' me everything. I don't know how you could do it, Joe, to this poor lass.'

'Do what?' Joe glared at her but a cold feeling invaded his chest. 'Av done nowt.'

'Tha's put this girl's life in danger wi' thee silly antics. It'll be the noose for all three o' thee if tha's caught, and Ginny'll go to jail for her part in it too.'

Joe loosened his collar. 'Well, if tha must know, I've got friends in 'igh places who've just told me the trail's gone cold.'

'Maybe their information's wrong,' said Jemima.

Joe waggled his hand at her dismissively. 'We keep our gobs shut,' he shot meaningful looks at Seth and Louisa, 'and nowt will come o' it. Lou, tha really needs to go an' see Ginny an' make sure she's keepin' quiet.'

'Don't thee order me about, Joe. I've 'ad enough o' thee.' Louisa said. 'Jemima came to tell us she's 'eard summat. It's about me, not thee. Tha should go an' see Ginny. Silas'll 'av thee guts for garters.' She put her hand over her mouth and her eyes filled with tears.

'A police-detective will be callin' on Louisa,' said Jemima. 'He reckons she was seen leavin' here wi' two men in the early hours of that mornin'.'

Joe made a scoffing sound. 'They can't rely on some drunkard who's prob'ly seein' elves and goblins hoppin' about in the night an' all.'

Jemima glanced at Louisa, then looked back at Joe. 'That's more or less what I said. But this weren't somebody in 'is cups. This were a furnaceman comin' off his shift early wi' a gash in his arm, an' cutting through 'ere to get to the infirmary. He knows her by name and by reputation.' She reached to touch Louisa's hand. 'Am sorry, love.'

Joe blew air out of his cheeks. 'Reight, so it'll be 'is word against thine, Lou.'

'What's my word worth?' Louisa smiled bitterly.

'I don't care about either o' thee,' said Jemima, looking from Joe to Seth.

Seth nodded his acknowledgement.

'Feelin's mutual,' said Joe.

'She's to say she stopped at mine that night. She's comin' to work for me, I were showin' her the ropes that night an' it got too late for 'er to get home safely.'

Joe rubbed the dark stubble on his chin. 'Reight then. It's simple enough. All tha has to do, Lou, is keep thee nerve.'

17

The tapping of the knocker-upper on her neighbour's window woke Louisa. She hadn't been in a deep sleep — she wouldn't have heard the stick hitting the glass if she had been. The woman who went from house to house rousing the workers charged sixpence per client and had started using a pole when she realised that, by banging on the front door, she was knocking up other workers who used her for their alarm but weren't paying for the privilege.

The steel worker next door started his shift at seven, so it must be around six in the morning. Louisa rolled away from the light filtering through the net curtain, intending to snatch another hour of restless sleep, but a burning sensation welled predictably in her throat and she struggled into a sitting position then held herself still, taking shallow breaths, the quilt puddled around the waist of her flannel nightgown.

She was waiting for a knock of her own to come. It had been four days since Jemima Greaves had warned her to expect a call from a police-detective. Louisa hardly dared hope that Joe was right, that the trail had gone cold. All the talk now was of the confessions being made, on an almost daily basis, to the judge presiding over the inquiry into the outrages. Not even a travelling circus could compete with the entertainment being laid on at the town hall. The building couldn't hold the number of people wanting a ringside seat. Jemima Greaves had told her there was more scandal being revealed in that dusty council chamber than could be found in the most salacious penny dreadful.

She was wringing out a bedsheet to hang in the warm breeze blowing through the backyard when the dreaded knock finally came. Three heavy raps on the front door. Louisa's heart lurched. She dropped the sheet in the tub and dried her hands on her apron as she walked slowly from the lean-to and through her front room, her heart shrivelled by an overwhelming sense of futility, as if she was already walking to the gallows. It was hopeless. How could she lie to a detective when she knew her eyes, her face, her whole body would betray her? She was not that good an actress.

She inserted the key in the door with shaking fingers and opened it slowly, ignoring an urgent instinct to run, to hide herself away. If only she could shrink to the size of a mouse and disappear into the wall. She envied mice, or any dumb creature. She would not be allowed to remain dumb.

Joe stood on the pavement, his brows drawn together in an impatient frown, Seth alongside him.

'What took thee so long?' said Joe, shouldering past her.

Seth grimaced sympathetically. 'No bobbies turned up yet?'

Louisa took a deep breath, trying to calm her racing heart. 'Tha shouldn't be 'ere,' she said. 'What if he turns up now, an' decides he'll tek an interest in the pair o' thee? I were seen wi' two men, and here's two men makin' themselves comfy.'

Joe sat at the table. 'Not unusual in tha line of work, though, eh? Men hangin' about?'

'Give over,' said Seth. 'Summat smells good, Lou.'

Louisa sighed. 'Stew.'

She closed the door behind them and locked it.

'We were goin' to the Blue Pig for us dinner but stew'd fit the bill,' said Joe. 'I were wonderin', Lou, if tha's seen owt o' Ginny yet? I've a mind to call on her meesen, or send our Seth 'ere.'

Seth rolled his eyes and Louisa guessed Joe had already broached this idea and been given short shrift.

Joe continued, 'It weren't 'er fault, Lou, that tha's ended up wi' all this on thee plate.'

'An' the rest,' she said quietly. 'I know that, Joe Crookes. Am blamin' thee.'

Joe shrugged. 'Fair enough.'

'Am just not in the mood to put on a glad face for Harriet an' Silas an' pretend all's well, when it's not. It's wearin' me out.'

Seth clapped his hands together. 'Tell thee what, me an' Joe'll nip out an' get us a fresh loaf o' bread an' some cakes an' a few bottles o' ale if we're sharin' tha stew. Let's forget about our woes for a bit, eh?'

Louisa was surprised to find herself cheered by this idea. She locked the door behind them and moved her rocker to the window. If a police-inspector called, she would run upstairs. She could count on the brothers to make themselves scarce if they got wind of a bobby in the area.

They were back in no time. Seth ladled out dishes of stew and they shared their flood stories. Louisa learned that Joe and Seth had been on higher ground the night Dale Dyke exploded — they didn't explain why they were still abroad at midnight but Louisa caught the warning glance Seth gave Joe and could guess they were up to no good — and had heard the great wave as it crashed invisibly through the valley beneath. 'I thought the world were endin',' said Joe. Louisa told them about working as a maid in the household Harriet ran for her uncle and aunt, about being caught by the great wave and almost drowning, and how she still suffered the effects of it. And how Harriet's cousin, poor little Alice, was one of the hundreds who had perished. 'Alice was only six,' she said. 'And Ginny's brother-in-law, Silas Hinchcliffe, he'd only arrived in town the afternoon before it burst, from the same farm as Ginny. No more than a kid, he was.'

Joe pricked up his ears. 'There's a farm?'

'Aye, but it belongs to Silas's folks, not Ginny.'

'She's got a boy, though,' said Joe.

Louisa shook her head. 'It'll go to Silas an' he's not taken kindly to thee, Joe.'

''e would if he met me,' said Joe.

She laughed. 'Tha's a hoper, I'll gi' thee that.'

The brothers departed in the early afternoon. Joe — bolstered by ale — proclaimed he would go to Ginny *here an' now an' make sure she's not spillin' her guts* and Seth gave Louisa a resigned look and raised his eyes heavenwards.

She leaned against the doorframe as the brothers walked away, closing her eyes to enjoy the comforting warmth of the light on her face, listening to the distant sound of carriages rattling down the main street and the calls of street hawkers. She felt a flutter low in her abdomen, a reminder of her plight, and squeezed her eyes shut more tightly.

'Miss Leigh?' said a deep, male voice.

Louisa gasped and opened her eyes to find a man standing in front of her.

'Miss Louisa Leigh?'

His face was framed by bushy mutton-chops and his eyes drooped at the corners, as if they had lost their fight with gravity. He wore a double-breasted jacket, matching brown-coloured cravat and topper like any gentleman caller, but Louisa realised immediately who this must be, despite the absence of a uniform. He carried a cape over his arm, the sort of cape a watchman might wear on a spring night as he patrolled the high street, on a regular nightly route that took him past the spire of St Peter's and St Paul's and down to the marketplace, whistling a tune under his breath while his feet marched him towards his death.

He repeated himself, more loudly this time. 'Miss Leigh?'

She recovered herself. 'Aye.'

The blood roared in her ears so that she didn't hear, or in her panic, immediately forgot, his name. The man explained he was investigating a manslaughter that had taken place in Change Alley. Or perhaps he had said murder. Louisa's name had come up in relation to the investigation. He had smiled at her encouragingly.

'We have to pursue all lines of enquiry.'

'Aye, I understand thee,' she said. 'Tha'd better come in.'

He peered past her but remained where he was. 'I thought perhaps you'd accompany me to my office at the town hall, if you are at liberty to do so now?'

This wasn't a request. Louisa nodded. 'I'll just get me key.'

'Lock up nice and tight. You can't be too careful, especially around here.'

They walked in silence through the streets, the

detective occasionally hailing a passer-by cheerily. Every time he did, Louisa quailed inside. What would the neighbours think, witnessing her in the company of a police-detective? They would think that she had been arrested for prostitution, that she was diseased and being taken for examination by a doctor, and that she would be locked in a cell for a few days, until the space was needed for another criminal. Before she was thrown back on the street, a chaplain might visit and she'd be given a bible and advised to mend her ways. It would be preferable to this.

The town hall sat near the top of a steep road with Lady's Bridge at the bottom of it. How would it be to take off down this road, Louisa thought, as the officer stood aside to allow her to enter the building first, to run across the bridge and leave the town behind, take her chances on the open road. She might get as far as Ecclesfield village. But if this stout fellow caught her, if he surprised her with an unexpected fleetness of foot, it would set the seal on her guilt. She stepped inside, barely noticing the knots of people crowding the foyer. Uniformed policemen milled around and her detective — she now thought of him as 'hers', she realised — acknowledged each of them with a grave nod or a smile, depending on rank.

The basement of the town hall contained the cells where prisoners were held before transportation to the assizes in Leeds or York. Louisa had an appointment to keep later, at Barber's chemists. Would she be free to attend or locked in a damp cell? She wiped sweat from her forehead with shaking fingers. She'd forgotten her alibi. She knew she would tell the truth if the detective asked her a direct question, she had no doubt of it. Or she'd be struck mute, and he would know her guilt from her silence. She heard Jemima's voice in her head. *Calm theesen. He's watchin' thee like a hawk*.

She lowered her gaze as they exited the foyer, focusing only on putting one foot in front of the other. The detective put his hand on her elbow to direct her down a wood-panelled corridor, the chatter becoming fainter, and into an office, closing the door behind her. Louisa's ears whined in the sudden silence. There was a desk with two neat stacks of paperwork on either side. *Damning confessions, no doubt*. Jemima's voice in her head again. Don't add yours to the pile. It helped, somehow, to imagine Jemima's reaction to her plight. The detective sat in the chair behind the desk and drew a fresh piece of paper from a drawer, then blotted his pen before holding it, poised, over the blank sheet. *He won't ask thee to sit. Sit down anyway. Remember, tha's done nowt wrong*. But she had. She had.

Louisa sat in the chair, facing him. He looked at her and smiled.

'Shall we begin, Miss Leigh? Terrible business, isn't it?'

'Aye, I 'eard of it.'

She swallowed and held her hands still in her lap. Her mind was racing, still trying and failing to locate the story she had so carefully practised. The cells were beneath her feet; she wondered how many were occupied and how cold and lonely those prisoners must be. She might join their ranks today. She felt a stutter in her heart and an answering flutter from her lower belly, reminding her again of the desperation of her situation.

'You'll be aware of our investigation into the tragic events that transpired in Change Alley.' He gave her a kind look and now her heart leapt. He would not bestow such a look on her unless he believed her innocent. Would he? 'You were abroad that night, I'm told.'

Tha were at Greaves' hansom cab and funeral hearse establishment. Tha'd been learnin' the ropes for tha new job and it got too late to go 'ome safely.

'I were at a friend's house, stayin' the night,' she said. She twisted her hands in her lap. *Ask him why he's so interested in tha whereabouts that night?* 'Am I being accused o' summat? Or might I 'av seen summat and not realised it?' *Shut up, Lou!* That was Joe's voice.

'Are you sure you have the correct night? The night you stayed at your friend's home?'

He'd ignored her babble. Her face burned. 'Aye.'

He scribbled a note on the paper, then looked up at her expectantly.

'Aye,' she repeated. 'Am sure.'

'It's only that, had you been abroad that night and gone to the area around the King's Head on business that we are most certainly *not* here to discuss,' he paused, 'you might have been a witness to something that you are afraid of disclosing, fearing the consequences to a woman in your, what shall we call it, your trade?'

Louisa flinched. 'Am tellin' thee the truth.'

'The witness I'm speaking of, he's a godly man to all intents. But he knows you by name and occupation, so to speak. How might that be?'

Louisa shrugged. 'How should I know if tha's not tellin' me 'is name? P'raps he bears me a grudge, me bein' a fallen woman.' She twisted her hands together. Calm down.

‘Something you freely admit.’ He scribbled on the paper. ‘You’ll be aware, no doubt, I have the power to detain you under the contagious diseases act . . .’

‘I’m clean.’ Tears sprang to her eyes.

‘I’m sorry I cannot spare your blushes.’ He fished in his trouser pocket and handed over a handkerchief. Louisa blew her nose into it, furious with him, with herself. ‘You’ll also be aware that I can arrest you, based on the confession you have just made before me, and you might find yourself sentenced to a month’s hard labour. You know that it is an offence for a woman to sell herself.’

‘I were at me friend’s place,’ Louisa said slowly. ‘So I can’t ’av been near the King’s Head, could I?’

He sighed and put down his pen and patted the pockets of his jacket, bringing out a curved-handled pipe, tamping tobacco into the bowl and lighting it, puffing into the stem then sitting back and rubbing his hand over his mutton chops. He was enjoying himself at her expense.

‘Still, you’ve admitted it, committing illegal acts.’

‘I’m sure the gentlemen that call are aware o’ that, an’ all,’ she said. ‘Some o’ them that call are the same ones that write these laws into bein’.’

‘You’re a clever girl.’ He put down his pipe and picked up his pen. ‘And you are correct. I am interested solely in that particular night, and your whereabouts on it.’

‘Like I said, I were at a friend’s, learnin’ all about the layout o’ the town, and bookin’ drivers an’ findin’ out which customers need special attention and which’re poor payers, an’ who gets credit and who dun’t. And funeral hearse hire, an’ all. It’s Jemima Greaves’ cab business I’m joinin’. It’s legitimate.’

'Ah, yes,' the detective smiled again, as if they were passing the time of day in a coffeehouse. 'A formidable lady. I've made her acquaintance. Mrs Greaves was most sympathetic when I organised my dear mother's funeral.'

'It's a small world.'

'Well.' He rapped both knuckles on the desk, startling her, then got to his feet and Louisa did the same, trusting her legs would hold her up. 'Thank you for your time, Miss Leigh. I'll probably call on you again, in the next few days. I hope that won't be too much of an imposition.'

'Not at all.' She decided against asking what type of call he'd be making.

He walked her to the town hall entrance, his hand cupping her elbow. Once outside, Louisa nodded to him and walked briskly away, up the hill towards home, the skin on her back prickling with the certain knowledge he would continue to watch her until she was out of sight. She turned the corner, approaching the end of Change Alley, keeping her eyes averted.

A chill ran down her spine. She knew that if she looked down that road, towards the splintered façade of the print-works, she would see him, a bloody sacrifice sitting in the folds of his cape, his hand outstretched, his knowledge of her guilt written in his eyes.

18

Ginny dropped the bowl of peas onto the grass and her hands flew to her throat. A figure had appeared on the other side of the trellis, half concealed by the climbing plants.

Joe stuck his head around the frame. 'Ey up, love.'

She gasped, at once elated and afraid. The last time she had seen Joe he had been furious with her, had shaken her so that her teeth rattled. But here he was, grinning at her, and nodding a greeting to Isaac who had run up from the bottom of the garden with the dog, skidding to a halt and sticking his thumb in his mouth. The boy regarded Joe solemnly. Ginny told him to say hello to Joe but he just continued to suck his thumb.

'Gerroff me,' Joe said, pushing Shandy down. He brushed his trousers. 'Bleedin' dog's makin' a reight mess o' me.'

Ginny moved towards him, to touch him, to confirm he was really standing before her, but was halted by Isaac, who wrapped his arms around her skirt and almost toppled her. Joe reached out to take her elbows. 'Steady on.'

Isaac said: 'Mam, you dropped the peas.'

Joe laughed. 'Tha looks flummoxed.'

'Well, I am!' She shook her head in disbelief. 'I've been waiting, for you or Louisa, to come. It's been hell. Oh! If Silas finds . . .'

'Av been waiting an' all, behind that wall,' he

gestured over his shoulder with his thumb, 'an' my patience 'as finally paid off. They've just gone out, both o' em.'

'Yes, they've gone to look at new premises, on Kelham Island.'

'On shanks' pony.'

Ginny squinted at him. 'Yes, Harriet did mention it would be nice to go for a stroll in the sunshine.'

'Mam, you dropped the peas,' Isaac repeated more forcefully.

'Pick them up then! Here.' She bent to retrieve the bowl and shoved it into Isaac's hands. She straightened, sweeping her hair back with both hands, then folding her arms over the old, stained blouse she wore to do the gardening. 'I look a sight.'

'A sight for sore eyes,' said Joe.

Ginny put on a modest smile and looked down at Isaac. He was cramming more peas into his mouth than were going in the bowl. 'Isaac. We'll have none left for tea.'

Joe leaned closer and whispered deliciously in her ear. 'Can we talk, me an' thee, wi'out this little 'un earwiggin'?'

Ginny tucked a strand of hair behind her ear and played her fingers over her lower lip. Gratifyingly, Joe's gaze dropped to her mouth, as she'd intended. She was thinking furiously. If Silas caught Joe there'd be ructions but she couldn't bring herself to send him away. The sight of him was like unexpectedly coming across the first violets of spring, those blues and purples that warmed her right through. Isaac would tell his uncle, no doubt, that a man called Joe had turned up on the doorstep — or from behind the pea trellis — so she supposed the damage was already done.

'Ginny, can I come in?' Joe sounded impatient.

'You can,' she said. She took Joe's hand. His warm fingers squeezed hers, sending a delicious tremor through her body. 'Isaac, will you go and play in the front parlour?' The boy looked up at her and made an 'umph' noise through his mouthful of peas. 'You can take Shandy with you. And the peas. Finish them off, if you like.'

She closed the parlour door on Isaac and the dog before guiding Joe up the stairs and into her bedroom. He arched one eyebrow.

Ginny giggled with delight. She sat on the bed and patted the mattress. 'I'm not to see you.'

'Tha knows I won't be told who I can an' can't see.'

'They're sending me home, back to the farm.'

Joe shrugged. 'Tha's mine now, Gin. Tha dun't need to listen to what they 'av to say, or do what they tell thee. Just keep thee trap shut and it'll all come reight.'

'I've not said anything, Joe. I promise. Tell me what's happening. Is Louisa alright? Does she hate me?' She gazed up at him appealingly. 'She hasn't been to see me.'

Joe sat beside her. He nuzzled her neck. 'Am sorry tha's been on thee own wi' this.' He kissed her and she returned it hungrily. He lay back, pulling her with him, climbing on top of her and fiddled with the buttons on her blouse. 'What about the boy?'

Ginny was too breathless to speak. She shook her head and reached down to put her hand on him. He pushed her skirt and petticoat up and then sat up, on his knees, to unfasten his trousers, his eyes on her sex. She bent her knees and moved her legs apart.

'Tha does gi' a man a fine welcome,' Joe said, moving over her, his mouth roaming over her throat, her earlobe, finally settling on her mouth, kissing hungrily. She moaned.

'Only you, Joe. I thought you were angry with me.'

He lifted his head to look into her eyes. 'This'll 'elp me to forgive thee.'

Afterwards, she lay on the bed watching Joe hop around trying to get his feet into his trousers. When he lost his balance and fell back onto the bed, Ginny straddled him and bent to kiss him. He brushed her hair out of his face.

'What if they get back an' I'm still 'ere?'

'Are you afraid?'

'No, course not.' He nibbled her lip, gently. 'But I am in another man's 'ouse ravaging 'is sister, a man that's already got it in for me.'

'Five more minutes,' she said, resting her hand on his shirt, feeling his heartbeat beneath her palm. 'I've missed you.'

He smacked her rump. 'Come away wi' me then, out o' this stinkin' town, find us a new life.'

Ginny hesitated, frowning. He was joking, of course. She recovered herself, smiling down at him. 'Alright then, where to?'

'America. Seth gi' me the idea. Am bein' named an' shamed by this bleedin' union stuff. I won't stay in this town, am tellin' thee.'

He was serious. Ginny got up off the bed and walked over to the window, staring down on the garden and river beyond. Finally, she turned to face him.

'I have made a commitment to you. I want us to be married, Joe, but I want to stay here, in this town.'

He sneered. 'An' 'ere I was, thinkin' tha couldn't resist old Joe 'ere when really tha were doin' thee womanly plottin'.' He got up. 'I'd best be off.'

Ginny forced a teasing smile. 'You don't like being alone, Joe. I know you.'

He took her by the shoulders — for an instant, she was back in the street outside the yard, being shaken like a ragdoll — and kissed her on the mouth. 'Come wi' me then.'

The front door banged, startling them both. They stared at each other, wide-eyed, then Ginny ran from the room and peered over the banister.

Harriet stood in the hallway, pulling off her gloves. 'Ginny, there you are. What are you doing? Isaac's making a mess of the windows in the front parlour. There's green muck all over them.' She disappeared from view then returned, bonnet-less, to check her hair in the mirror. 'He gave me a fright.'

'I was napping.' Ginny raised her voice. 'You're back early, sister.'

'There's no need to shout. Come down then. I'll tell you all about the new place we're thinking of taking on.'

'Alright.' She turned to see Joe standing on the threshold of her room and bit back a scream. She signalled for him to get back inside, pleading with her eyes, and could see he was struggling against an urge to dart downstairs and out of the house. But he retreated enough for her to close the door on his face. She ran back to the staircase. 'Where's Silas?'

'Over in the yard. He'll be back for his dinner in an hour or so. Oh, Isaac, what on earth have you been doing with those peas? Come on, let's get your clothes changed.'

Ginny ran downstairs. 'He just needs a wash. In the kitchen. Then I'll tidy up his mess while you put your feet up, sister. You were quick.'

'We got a lift back in Hal's cart. Are you alright? You look a bit harried.'

'Oh, it's been a long morning with this one. It's why I needed that nap.' Ginny took hold of Isaac's wrist to pull him into the kitchen, where she would tell him Joe's visit must remain a secret from Aunt Harriet and Uncle Silas. Joe was there in the house. What if Silas decided to search her room? She could tell Isaac the man he met was an entertainer, that she was planning a surprise for the family, and especially for Isaac, if he could be good and keep a secret.

'Where's that man gone?' he said.

'What man?' said Harriet.

Ginny's gut lurched. 'Oh, yes,' she said. 'I was going to tell you, yes.' Why not tell the truth? She and Joe were engaged now. But he might deny her, still. And now he was caged, and unpredictable, like a wild animal, and might lash out. Silas would likely put her and Isaac on a train that very day.

'Yes,' she repeated. 'A man did call, earlier. He's started a grocery, in . . . in Bardwell Road, I think he said, and he's offering to make deliveries twice a week.'

'How much will he charge for that?'

'I can't remember what he said.'

She glanced upstairs, she couldn't help herself, but Harriet was already walking into the parlour and didn't notice.

At dinner time, Ginny pushed her food around her plate, her stomach churning with fear. She strained to hear noises from above but all was quiet. She was terrified Joe would run downstairs and out of the house, not caring whether this was witnessed, and leave her to face Silas's fury and Harriet's disappointment. She'd repeated her lie when Isaac told Silas about

Shandy getting dirt on the stranger's trousers. Silas had shrugged; grocery shopping was a household issue and therefore Harriet's domain. The half-hour Silas was in the house felt like the longest thirty minutes of Ginny's life. After he had left, she suggested to Harriet that they go into the garden. There was some weeding to be done, or they could sit and enjoy the sunshine.

All she could think was that she had to leave a clear path for Joe to make his escape.

'I'd rather sit in the parlour. I haven't read the paper yet,' said Harriet.

So that was where the three of them sat. Isaac curled up in a corner of the settee, sucking on a sugar pig Harriet had brought home for him. Ginny got up to close the door but Harriet asked her to leave it open, to air the room. 'Let's have an hour of idleness,' said Harriet. *The devil makes work for idle hands*, Ginny's mother-in-law told her every time she caught her sitting in a chair. She took out her mending and looked at it hopelessly. She was using all her energy to appear unruffled. Darning stockings was beyond her.

'Oh my,' said Harriet. She did not believe in Ginny's mother-in-law's mantra and took every opportunity to read a book or a newspaper. Ginny loved that about Harriet, ordinarily, but it was an attitude that wouldn't get them into the garden and safely digging. 'Listen to this, Ginny.'

Ginny darted a glance through the open door at the hallway and the foot of the stairs that were visible beyond. 'What is it?'

'The matron at the Sheffield workhouse — I know her vaguely but can't remember how — anyway, she's appeared in court if you can believe it. The guardians say she called the cook a *dame*, but she says she didn't appreciate dame is an offensive term and that the cook had been impertinent and should know her place. Goodness me, it gets worse. She called the cook . . .' Harriet glanced at Isaac and whispered the words to Ginny '. . . a brazen hussy!'

Harriet put her hand over her mouth but her eyes were sparkling. Ginny laughed, then glanced again into the hallway. Was it her imagination or did she hear a creak from the staircase, the sound of feet descending as quietly as possible? If Harriet was reading the newspaper she wouldn't see Joe if he sneaked past the parlour. Ginny looked anxiously at Isaac. He'd nodded off.

'What else?' she said. 'Read me some more.'

'Let's see. She's accused of stealing from the stores, too. Soap and glasses and, oh, the treacle barrel *and* a panshon. She must have deep pockets.' Harriet laughed and turned the page. 'What else indeed? Six girls escaped from the Glossop convent. They've been rounded up and returned.'

'I think Silas would like to send me to a convent,' said Ginny, then blushed deeply, remembering what she'd been doing only hours earlier. How long had Joe been cooling his heels now? An hour or more, she thought. His patience would soon run dry.

'Oh hush, Ginny. Let us have one afternoon where we do not argue.'

Harriet returned to her newspaper. Ginny got up and went to the upright piano. It faced the window. 'Will you play something, Harriet?'

'Yes, of course. What would you like to hear?'

'Anything. I don't mind. I just love to hear you play.'

'You flatter me. I'm not very good.'

'Well, I have never heard anybody play better.' This was true. There was no piano at the farm and the church organist made up for a lack of skill with deafening over-enthusiasm. 'I'd like to hear a gentle tune, sister.'

She glanced over the newspaper while Harriet played. A headline caught her eye. *More Astounding Disclosures*. It was the ninth day of the inquiry Joe was so het up about. A witness had given evidence about a shooting in which a man had died a slow and lingering death. Ginny shivered. Joe could not have anything to do with this. He and Seth were ratteners, not assassins. No, they could not be involved in this particular outrage. Ginny looked closely at the small type. She could read but not fluently. The letters sometimes jumbled themselves up. She found it helped if she followed each line with her finger. She came to a name she knew and paused, keeping her face carefully neutral. Joe Crookes, named by a witness, in connection with the Linley shooting.

She realised the music had stopped.

'What are you reading?'

'Nothing.' She put the newspaper down but another shudder ran through her body.

Harriet had a concerned expression on her face.

'You're rather pale.'

'I think I'll fetch a shawl,' said Ginny. 'I'm feeling chilly.'

'I hope you're not coming down with a summer cold.'

The hallway was deserted and still. Ginny could hear only the usual noises coming from the factory yard. She breathed out slowly and climbed the stairs. As she entered her room, she put her finger over her lips but let it drop when she realised the room was empty. A breeze from the open sash stirred the curtains. He was gone.

19

Joe jammed his hands in his pockets and lowered his head as he pushed through the crowd jostling on the pavement outside the town hall building. What he would give to be one of these bystanders eager for a glimpse, finally, of the villains behind a decade of bloody crime. Instead, his was one of the faces they were seeking out. How grand it would be to gossip along with the rest, to boast of waiting for the opportunity to land a good thump on William Broadhead's nose, of walloping one of his henchmen. Joe would give up all the sovereigns he'd earned to walk in the shoes of these self-righteous folk.

He could hear Seth now. *Easy for tha to say. Tha's spent all thee coin. Runs through tha fingers like watta.*

Seth hadn't been named by any of the witnesses; he had cleverly kept himself in Joe's shadow and would never be called out for the crimes they'd committed together. Joe was the silly bugger who'd been too keen to show off his status as the gaffer's man. He smarted from the injustice of it.

Inside the town hall, it was no less crowded. Joe had been instructed to report to the clerk's office. He stood in the foyer, at a loss. Behind the people going hither and thither, a man stood by the fireplace, smoking a pipe and observing the room in a disinterested way. Joe approached him.

'Can tha tell me where the clerk is?'

The man looked Joe up and down and curled his

lip. 'How should I know that?'

Joe reeled away, towards the stairs. He wanted to lamp the man but he was out of his depth here, in this place he'd never set foot in before, and it knocked the confidence out of him. He bumped into somebody and muttered an apology. He climbed the staircase, which was lined with knots of men talking in low voices or hailing each other, or somebody down in the foyer, loudly. Not recognising any of their faces, he didn't want to search them too closely in case he himself was recognised. He stopped on the landing where the first set of stairs ended. Two men were consulting a ledger one of them held in his arms.

'Recall today for . . . let me see . . . I can't find his name.'

'I can't hear myself think. I must have already turned a hundred people away.'

'I've not seen anything like this since the flood. Remember them all round the fire?'

'And queueing up for compensation.'

The flood. A disaster the town had tried to forget as quickly as possible. Joe hoped his role in the outrages would be as quickly consigned to history.

''Scuse me,' he said.

The men looked up, and said in union: 'Yes?'

'Am a witness, told to report to the clerk's office.'

'Well, that's downstairs. Wait a minute. You'll be on this list. Name?'

Joe lowered his voice. 'Joseph Albert Crookes.'

'Here you are. Go up, left at the top. Door at the end. Wait outside. You'll be called for.'

Joe waited for a group of men to finish descending the top flight of stairs. He recognised the man leading them, a short, compact figure with a knot of scar tissue running from his mangled earlobe and disappearing under the collar of his shirt. He was a surgical instrument maker who'd got on the wrong side of the gaffer two summers ago and been done over. Not by Joe, but Joe had been with William Broadhead when he'd paid a visit to this man in the infirmary. The gaffer had shaken his hand and advised him to let bygones be bygones for the sake of his family. *Reight enough, I were an ugly bugger before tha came along*, the man had joked weakly. You must mean before the unfortunate accident that befell you, the gaffer had said, and Joe had laughed along with them.

He kept his eyes on the banister he was clutching and braced himself for the inevitable encounter. But the surgical instrument maker looked right through him and continued on. Joe let out a shaky breath. The corridor at the top of the stairs was busy but he glimpsed the oak door at the end. Men were sitting on benches on either side of the narrow passageway, making it even more difficult to negotiate. Those standing nearest the closed door were silent, heads tilted as if that might help them hear more clearly what was going on inside. He could hear raised voices, authoritative tones coming from the chamber, but not what was being said.

Joe cleared his throat. 'Am I to wait 'ere? Am givin' evidence.'

'Aye,' said the man beside him, 'somebody'll come and fetch thee when it's time.' He sized Joe up. 'What did Broadhead do to thee?'

'Stole me tools,' said Joe. He gave the man a sideways glance. He didn't recognise him. 'What about thee?'

'Just a rattening? 'e blew my place up, failed on all counts.'

'Why?'

'Because he employs shite that don't know what they're doin'.'

'I meant, why'd he try?'

'I got mesen a new bit o' kit to grind straight saws an' he reckoned it interfered wi' hand labour. Then 'e threatened me missus, wrote her a letter.'

Another man who had his ear pressed to the door turned to them. 'Shush!'

Joe lowered his voice to a whisper. He knew who this man was. 'Then what?'

'Well, I had to get rid, didn't I? Sold it on. But av ordered another now. This inquiry'll put a stop to the likes of William Broadhead. Oh aye.' He stuck out his hand. 'Wheatman. I own the . . .'

'I've 'eard o'thee.' Joe shook the man's hand. 'Sydney Parker.' The false name sprang to his lips without hesitation.

'Will tha pair be quiet?'

The factory owner nodded towards a spare bench and Joe followed him, pulling his cap down over his brow. He'd walked into a bearpit. When they were seated, Wheatman resumed his one-sided conversation.

'So, Broadhead were givin' evidence yesterday an' all, and I got 'ere early, managed to get into the public gallery. Packed, it were. An' here comes this man, full o' himsen, puffed up like a parrot. Braggin' about 'ow he's treasurer of the organised trades association with sixty thousand members.' The man snorted. 'An' listen up. He had his supporters, gentlemen who reckoned 'e were a popular an' experienced unionist. Well, this so-called defence committee were in attendance, on behalf o' all the unions, tha knows?'

Joe nodded.

'An' they left in disgust when they 'eard what he'd been gettin' up to. Walked out o' the inquiry! Said they couldn't be associated wi' him. And then what 'appens?'

Joe shook his head.

'Broadhead needs a police escort out o' the building or the mob would've 'ad him. Nob'dy were expectin' him to admit to everythin'. He'd lost count o' all he'd ordered to be done to folk over the past ten years. Course, he'll get away wi' it. His sort allus does.' Wheatman sighed. 'Upshot is I can't even get in the place today. Must stand out 'ere an' wait me turn to gi' evidence. I'm lookin' forward to that though. Bet tha lookin' forward to it? Havin' tha day in court.'

'Aye,' said Joe. He rapped the wooden seat with his knuckles, feeling as hollow as the sound it made. 'Too reight I am.' He hesitated. 'It's not a proper court though, is it?'

'As good as. It's all comin' out and 'e might get away wi' it but 'is henchmen'll be run out o' town, mark my words.'

Fear curdled in Joe's gut. 'That don't seem fair to me.'

Wheatman shrugged. 'Well, 'e could be dragged down wi' 'em. The judge is sayin' he's not given up all he knows, that he's not named enough men. He might go down for that.'

There was a flurry of activity by the door. A young man had come out and was calling in a reedy voice for a witness. He repeated the name and Joe sagged in relief. It wasn't his. If it had been, he would have had to ignore it or who knew how Wheatman might have reacted, and where would he end up then? Arrested?

He was cornered. Then four or five people emerged and there was some debate about whether that freed up space in the public gallery. The clerk allowed the same number inside, found his witness, and the door was closed once again.

Several men crowded around those who had emerged from the room. Joe got up to linger nearby.

'Not quite as bombastic today,' said a portly gentleman. He was wearing an expensive-looking double-breasted coat and a silk spotted cravat. His sharp eyes found Joe, and moved on.

'Who's that?' said Joe to Wheatman.

'Leng. He owns the *Telegraph*. He's a foreigner, I believe from Hull, originally. But it's thanks to 'im we're 'ere. He's against the unions and ran a campaign in the papers.'

'He is arguing now that his hand was forced,' Leng was saying, 'that he committed these heinous acts because unions aren't recognised in law and therefore workers are not compelled to support their fellow men, and they must be made to do so.'

Seth would agree with the gaffer there. Joe watched the newspaperman walk down the corridor, accepting handshakes and pats on the shoulder as he went.

Then the door opened again and all heads turned towards it eagerly. It was the clerk again.

'We won't be calling any more witnesses today,' he said to a chorus of groans. 'Please return on Monday at ten sharp.'

Wheatman clapped Joe on the back. 'They must think we've nowt better to do, eh?' he said cheerfully. 'I'll si thee then.'

Back on the pavement, Joe closed his ears to the chatter around him. He'd spend all weekend stewing in his own fear, a miserable prospect. He set off up the hill towards Seth's place. Joe's too, now he'd dropped all pretence of renting the room he'd been thrown out of. Homeless and jobless to boot. There was work to be had, though. He'd been approached while drinking in the Blue Pig by somebody who reckoned to own a portfolio of properties — houses, shops, factories — and was looking for a man to help collect rent from reluctant tenants. Was Joe interested? He'd shaken his head, overcome by the bitter realisation that this man saw only a thug when he looked at Joe, not the charming rogue he'd always considered himself to be. Thirty-five and nothing to show for it. At least Ginny still believed in him. She'd follow him to the ends of the earth. He was counting on it.

By Baker's Hill, he stopped and turned to look back down into the basin of the valley, the bridge over the Don, the railway line on the other side, the canal dropping down from Tinsley and the eternal smokestacks. His town. He was sure there were prettier places but did he have the guts to leave? Yes, Ginny would go with him. All he had to do was click his fingers. It was Ginny who'd pointed out he hated to be alone. It smarted, but it was true.

He couldn't run now. They'd be after him if he failed to turn up. But Monday was two days off and anything might happen in the meantime.

20

She would divide this day into manageable chunks. It didn't pay to think too far ahead. Louisa rose, pushed her feet into her slippers and took the blanket from the bed and the potty from underneath it. Wrapped in the blanket, she stepped carefully down the darkened stairwell. There were women in her position who would deliberately throw themselves downstairs, or have a man punch them in the stomach. Sometimes they had no choice in the matter. She shuddered and padded into the backyard, avoiding the shallow puddles that were just distinguishable in the pearly light of the dawn. She felt the light rain as a gentle mist on her face. She put her hand on the latch of the privy and paused. Something was up. She breathed in sharply. The nausea that had plagued her had disappeared, snuffed out seemingly as easy as extinguishing a lamp. She felt as if her old capability had been restored and wondered whether this was a temporary thing, like the sun emerging from behind a cloud only to be swallowed up again in a moment.

She made porridge for breakfast, adding a generous dollop of sugar, and dipped oatcakes into the mixture, chewing and swallowing quickly. She recalled there was a bottle of dandelion and burdock in the cupboard and got up to find it. The mere thought of it would have set her teeth on edge yesterday. Now, she drank it down. Energised, she decided she would tidy her messy bedroom. The men who visited didn't care about her clutter and nor had she, until now. She put on a flannel vest a customer had left behind, instead of the stays that were impossible to fasten, and a petticoat that, even left untied, was tight around her middle. Her mind skidded away from the reason for this and she tugged the net open, enjoying the warmth of the morning light on her bare arms. She picked up the clothes scattered over the floor, bed and chair and hung them in the wardrobe or folded them neatly in the chest, carefully pushing closed the rickety drawers.

She washed and dried her face and then put on the dress she would wear to her appointment, a grass-green blouse and skirt that had belonged to her mother. She wrapped a darker green shawl around her shoulders and bent to check her reflection in the dressing table mirror. Her cheeks were rosy, her eyes clear. She frowned; she had never looked better while inside she was battling a growing terror of what lay ahead.

Downstairs, the clock on the mantelpiece told her there were still two hours to go before her appointment. She brewed a pot of tea, although always there was that gnawing desire for something stronger, something that would take the edge off, and sat in her rocker to drink it. She rested her hand on her belly. Even through the material of her dress and petticoat she could feel the stone-hard mound. She stroked it and pressed her hands against it — and felt the by now familiar answering flutter, deep in her abdomen. Louisa pleated her lips and got up and took her purse from its hiding place under the yellowed paper bags, bits of string and rags that filled the top drawer of a small bureau that sat at the foot of the stairs. She kept a bowl on top of the bureau for those gentlemen guests who were too delicate to acknowledge they were paying for her services, who preferred to keep up the pretence in the bedroom and drop their coin into the bowl on their way out.

She opened the purse and tipped the contents into the palm of her hand, separating out the silver and the coppers. These went into one of the yellowed paper bags. That left her with ten gold-coloured coins, which she poured back into the purse. Ten sovereigns. Five handed over by Joe; five loaned from Jemima Greaves. Louisa would pay the loan back at the rate of one shilling a week over her first twenty weeks of employment at the Greaves hackney cab and figured, funeral hearse company. She would start her new job in a week's time; Jemima believed she would be recovered by then. The prospect was daunting but all she had to do was conjure the face of the night watchman and her resolve to turn over a new leaf was hardened. She was re-making the lie she had told the police-detective into truth, or half-truth at least.

She clutched the purse in her hand and returned to her rocker and sat, and rocked, and watched the hands of the clock. She couldn't detect their movement but, somehow, the time passed.

* * *

The bell over the door tinkled like the sound of breaking glass when Louisa let herself into the shop. Sunlight glanced off the myriad glass jars of potions and powders. A bunch of lavender sat in a vase on the counter, giving off an overpowering scent that made her nostrils twitch.

She was relieved to see Milly Barber behind the

counter, serving a customer, her father nowhere in sight.

She caught Louisa's eye and smiled. 'Be with you in a minute, love.'

Louisa nodded. She wandered to the back of the shop and pretended to examine a tray of lavender drawer sheets. The shop bell rang, signalling the exit of the customer, and Milly came over. She picked up a basin of pills. 'These should be in the laboratory, not sitting out here for anybody to take. Father has forgot himself again.'

'What are they for?' said Louisa.

'Toothache, headaches, coughs,' said Milly. 'All manner of ailments.' She shrugged. 'Coca is very popular.'

'Are tha a chemist?' said Louisa.

'Apprenticed to my father.' She smiled at Louisa. 'He has no sons. Shall we go through?'

Milly took her into the room with the green chaise longue and the black-tiled fireplace. Louisa wondered how many women had been shown into this room since she was first here. A lump rose in her throat.

'I have the ten pounds,' she said.

'I'll take that from you now,' said Milly.

Louisa handed over the coins. They made a soft chinking sound as they fell into Milly's palm. Milly dropped them into her apron pocket as if there was no more import to the exchange than if Louisa had been buying sausages at the market.

'Thank you,' she said. 'Please sit. Can you drink this tincture?' She pointed to a stoppered bottle and a glass that sat on the mantelpiece.

'What's in it? Will it . . .'

'Oh no, nothing like that. The time for a potion has

come and gone.' Milly poured some of the liquid into the glass. It was the colour of dead leaves. 'This will help to relax you.'

'How much does it cost?'

Milly smiled gently. 'I won't charge you for it.'

Louisa took a careful sip. The taste was bitter.

'Better to drink it down at once,' said Milly.

She did.

'Now, I'll return shortly.'

Louisa nodded. She was holding at bay a brimming lake of tears and couldn't trust herself to speak. She had just begun wondering how long she would be kept waiting when Milly returned with an older, greyer version of herself, the same kindly smile and round cheeks. 'I'm Mrs Barber,' the woman said.

Louisa made to stand up but Milly put a hand on her shoulder, gently but firmly preventing her from rising. She wanted to look up at Milly, to ask her where it would be done, but her head was so heavy and yet light at the same time, as if she might float to the ceiling were it not for the anchor of Milly's hand. The other woman had crouched before her and was opening a valise Louisa only now noticed she had been carrying. Her heart raced; what instruments would be used on her body? At the same time, she was curiously unconcerned, as if all this was happening not to her but to somebody whose body she was temporarily inhabiting and could safely ignore. She studied the oblong of light at the end of the room. She couldn't remember what it was called, the thing that let in the light. This amused her and she giggled.

'What were in that tonic?' she said to Milly, who was far away, miles away, but managed somehow to still be cupping Louisa's shoulder in her hand. She didn't respond and Louisa wondered whether she had even said the words aloud. It didn't matter, nothing did.

'Are you ready, love?' Milly's voice was soft as a down pillow.

Her eyelids were lead weights. She closed them. That was better. Voices arrived like ripples on a pond.

'How much did you give her?'

'The usual amount, but she's probably not had it before. I imagine she can't afford to treat her ailments with laudanum and hemp.'

'That reminds me . . .' the voice faded away for a while and then returned '. . . your father. I'm at my wits' end.'

'It's alright, mother. I'll order more on Monday.'

She wondered, idly, why the side of her face was squashed. She opened her eyes, which made her dizzy so she closed them again, but at least that glimpse had told her that she was now lying on the chaise longue, on her side. The seat was too hard to be comfortable, she would have preferred to sink into a soft mattress, but it was gratifying to lie down. The voices returned.

'. . . and try to relax . . .'

'. . . help lift up your dress?'

'. . . and bend your knees . . .'

'That's it. Curl up . . . you won't fall . . . here.'

Louisa drifted away. She wondered if all the material bunched around her waist was a blanket and tried to pull it down over her legs, which were cold. She felt her hands taken and held and panic rose in her gut. She opened her eyes fully and the room swam into focus.

Milly was sitting on the floor by Louisa's head, holding both her hands in hers. 'What can you see, out there?'

Louisa was confused. Did Milly mean the square of light at the end of the room? She looked. She could see tree tops swaying behind chimney pots that billowed smoke into a peacock-blue sky. It was summer. Perhaps they'd leave her here to sleep. Is that what she was here for, to rest? She stared at the light then closed her eyes. A black shape filled the world, black as a watchman's cape as it settled on the ground. She smelled the coppery scent of blood.

With a gasp, Louisa sat up, her heart pounding in her throat. The older woman concealed whatever instrument she had just lifted from the valise behind her back, and Milly crouched beside her, reaching up to place her cool hand on Louisa's forehead, a concerned frown on her face.

She was swallowing repeatedly and could not stop.

* * *

Milly guided Louisa down the steep, darkened staircase at the back of the shop, through a heavy curtain and into an equally dark, short corridor with a door at the end. She fiddled with the latch and opened the door, stepping outside into the early evening light. Louisa followed.

A lingering warmth rose from the ground that had been baked in the day's heat. Louisa breathed in deeply, enjoying the heady mix of sweet pollen, brick dust and smoke. She would not think yet about what she had done.

Milly pointed to the top of the sloping yard. 'Go up those steps and along the ginnel. It'll bring you back onto the main street. Here. I've got something for you, Louisa.'

She handed Louisa a paper bag, folded over at the top. Louisa looked inside. Pastries. They smelled delicious and set her stomach rumbling.

'Thank you,' she said. Milly smiled and stepped back inside, raising her hand in farewell and closing the door behind her.

The journey home was busy with pedestrians and hawkers — all brought out by the fine evening like chattering nightjars. A woman stood on a busy intersection, a small girl at her side, displaying a tray of greengages. Louisa felt a sudden craving for the sweet fruit — she could practically taste the luscious burst on her tongue — but had no small coin on her. Evenings like this also brought out thieves and pickpockets. She strolled on up the hill towards home, enjoying the ache in the muscles of her thighs and calves. She was almost euphoric but mistrusted the feeling; whatever she had drunk at the chemist's was still in her, she knew it from the slight disorientation she felt, her strange detachment from what had occurred in the back room of the chemist's shop.

It was getting dark by the time Louisa reached the end of her terrace.

A gig came up alongside her and she stepped back out of the way of the panting and snorting horse pulling it.

'Louisa!' The round and broken-veined face of an over-imbiber of fine wine emerged from behind the hood of the vehicle. 'I thought that was you. Excellent timing, my dear. Excellent.'

She smiled at him mechanically. 'Mr Godfrey, I weren't expectin' thee tonight.'

'I know that,' he said, his eyes twinkling in the gloom. 'What do you think of my new ride? Fancy a spin in her?' He began to cough and reached down to retrieve a bottle of wine, drinking noisily from it.

'Are tha drunk agen?' said Louisa. He was bad enough when sober.

'You can be too. I've got another bottle,' he said, bending again to come with a bottle in his other hand. The horse stamped and whinnied. 'Come on, come and sit by me.'

'No thanks.'

'Are you sure? You're no fun anymore.' He pouted grotesquely. 'If you're busy, if you're tied up, haha, I can return later?'

'No,' said Louisa. 'I just told thee. Not tonight, or any night. Am done wi' thee, wi' the whole lot o' thee.'

She reached her front door and fumbled with the key.

'Hey!' he shouted. 'Are you rejecting a carriage ride, or all rides? Giddy up, girl! Hahaha.'

Louisa let herself into her cottage and slammed the door on his hoots of laughter. She locked it and rummaged in a drawer for a match to light the lamp. She sat down to take off her boots. She was hungry. Tucking into the pastries, she tried to keep her mind blank. She'd made a momentous decision; she would think on it tomorrow, not now.

But, later, laid in bed, her hands crept to her stomach and she replayed those final moments before she left the chemist's house. Milly had put her hand in the pocket of her apron and brought out the sovereigns. 'I almost forgot to return your money.'

Louisa had taken them. 'I'm sorry for messin' thee about.'

And Milly had shrugged. 'It's your choice, and that's how it should be. Not everybody gets to choose.'

21

Ginny perched on the edge of the bed. She'd slept here every night since mid-March under a thick white quilt, resting her head on clean plump pillows, drifting off to the sound of Isaac's animal-like snuffles from the cot in the corner.

It was early summer now and she wondered whether she'd ever see this room again.

Peter's folks had requested her return. In fact, to add insult to injury, Ginny's mother-in-law was coming to collect her five days from now. Her letter had asked whether Harriet would be so good as to accommodate her for a single night. She would arrive by stage coach and leave for the return journey with Ginny and Isaac the next morning. Ginny had watched Harriet's face fall as Silas read the letter aloud to them. Harriet had pulled Isaac onto her lap and given Ginny a tremulous smile. 'You have been with us a long while and Isaac must be missing his grandparents.' She had tightened her arms around Isaac and kissed the top of his head. 'You'll visit us again.'

Not likely, thought Ginny. She'd been the olive branch extended to Silas by his estranged parents. Let him meet his nephew and feel kindly towards his family again. Silas might agree to pay a return visit, with his fancy wife, and mend the bridges he had burnt. He was their only son and heir, after all. Ginny reflected bitterly that she was no better treated than a farm animal — useful, valuable even, but under the yoke.

Her dreams and desires were irrelevant. She stroked her fingers over the counterpane. The daisies Isaac had presented her with, that he had arranged in a jam-jar with Harriet's help and placed on the bedside table, were a distorted bundle of yellow and white, blurred by the tears in her eyes. Harriet would make a wonderful mother; she had the patience Ginny lacked, and she doted on Isaac.

Silas loved him too. He saved his harsh words for Ginny. *Tha's got theesen tangled up wi' a proper crook. Crook by name and nature. Silly girl.*

She would show him. She'd show them all.

Ginny got up and pulled open the wardrobe door. Her country smock hung alongside the woollen dress she wore around the house, a lightweight summer skirt and blouse donated by Harriet and a pale green dress, the skirt decorated with narrow bands of navy-blue velvet, the bodice cut in the new style, that Harriet had stood for at the Norfolk Market tally shop. Ginny had been paying for the second-hand dress in instalments from the wages Harriet gave her. It was almost hers. There were also three beautiful satin gowns Harriet had inherited from her aunt, hanging there like precious jewels, and a dove-grey taffeta Harriet said she had worn only once. The colour was drab on Ginny but she could see how stunning it would look on Harriet, with her red hair. Harriet said she was saving these gowns for a time when they had the money to spare to host supper parties, although the garments would probably be out of fashion by then. Practically every penny they earned was ploughed back into the business. Ginny thought it was a shame to see these dresses go to waste.

She raised her gaze to the shelf above and the beribboned bonnet that sat there. Her father-in-law would burn this bonnet if she took it home. Only wealthy women were entitled to ribbons and velvet, he said, not the likes of her. And only the rich could afford to bare their arms, shoulders and bosoms in the sort of dresses Harriet was storing in this wardrobe. Men couldn't be accountable for their actions when women tried to rise above their station and flaunted themselves. These women were *asking for trouble*.

She took down the bonnet and put it on, admiring her reflection in the rosewood-framed mirror on the wall. It was the nicest thing she'd ever owned. She replaced it on the shelf and ran her hands over the dresses before selecting the summer dress donated by Harriet. She put the blouse and skirt on over her shift, petticoats, stockings and stays, then put her feet into her boots and tied up the laces.

Downstairs, Isaac sat at the kitchen table, swinging his legs. He beamed when he saw her.

'When will Uncle Silas and Aunt Harriet be back from the market?' he said, his piping voice piercing her heart. 'Am hungry.' He sneezed. 'Can you make me summat?' He sneezed again.

'Have you been rolling in the grass?' said Ginny. She knelt and wrapped her arms around him, inhaling the heady scent of summer. 'You are my good boy.'

Isaac patted her back. 'Am reight *reight* hungry.'

'Let's see then.' She rummaged in the pantry and came out with a covered tray. 'Look! The scones your aunt baked. And we have jam. Blackcurrant. Your favourite.'

'Are they to eat now?'

'Why not? A special treat!'

She tried to laugh but it came out more like a sob. 'You can spread the jam if you like.'

'Can I?' His eyes were round as saucers. 'With a knife?'

'Here you are, love.'

Ginny put a plate, the scones, a pot of jam and a blunt-edged butter knife on the table in front of Isaac. She checked there were coins in the pocket of her dress and took down the shawl that was hanging on a hook behind the pantry door. Her chest was tight, as if there was not enough air in the room, and the urge to escape was bringing her close to panic, but her eyes misted over when she looked at her son.

She wavered, her hand on the door that led into the garden. 'I'm just going to get a breath of fresh air.'

That might be all she did. Who was to say?

Isaac nodded without looking round, now fully engrossed in the task of transferring jam from the bone-handled knife onto the scone she had cut in half for him.

Outside, Ginny leaned against the trellis that was supporting a climbing rose and took a deep breath. Here she was, getting the air she had said she needed. She could go back inside in a moment. She looked to the left, to the path that led towards the yard, then turned her head back to the kitchen door. She had closed it behind her. The dog padded around the corner of the house towards her.

'Come here, Shandy.' She opened the kitchen door to let the dog in. 'Isaac, Shandy'll look after you while I . . . while I just . . .' closing the door again without finishing the sentence.

She walked slowly along the edge of the yard, shutting her ears to the clangs and shouts from the forge, the gurgle and chatter of the wheel. She trailed her fingers along the mossy top of the hip-height wall that began in the yard and curved around into the street, and kept walking until the factory clatter was as remote as the bleats of distant sheep.

* * *

'He's not 'ere.'

Seth appeared unsurprised to find Ginny on his doorstep. 'Come in. Louisa not about?'

Ginny felt deafened by the drumbeat of her heart. She looked up and down the street. She patted her cheeks, which were damp with perspiration, and touched her hair where it grazed her temple. Seth was gazing at her with a mildly curious expression on his face. She looked quickly away from him.

'She's not in. Where is he?' said Ginny.

'No doubt drownin' his sorrows. Are tha comin' in? It's not a lion's den. A bear's cave, maybe. Your bloke's the bear wi' a sore arse. An' I'm partly the cause on it.'

She stepped over the threshold, pleased that Seth had called Joe her bloke. 'Fiancé, if you don't mind.'

Seth's eyebrows shot up. 'Oh aye? Then tha might tell thee fiancé to stop wi' the narkiness.'

'What have you done to him?'

'Nowt. I've done nowt, seemingly. That's the problem. Accordin' to them that have been spillin' their guts I'm clean as a whistle. Joe's not.' Ginny dropped into a chair and Seth stared hard at her. 'So tha's come to check the lay o' the land?'

Ginny nodded. 'I can't afford to wait around.'

Finally, she was able to meet Seth's eye. 'I'm sorry I interfered, in that job you and Joe did. I shouldn't have.'

'What job?' His eyes were innocently wide. 'There's been no job that I know of.'

Ginny laughed. 'Is this why you're not being dragged to the town hall along with Joe?'

'Joe likes to brag.' Seth shrugged. 'Tha must know what he's like by now. Am surprised tha family's allowin' this engagement, after all that's 'appened.'

Ginny pulled a face.

'Ah, it's like that then.'

She got up and paced the room, eventually going to the window. The pane was greasy and the frame infected by spreading blooms of mould. Looking out, she willed Joe to appear from around the corner, to spot her in the window, and for the faint smile that seemed always to play about his lips to widen into a delighted grin. She sighed.

'Look,' said Seth. 'We can go an' see if he's proppin' up the bar at the Blue Pig. It's not far.'

'I've walked miles today,' she said. 'I can do a few more.'

She waited on the pavement, hugging her arms tightly to her body, a jittery feeling in her stomach, while Seth knocked on Louisa's front door and tried the handle. It was locked.

'She's never in these days.'

She kept her voice light. 'Is she cross with me, d'you know?'

'I shun't think so,' said Seth, 'she's not the type to be cross wi' anyone, 'cept herself. No, she's bin comin' an' goin' I don't know where. Not seen much o' her since . . .' he trailed off.

Ginny bit her lip, trying to quell the doubts that assailed her. She needed Louisa's help for what came next. Silas and Harriet would have returned home by now and found Isaac alone, and her gone. She could picture the scene; Silas's fury. *She'll 'av gone to that good-fer-nothin', or to Louisa's. I'll fetch 'er back, kickin' an' screamin' if I have to.*

Harriet, sorrowful. *Don't go off in a temper, Silas. You'll only make it worse.* Pulling Isaac onto her lap, imagining that Ginny had deserted her son.

She paused on the threshold of the public house then straightened her back and followed Seth inside.

The interior of the Blue Pig was dimly lit but she was aware of the looks she was getting, both salacious and disapproving, from the handful of men there. Then she spotted Joe, standing at the end of the bar. Gratifyingly, his face lit up when he spotted her. He patted the arm of the man he'd been talking to and came over to them.

'Ey up, lass. Can't I even enjoy a pint o' porter in peace?' He nodded at Seth. 'Alreight.'

'Aye.' Seth said. 'Yer fiancée turned up at the door, eager to see thee.'

Her nerve was deserting her. 'I had to see you. Shall we go in there?' she said, pointing to the door to the snug.

'Men only in this establishment,' said Joe, 'an' last time I 'ad the pleasure o' looking, tha were a woman. This'll do.' He pulled out one of the chairs around a small table near the door and sat down. 'What's up then, love? Can't stay away from me, eh? I do 'av that effect on the female population.'

'Same agen?' asked Seth. Joe nodded and Seth went to the bar.

It was now or never. Ginny sat down next to Joe and took hold of his hand. 'I'm staying with you, if you'll have me.'

'I'll 'av thee, happily,' said Joe. He leaned towards her for a kiss. She turned her head away impatiently. 'What's up?'

'Listen,' she said. 'I'm not going back, or if I am it'll be to tell them I'm getting wed. They want to send me away, Joe, and I'm not going.' She squeezed his hand. 'I've made up my mind. I'm with you now.'

'Are tha proposin' marriage to me?' He laughed. 'No, tha tellin' me 'ow it'll be, aren't tha? These schemin' women'll be the death o' me.'

'What's wrong with that? I could be carrying your child, right now.' She tried to calm her breathing. 'Joe, I want to stay here, with you. I need to marry again. I *want* to marry again.'

'What if I'm gettin' away from all o' this?'

'What do you mean?'

'The truth's comin' out. Am not stayin' in this town to be gawped at.' He leaned close so their noses were almost touching. His dark eyes and sensuous mouth filled her vision; his breath smelled of ale. 'Why dun't tha come wi' me? Me an' thee, gettin' out. What d'you say?'

22

Jemima Greaves lived in a house attached to a large stable block and yard on Furnace Hill where she kept her horses, licensed cabs sprung on two or four wheels and a polished glass hearse for rental to the wealthier class of mourners. She had passed on to Louisa the rumour that her cottage was in the path of a new development, and she ought to find alternative accommodation. She'd be lucky to get a cottage to herself, but there were respectable rooms for rent — here, her eyes had dropped to Louisa's belly — and hadn't Louisa once lodged in Malin Bridge with a kind family? Jemima was sorry she couldn't accommodate her in a house that contained all six of the Greaves children, ranging in age from seventeen — the oldest, a girl, who worked at Jackson's file grinders and brought her wage home to her mother — to eight, the only boy who would, Jemima hoped, inherit a business that was still going strong when he came of age.

'You're to be my right-hand man,' Jemima said to Louisa. 'I hire out to six drivers an' have a couple of boys who help clean the cabs an' mind the horses, so as I said to thee before, there's no physical work for thee to do. I mostly need help keepin' track o' everythin' an' a girl with your sweet face and kindly manner is just the ticket for dealings with the customers.'

Louisa knew she was being flattered. Sweet and kindly were not descriptions she'd allow herself. But Jemima Greaves was offering her a lifeline and she would take it, whether she felt she was deserving of the older woman's help or not.

They sat in the office above the stable block that was now her domain, drinking tea. Shame coloured Louisa's cheeks. She had embraced the whirlwind that was Ginny but taken this quiet woman's many kindnesses for granted. Worse, her late mother's friend knew all about her, about how she'd been carrying on, the many men that meant she would never be able to identify the individual whose seed had stuck, whose child she was carrying. And Jemima had not abandoned her.

On top of the desk sat a pair of knitting needles, spearing a ball of soft cream-coloured yarn. Louisa picked the bundle up, thought about how knitting needles could be employed to lethal ends, and put it down again.

'Am reight grateful to thee, Jemima,' she said.

'Oh, hush. You're not a charity case, love. I need the 'elp and I can tell thee now that tha'll be workin' hard for thee wages.' She nodded at the knitting. 'It gets a bit quiet in 'ere sometimes. I started a scarf for me eldest. P'raps you'll cast on a few rows every now an' again.' She tipped back in her chair and cackled. 'Should be done by winter. Millicent taught thee to knit, I hope?'

Hearing her mother's name reminded Louisa of another Milly, who had also been kind to her.

'What about when I've a kid in tow?' she said.

Jemima smiled. 'We'll work it out, love, don't thee worry about that just yet. It's still early days.'

Which meant that anything could happen.

Louisa took the omnibus home, paying fresh attention to the hackney cabs on the road, to the drivers sitting on the box, craning her neck to look back when the bus passed stationary cabs, trying to spy the people inside, those wealthy paying customers. 'The rich man doesn't seem to have the same use of his legs as the working man,' Jemima had told her. 'He'll take a cab for a ride of a mile if it suits him.'

Louisa settled back on the bench, swaying along with her fellow passengers, bracing herself against the sudden jerks and bumps and enjoying the mindless motion, the warm feeling of contentment that was spreading through her body. She couldn't remember when she had last felt happy. Was this happiness, now? Or was she deluded to believe she had turned over a fresh page, that she was rewriting her life to include a fatherless child, a legitimate job, the renewal of her friendship with Harriet, with Silas. Was it possible she was regaining her old self? Whatever the case, she would savour the moment. Such moments, she knew, were few and far between.

She got off the bus in Surrey Street and waited for a cart filled with iron girders to pass, the horses yoked to it slipping on the cobbles, straining with the weight of their load. She crossed the road towards the grocer's shop that was sandwiched between a chandlery and a shoemaker. She'd be able to afford to get new soles on her boots now. Or a new pair of boots, if she could put some money by. That would be a treat.

She bought bread, milk, cheese and ham, and a packet of sugar from the aproned youth behind the counter and walked home briskly. She was ravenous. A man was waiting for her on the corner of Barker Pool. Louisa slowed her pace. She'd known she would have this to deal with but fear clenched her throat. She would never be allowed to escape the life she had fallen into.

'Ey up, Lou,' the man said as she got nearer. 'Are tha in tonight, ten o'clock?'

'Not anymore,' she said. 'Not at ten and not ever.'

His eyebrows shot up.

She spoke before he could. 'Av found a new job, am not doin' . . . that . . . anymore.' She lifted her chin, challengingly. 'Alright?'

He shrugged and sauntered away. 'P'raps I'll see thi around, then.'

Louisa stared after him, her heart pounding. She had expected more trouble than that. She collected herself and walked on.

The warm day had baked the stones of the pavement but it was cold and damp inside her cottage. When the knock came, she was on her knees building a fire with kindling and coke. She went to answer with trepidation in her heart; it would be a client who had decided he wasn't taking no for an answer, or the police returned to command her to revisit the town hall, and end up in a cell, or the detective, wanting something she would be unable to refuse. Jemima had told her she was in the clear, that no evidence of her presence in Change Alley had been found, and that the authorities were chalking it up as the final union outrage, content it was the last to be perpetrated. But Louisa supposed she would be always dreading every knock on the door. If this was to be her lifelong punishment, she could not complain.

On the doorstep stood Ginny, Seth and Joe. Alehouse fumes came off them like tannin from a sheep's hide.

'Been celebratin'?'

Ginny gave her a sheepish look but her eyes were

shining. She spoke in a rush, stumbling over her words. 'Lou, I'm glad to see you. I've been wanting to tell you I'm sorry for everything. It should've been me. I can't think what you must have . . .'

Louisa ushered her inside. 'Let's not tell the world an' his wife our business, eh?'

The men followed, Seth thrusting a package into her hands. 'Fish! Fresh from the market,' he said. 'Enough for all on us.'

'Got taters?' said Joe.

Ginny offered to light the stove and bustled around laying out plates and cutlery. She was merriness itself, spots of hectic colour standing out on her cheeks. Louisa looked on, suspiciously, but decided she'd hold her tongue until they were sitting down and eating, when she could look each of them in the eye.

The fish was poached, potatoes peeled and boiled and the cheese Louisa had purchased melted on top. Joe produced bottles of ale seemingly out of thin air. Louisa declined. Her craving for alcohol was always there, like a nagging toothache, but that was a path she'd not slide down again. As they took their seats around the table, she saw Joe had hung his coat on a hook on the wall and her heart stuttered in her chest. It could be a lifeless body, hanging there. Or a watchman's cloak.

Joe's voice startled her back to the present moment. 'Now that's a tea fit for a king!'

'I suppose tha's the king,' said Seth.

Joe ignored him. Louisa had already noticed tension between them; the last thing she needed was a clumsy beer-fuelled fight kicking off in her cottage.

She caught Ginny's eye and asked the question that had been on her lips since she had opened the door to them. 'I thought tha were under house arrest? What's goin' on?'

Ginny's eyes sparkled. 'I'll tell you everything, Lou. Are you ready?'

'Well, I did ask thee so, yes, I should say I am.'

'Me and Joe are to be wed.' Ginny leaned back triumphantly, looking from Louisa to Joe and back.

Seth said, 'He's finally realised the benefits of havin' a wife to cook 'is dinners and wash 'is britches.'

'An' the rest,' said Joe, putting his arm around Ginny and planting a kiss on her lips.

'Congratulations to the pair o' thee,' said Louisa. 'I'm wonderin' . . .'

'Don't look so concerned, Lou. We'll find you a man,' said Ginny, 'and have a double wedding.' She blew a kiss to Seth. 'I know a man not a million miles away who'd . . .'

'I think tha's drunk theesen stupid,' said Louisa. 'I can fend for meesen, thank you.'

'Good for you.' Ginny snuggled into Joe's side and he patted her arm absently. 'I know I need a man's protection. This man.'

Louisa turned a frosty gaze on Joe. 'What did Silas make o' it when tha told him?'

Joe frowned and swigged from his bottle of ale.

Ginny pushed her plate away. 'Silas will be glad to be shot of me. He was going to send me away, did you know that? Back to be a slave for . . .'

Louisa interrupted her. She'd had enough of Ginny's familiar refrain. 'What about Isaac?'

Ginny bit her lip, suddenly on the verge of tears.

'I'll tell thee what,' said Seth, 'me an' Joe will scarper so you ladies can 'av a natter. Put the world to rights. Eh, Joe?'

‘Good thinkin’,’ said Joe, blurrily. He stumbled as he rose from the table, knocking his bottle over, and fumbling to catch hold of it. It slipped through his fingers, smashing on the floor. ‘Buggery.’

‘Leave it,’ said Louisa. ‘I’ll clear it up.’

She was aware, as she ushered the brothers out of the house, of Ginny tidying up quietly behind her, mopping up the broken glass and carrying the plates into the leanto. Louisa sat by the fire and when Ginny reappeared gestured for her to sit down too.

‘Can I ask thee agen, Ginny, what’s goin’ on? Has tha thrown tha lot in wi’ Joe, then?’

‘Yes.’ Ginny looked defiant but she was twisting her hands in her lap. ‘This will sound terrible but please hear me out. I want to be with Joe and he agrees . . .’

‘. . . that’s big o’ ’im . . .’

‘Lou, please let me finish. Joe’s not keen on raisin’ another man’s boy and I don’t want to push it, not just yet. Anyhow, Isaac will have a better life with Harriet and Silas. They love him and they’ve no children. Oh!’ Ginny sat bolt upright, as though the idea had just occurred to her, though by now Louisa knew her well enough to know better. ‘Do you know, she might be barren! Poor Harriet. It would be a crime to take Isaac off her.’

‘Don’t play me for a fool.’ At least Ginny had the good grace to look ashamed of herself. ‘Isaac’s thine and that’s the end o’ it.’

‘I know that!’ Ginny’s eyes flashed. ‘I’ve been reminded of it every day since his father died. You don’t know what it’s like.’

‘I know tha thinks there’s summat glamorous about our Joe. He’s a feckless man.’

‘I’ve made my mind up.’

'An' Joe's all for it? The eternal bachelor boy?'

Ginny looked into the flames. She was in a subdued state now and it was a few moments before she spoke again. 'It's better than going back to Peter's folks, which Silas is set on. I'm to be collected like a child who's not to be trusted. And the funny thing is, Silas was a runaway himself.' She looked back up at Louisa, appealing for her sympathy. 'You'd think he'd be more understanding.'

'Different rules for women. Tha should know that by now.' To soften the harshness of this truth, Louisa reached forward to squeeze Ginny's fingers before settling back into her chair with a sigh. 'Make the best o' it, love. That'd be my advice.'

'I'm not going back.' Ginny's lips were set in a thin line. Louisa shook her head in exasperation; this girl was as stubborn as a donkey.

'I'll tell thee what,' she said, 'why not return for a bit, so your boy can see 'is grandparents again, an' let the dust settle, an' tha can even come back and stay wi' me?' A bubble of optimism rose inside her and she couldn't contain it. 'I've got a job, tha knows, a proper job, an' I'm soon to be a . . .'

Ginny interrupted her impatiently. 'No, you don't get it, Lou. I'm not talking about the farm. It's Silas and Harriet's I'm not going back to, and I need you to tell them.'

23

He'd breakfasted at the Blue Pig with an old mate who reassured him there'd be nothing to worry about. So when Joe strode into the town hall he was feeling confident, cocky even. All he had to do was confirm the names of a handful of fellow culprits, just as those fellow men had dished out his name, admit to the acts he'd carried out on the gaffer's say-so, and he'd be free, and nobody could touch him, not a constable nor a courtroom judge. Rattenings were commonplace, accepted in the trades. There was no shame in admitting to those, and he would, as freely as previous witnesses had done.

The strong beer he'd drunk that morning wore off around about the same time as the questioning became more difficult. It wasn't that he didn't know the answers, more that he was being asked to articulate his actions for the first time. Telling the unvarnished truth wasn't as easy as he'd thought it would be.

Joe's neck began to itch when he was asked how the bomb that had exploded in Wheatman's factory was created. He told them he had purchased twenty-four pounds of powder from a place at the bottom of Pinstone Lane, a tin bottle from Milner's and a fuse from a shop in Snig Hill. No, he couldn't remember the name of the shop. No, nobody had been injured in the explosion. It was a warning, only, delivered on the gaffer's orders.

Wheatman had wanted to bring in a new machine

to do the job of several workers.

Joe missed the next question because he was reflecting that the blow-up had worked, for Wheatman had not purchased the new-fangled machine after all. He rolled his shoulders back, his earlier self-assurance partly restored.

'Sorry, I missed that. What did tha say?'

'Do you recollect the time when James Linley was shot, and his death from the wound, six months later?'

It was like being slapped across the face. Joe breathed out hard, through his nose. It sounded harsh in his ears.

'Aye.' His voice was so faint he could barely hear it himself.

'Speak up please.'

'Aye,' he said, only slightly more loudly. He coughed to clear his throat but began to retch instead. He bent towards the polished wooden planking but it seemed an impossible distance away. He was puzzling over this when the floor came up to meet his face with a slam that should be painful but somehow wasn't.

Now there were hands in his armpits, hauling him away from the planking, fingers digging painfully into his flesh. A chair appeared behind him and he was pushed down into it. He'd escape the noose but the gaffer would get to him if he told the truth about Linley, if he even suggested the shooting had been the gaffer's idea. Joe would have his throat slit while he slept, or be shot through the head.

Like Linley.

He accepted the brandy being thrust under his nose with both hands but they were shaking so hard he couldn't drink, although he was desperate for the liquid that sloshed and glinted in the crystal. The glass clattered against his teeth and was taken from him. Somebody was muttering in his ear — he could feel their breath tickle his cheek and was faintly aware of the smell of garlic — but he couldn't make out the words.

Calm theesen down. It were Linley's name being spoken so sudden that got to thee.

He shuddered and rubbed his hands over his face. The brandy was presented to him again and he took the glass and downed it. He could hear the murmurs coming from every corner of the room and considered asking for more brandy. He'd stopped shaking and his mind had cleared but all that meant was that he was all too painfully aware of where he was, and what he had still to endure.

Others have spoken about Linley, in connection with thee. Make a full confession. But that would mean admitting the gaffer had ordered the shooting. None of the previous witnesses had pointed this out. That was because none of them had been given the order. Only Joe Crookes.

'Are you ready to resume?'

Joe nodded, croaked out an 'Aye', and walked unsteadily to where he had been standing when he had swooned — *swooned like a bleedin' woman* — before the judges of the inquiry and the packed chamber. His humiliation was complete and this was, conversely, a brief comfort to him — for things could not get any worse — until he remembered the thought that had brought him to his knees. The gaffer would kill him and if not the gaffer then a relative of one of his victims. A flimsy piece of paper wouldn't save him from that sort of justice being meted out.

Now, he was aware of the inquisitive faces all turned

his way. The brandy still burned in his throat. The question was put to him again.

'You were seen by several witnesses, stalking Mr Linley, carrying a gun. For what purpose?'

He coughed into a clenched fist, praying he would not descend into another fit of retching. He dredged up the words he would speak; they were as heavy as lead weights in the pit of his stomach. He forced them out.

'To shoot Linley.'

Gasps and exclamations and calls for quiet rang around the room. Joe dipped his chin, trying to gauge the reactions of those closest to him without looking at them directly. He was aware of jostling behind him, more calls for order. The room fell silent again.

'I cannot ask you to continue,' said the judge from his platform, 'without letting you know the very great peril in which you stand. If you are guilty of this crime and do not confess your part fully then you will have to be tried for your life. Do you understand?'

Joe chewed on his lip and cursed his own stupidity. He hadn't appreciated that accepting an offer of immunity meant confessing his crime in front of a hundred men in this chamber, and all the citizens of the town when the next day's headlines were printed. But if he didn't continue, he'd be arrested before he could get out of the room, charged with Linley's murder, tried and hanged. He had a choice but it was no real choice.

'Can you answer?'

'Aye. Yeah, I understand.'

'You may do as you please, of course, but you will obtain security if you make a full confession. However, to receive your certificate, you must satisfy us that you have revealed the full extent of your involvement in these outrages.'

Joe glanced at the public gallery and, to his horror, met the eyes of the man whose factory he had bombed. Wheatman. Joe had introduced himself to this man as a fellow victim of the outrages. He looked away quickly but not before the man's furious glare was burned onto his retina. How many of his victims were here to see him, and was Linley's ghost among them? He would have asked Seth to come along, to stand in his corner, but he was cross with Seth, wasn't he? Seth hadn't to face this pack of jackals.

He'd missed another question.

'Pardon me, sir?' said Joe.

'What quarrel had you with Linley?'

'Oh, none at all! I 'ad no personal score to settle. An' I didn't . . . I did not intend to . . . The gaffer said Linley was doin' us — doin' the union — a great deal o' injury.'

'How so?'

'Settin' a whole lot o' lads on, tryin' to spoil the trade altogether. Doin' all the harm he could.'

Whispers rippled through the room. Joe had not known Linley personally but he'd known of him, and known that he was not liked in the town. Nobody had a good word to say about him until he got shot. Death had popularised him well enough. 'Gaffer said I were to wound 'im, to let Linley know he weren't doin' reight by the men. I were followin' 'is orders.'

'The gaffer's orders.'

'Aye.'

'And did this gaffer pay you for your trouble?'

'He gave me twenty sovereign.'

'And might this gaffer have a name?'

Joe squared his shoulders and again glanced at the faces filling the room. He couldn't see the gaffer's badger stripes.

He breathed in and held the air in his lungs, aware of the stillness in the chamber, of everybody's rapt attention. He gave his answer on the outbreath, as if the words were being forced from his body.

'William Broadhead.'

* * *

Joe pushed past the men who were crowding the corridor, the staircase and the foyer beneath, not daring to raise his head or pause in his flight. Was that derisive jeer as he left the chamber meant for him? Was that a deliberate shove on the staircase that made him stagger and almost lose his footing?

He'd been released from the chamber after sharing every detail of his crime with the judge, and warned he could be recalled to give more evidence and should not leave town. Then the next witness had been called and Joe scarpered. He released the breath he'd been holding when he reached the street. Marching up the hill towards Barker Pool, he fully expected to have his coat-tails grabbed, his hat knocked off, or his legs kicked from under him. He had a knife in his pocket and he curled his hand around the mother-of-pearl handle. Let anybody try to ambush him, he'd stick them without a second thought. He had a gun licence too, but that would soon be confiscated, he had no doubt, indemnity or no indemnity. The union scabs and the rabbits of Ecclesfield Wood would be safe. That the worst was over was a slow and delicious realisation.

Eventually, a grin spread across Joe's face. His steps quickened and he fairly flew the rest of the way to Seth's place.

Trust his brother to bring him hurtling back down to earth.

'So when does tha get this certificate?' Seth was sitting at his kitchen table, watching Ginny cook tea. Having a woman around had many advantages, Joe reflected. He kissed the back of her neck and wrapped his arms around her waist, aware of Seth looking away to stare gloomily out of the window.

'Judge said he'd read out a list o' who's getting one when it's all done,' said Joe.

'Will tha be on it?'

Joe hadn't thought of that. He blew his cheeks out. 'Why wun't I be? Gi' me some credit, Seth. Av told the whole truth, an' I've kept thee out on it when I could've named thee. So shurrup wi' thee mithering.'

He hooked his foot around a chair and pulled it out, sitting down and pulling Ginny onto his lap. She slapped at his hands, laughing — 'I've this tea to finish!' — and he reluctantly let her go again.

'Lou is coming round later,' said Ginny.

'She's bin busy on Ginny's behalf,' Seth said. 'Fightin' tha corner.'

'She's a sweetheart,' said Ginny.

Joe shrugged. 'I din't make Ginny come 'ere. It were 'er choice an' she can go back if she wants.'

'Joe!' Ginny threw him an aggrieved look. 'I'm just glad you've done your duty and now you can make a fresh start. With me.' She looked at him, uncertainly. 'Did anything get mentioned about . . .'

Joe held up his hand to stop her. 'It never come up. So we've no immunity from that, so I'd recommend tha continues to keep thee gob shut.' He turned to Seth. 'Crimes that deserve the gallows, that's what they were sayin'. Intimidation an' violence, even about the little stuff like takin' the bands. They'd 'av the hounds bayin' for us if they knew about Change Alley.'

Seth shook his head. 'Thought we weren't talkin' about that? Anyhow, it'll end well for the unions, I reckon. They've caught Westminster's eye an' I reckon it won't be long afore they're recognised proper, enshrined in law.'

Joe took the plate of meat and potatoes Ginny offered him. 'Tha does talk out o' thee arse sometimes but tha's the brainbox o' the family so I'll tek tha word for it. Wonder what's keepin' Lou? Hope she doesn't bring tha brother-in-law back wi' 'er.'

He patted the pocket that held his knife and decided he'd keep it on his person at all times now, just to be on the safe side.

24

It was Louisa's first time as the passenger of a hansom cab; she could be the wife of a town burgher, or one of the royal princesses exhilarated by an illicit drive through the centre of town. She could have Daniel Housley sitting alongside her, newly-weds out for a jaunt. She sighed.

Albert Rowbotham was on the box, negotiating street vendors, wagons and lumbering omnibuses with a flick of the reins and a few well-chosen words, all while driving the horse at a fair lick. The animal was a beauty, a long-legged ex-racer Jemima had purchased the previous August at the Brigg horse fair. Jemima had insisted on providing the transport, telling Albert he could keep all his takings for the next two days, provided he wait for Louisa for as long as was required. 'An' no slouching off to the nearest alehouse. I want 'er back in one piece, Al.'

They crossed the river Don at Lady's Bridge and Louisa reluctantly turned her thoughts to the unwelcome task ahead of her. She was cross with herself for agreeing to be Ginny's messenger — after all, this was the girl who had led her to Change Alley and the horror that was never far from her thoughts — but she couldn't help admire Ginny's spirit. Ginny would get what she wanted, one way or the other.

Albert slowed the horse on Harvest Lane and they trotted along gently. Louisa moved forward, out of the shadow of the cab's hood, so she could enjoy the warmth of the sun on her face. They passed a small dairy farm, the tall perimeter wall of an armoury and a row of brick-built workshops that were rented by little mesters, the specialist craftsmen who worked alone and whose skill at forging, grinding or finishing was renowned throughout the world. Louisa felt like she was seeing these familiar sights for the first time, savouring them as Ginny would. Here was a medium-sized foundry, probably employing two or three hundred people, the sort of place Silas aspired to. Louisa wondered if he would rise to the very top of the industry and end up in charge of a place like the Atlas Works in Brightside that employed thousands of people. She wouldn't be surprised.

All too soon, they were drawing up outside the Hinchcliffe factory. Albert guided the horse into the yard and towards the trough. The animal dipped its head to drink.

'I might need a hand gettin' out,' said Louisa. The corsetry she wore concealed her state but also restricted movement, and where in the past she would have swung herself to the ground from an omnibus without a second thought, she was afraid that now she'd end up sprawled in the dirt.

'Ah, reight.' He jumped down to help her disembark. She stumbled and he caught her in his arms and set her on her feet.

'There tha goes, love.'

He released her with a wink. He fancied himself, did Albert. He reminded her a little bit of Joe; they were around the same age, mid-thirties, their age showing in the crinkles around their eyes, and both believed themselves to be God's gift to women.

'I shan't be long,' she said. She adjusted the blouse

she wore over the corset and took a deep breath that only made the waistband of her skirt dig more painfully into her thickened waist. She was not only Ginny's message bearer; she had her own news to impart and hoped she was not doing her friends a disservice by fearing they would judge her and find her wanting.

She was halfway across the yard, and had just thrown a glance at the clerk's cottage, when Harriet and Silas emerged from the path at the side of the house and hurried towards her. Harriet was pale, her eyes red-rimmed. In rolled-up shirtsleeves, Silas looked like he was ready to punch somebody. Not just anybody. Joe Crookes.

Louisa spoke quickly, taking Harriet's hands in hers. 'She's alright, she's stayin' wi' me.' It was a small lie, in the scheme of things. 'She asked me to come an' tell thee —'

Silas interrupted her. 'That boy's upstairs ruwerin' for his mother an' nowt Harriet does will console 'im. Tha can tell 'er that.' He turned to Harriet. 'See? Not murdered, not under the wheels o' a cart. I told thee. She ran off to be wi' her fancy man, the ungrateful little . . .' he trailed off.

Harriet smiled weakly at Louisa. 'What a welcome we give you. Come into the house, Lou. Who is . . . ?' She gestured to Albert who was back on his box, watching them with an amused expression on his face.

'Albert brought me. He'll wait an' take me back,' said Louisa. 'Can he have summat to drink?'

Harriet called out to him. 'Would you like a cup of tea?'

'I'd rather 'av beer if tha's got any.'

'It's tea or nowt,' said Louisa.

'Tea, then. Thank ye.'

'Travellin' in style, eh, Lou?' said Silas.

'That's the least o' it. Wait 'til tha hears the rest.'

Silas mashed the tea while Harriet divided a sponge cake into slices, and Louisa sat at the kitchen table and told them about Ginny's decision to marry and stay in town. She did not tell them Ginny was living over the brush with Joe Crookes, or that she wanted to leave Isaac in the care of the Hinchcliffes.

When she had finished, Silas sighed and shrugged and looked at Harriet. She returned his gaze steadily. 'She's a grown woman.'

'She's got responsibilities,' said Silas.

'She won't leave Isaac. Lou, have another piece.'

Louisa wiped crumbs from her blouse into her hand and the dog leapt up from her spot by the fireplace to lick them from her palm, then sat on her haunches, gazing at Louisa hopefully. 'Ta, I will. Shandy, tha's a gannet.'

'Well.' Harriet spread her hands on the table. 'When are they to be married?'

'I don't know. I gather she asked 'im.'

'It's not 'appening,' said Silas. He sat back and folded his arms.

Harriet nodded slowly. 'Will she come and talk to us? Isaac needs reassuring.'

The three of them glanced up at the ceiling. Louisa had heard the boy's sobs when Harriet took a piece of cake up to him but now there was no sound from above.

'Maybe 'e can stay wi' thee for a bit? She'll calm down,' said Louisa, 'an' she'll see sense, I'm sure o' it.' She wasn't sure of it at all. 'No sense in tryin' to drag her 'ome against 'er will. She'll only tek off again.'

'I'm the one who'll get the blame for it,' said Silas.

Harriet snorted. 'Since when did you worry about what your parents think?'

'She's a widow wi' no means o' support and a child to raise. She's lucky we din't fetch a constable.'

'Oh, stop. You knew she'd gone off under her own steam,' said Harriet, 'that's why we didn't raise the alarm. And you were right about that, and Louisa is right about treading carefully now. You'll look after her, won't you?'

'A'course,' said Louisa. She sipped from her cup. 'Lovely tea. I've more news if tha's up to it.'

'Don't tell us she's carryin' that man's child,' said Silas. He laughed derisively, then stopped. 'What's up, Lou?'

She hadn't meant to cry but now the dam had burst she couldn't stop. Harriet knelt beside her, rubbing her back. Silas looked stricken. He took the hand that wasn't clamped over her mouth and held it tightly. Harriet whispered to her, meaningless sounds, comforting noises. Eventually, she caught her breath in a series of gasps and asked for a cloth. Harriet hurried away, returning with a handkerchief, and Louisa gently extracted her hand from Silas's and blew her nose into it.

'It's my fault,' said Harriet, 'I should have never introduced you. I put an unfair burden on you.'

Louisa let out a shuddering sigh. 'Don't be daft.' She knew the concern on their faces would harden after she had told them her news, that their expressions would become frozen in an effort to hide their disgust. She was terrified they would be polite to her, after the initial shock, and wave her off amiably enough. Harriet might even wrap up some cake for her to take with her. But the truth would prove too much for them. She was under no delusion she would lose these precious friendships for a second time, and this time it would be forever.

'It's thee,' Silas said. He was looking at her strangely. 'Tha's the one that's pregnant, not 'er.'

Harriet gasped. 'What? Louisa?'

'He's reight,' She got to her feet — it would be easier for them to ask her to leave if she did not have her feet under their kitchen table but was already halfway out of the room — and sniffed a few times to clear her nose, and wiped her hands over her face. 'I am. An' god knows who's the father, because I don't. It's a risk o' the profession.'

In any other circumstances, she would have laughed at the confused expression on Silas's face. Harriet understood her immediately, though; Louisa could see that.

'It's why I lost touch wi' thee,' she said. 'I were ashamed.' It was easy, now she had started, to continue, and the words poured out. 'I were given a choice an' I've made it. I'll 'av her, or him. I've got a proper job an' all. That man, outside, 'e's a driver for Greaves an' I'm 'elping run the firm. Tha could call me 'is boss, though he wouldn't agree.' She smiled tremulously. 'It's a fresh start. Your Ginny's an angel compared wi' me.'

In the stunned silence that followed, Shandy pressed her nose into Louisa's skirt. She moved away, resting her hand on the door handle.

'Has tha finished?' said Silas.

'Aye.'

He strode towards her and enfolded her in a hug so strong it took her breath away.

Then Harriet was telling him off for squeezing

Louisa too tightly and leading her back to the table, pressing her into a chair and crouching before her, wiping Louisa's cheeks, wiping her own cheeks with the corner of her apron, and all the while apologising for being a terrible friend.

'Harriet, tha weren't to know.'

'But you've been through all this alone.'

Silas patted her shoulder. 'Well, if she 'as, she's not on 'er own now. She's got us.'

'I'm mortified,' said Louisa, 'an' I don't deserve tha kindness.'

'Tha's wrong about that,' said Silas, 'an' tha's wrong about summat else.'

'What?' said Harriet.

'Ginny. She's no angel.'

***

They sat round the table with a fresh pot of tea and after a while began to talk of other things. Silas was now thinking of expanding the existing factory rather than relocate to new premises and Harriet was working out the costings. 'He wants to catch up to Tyzack's,' said Harriet, 'who has two hundred men making saws and scythes and files and steel.'

'Catch up and surpass 'im,' said Silas. 'It's meant takin' out a big loan. We belong to the Fitzwilliam building society now.'

They had looked at one of the new townhouses, where, said Harriet, there'd be a room for Louisa if she wanted one. Louisa's face coloured. Silas had obviously told his wife about the state of her rundown cottage. Harriet mentioned the merciful end to William Broadhead's reign of terror — here,

Louisa had shifted uncomfortably in her seat and Harriet mistook it for a physical discomfort, fetching a cushion for the small of her back. Finally, they remembered the driver was still sitting outside on his box. Silas excused himself to check the hull; he took another cup of tea and slice of cake out to Albert.

'I'd better get off,' said Louisa.

The two women embraced on the doorstep. 'Please come for tea on Saturday,' said Harriet. 'I'll be disappointed if you don't. Bring Ginny. Tell her we promise not to cage her up but she must come. Isaac is beside himself.'

'Don't worry, I'll tell 'er. Say bye to Silas.'

A voice called Louisa's name. She looked around to see Daniel Housley hurrying towards her and, despite herself, her heart soared.

'Ey up, Dan.'

'Good afternoon, Dan.'

Daniel Housley smiled awkwardly. 'Ladies.' He executed a jerky bow and blushed. 'I've been asked to accompany Miss Leigh home.'

'Don't be soft,' said Louisa, recalling her earlier daydream when they sat beside each other in the gig. She should stop being daft. It didn't help anybody, least of all her. 'I've got Albert, I don't need an escort. An' how would you get back?'

'Is this Silas's doing?' said Harriet.

He nodded. 'But I am most happy about it. I mean to say, I don't mind at all.' He wrung his hands. 'It would be my pleasure to travel with you, Miss Leigh. I need to visit the Norfolk hall to purchase a new pair of gloves for my mother, so really you are doing me a favour by providing transport. I can alight nearby.'

'Well, I can drop thee off reight outside the market . . .'

'Wonderful!' He beamed at her. 'Thank you, Miss Leigh.'

Louisa hugged Harriet. 'Bye, love.' She took Daniel's arm, leading him towards the cab. 'Dan, what 'av I told thee about callin' me Miss Leigh?'

Albert Rowbotham grumbled about the length of time he'd been kept waiting and wanted payment for carrying the additional passenger. Despite Louisa's protests, Daniel Housley handed over three shillings.

'It's a clement day for a drive,' he said, and instructed Albert to push back the hood. 'Miss . . . Louisa, will you be warm enough?'

'Aye.'

As the cab reached Harvest Lane, she closed her eyes briefly, overcome by drowsiness, and hoped Dan would not chatter on the journey back into town. He seemed to understand this and was content to sit in silence alongside her, swaying gently to the rhythm of the horse's clopping hooves, leaving Louisa with her thoughts. She was satisfied and gratified; she'd delivered a toned-down version of Ginny's message, had unburdened herself to her friends, and they remained her friends. It felt like a stepping stone safely crossed in her journey to a better life.

The man sitting beside her would not be in that life, not once he discovered her secret.

The cab pulled up on the edge of the busy square in front of the Norfolk market hall.

Daniel jumped down and held out his hand to Louisa. 'Accompany me? I know nothing at all about fashion, and my mother is bound to be unhappy with my choice.'

Louisa was surprised by his sudden boldness, and by herself for agreeing. 'We don't want tha presentin' the wrong sort o' gloves to thee mother.'

When they entered the building, she was momentarily dazzled by the shafts of light streaming through the iron and glass ceiling. They descended the few steps to the floor of the long hall. The flicker of lamps set at regular intervals gave the central feature, a ten-foot-tall moonstone fountain, an eerie glow, as if the world had turned upside down and she was underwater. She stopped beside a draper's stall, her eye caught by a tilted tray of buttons of every size and colour. She ran her hand over a bolt of midnight-blue silk, attracting the attention of the shop-keeper, who raised his eyebrows enquiringly. 'Can I help you, miss?'

'Oh. No, no, am just lookin'.'

She wandered on, aware of Daniel Housley at her side, and fantasised that they were newly-weds, choosing fabrics and trinkets to furnish their new home.

'Do you know,' he said, 'there are more than fifty shops in this hall.'

'Oh aye? Av never seen so many tranklements gathered up in one place.'

They strolled on. When a passer-by accidentally bumped Louisa's arm, Daniel crooked his elbow and they continued arm in arm. She smiled at him and his cheeks reddened.

'Tha seems shy around me, Dan.'

His blush deepened. 'Not at all.' He coughed. 'Do you know, where this hall stands was once the site of the largest public inn in the town? It was called . . .'

'The Tontine! Aye, I remember it, just barely. It were knocked down when I were about ten years o' age, I reckon. Me mother had a fancy patch box from the Tontine. I don't know how she got hold of it. I can't ask her neither. She died a couple o' years since.'

'I'm very sorry for your loss.'

'Aye. Well.'

'The Tontine was quite famous. Lord Surrey kept beautifully appointed rooms for his personal use. Those souvenirs are worth holding onto.'

'It were in her things. I must've lost it.' She wasn't going to tell him she'd pawned the elaborately decorated patch box long ago. 'I do remember her sayin' the Tontine should 'av never been demolished. It were a landmark. She told me about the postal coach that left 'ere precisely at eleven every mornin' for the journey to London that took a day an' a half.'

'It was one of the main staging posts. Ah, I see our destination.' He steered her towards a shop that seemed to sell only ladies' hats and gloves. 'It had stabling for sixty horses. It had a brewery and a banqueting hall that was the talk of the county.'

Louisa picked up a green velvet bonnet and stroked the nap. 'Tha's full o' facts, Dan.' He looked stricken. 'Am not complainin'! I like to talk wi' thee.'

'I feel the same.' He coughed into his fist. 'Ah, what would you recommend?'

She held up a pair of fur-trimmed gloves. 'I like these.'

'Splendid.'

Louisa wandered away while Daniel paid for the gloves. She'd return to this place, which was probably just as grand as the building it had replaced, when she had coin to spare. She would treat herself to that green bonnet. She stood before the water feature, the cooler air caressing her face. She would buy a small gift for Jemima Greaves, something frivolous that Jemima would never get for herself, to thank her for the kindness she had shown her, the lifeline she had thrown. She would buy some wool and knit a tiny cloak and a tiny pair of mittens . . . Louisa breathed in sharply. What was she doing here, flirting with Daniel Housley? She could imagine they were a courting couple all she liked, but she was fooling herself.

'Louisa?'

She whirled around.

'I'm sorry, I didn't mean to startle you.' Daniel Housley was carrying two packages tied with string. 'I've run my errand and,' he blew out his cheeks, 'now I'd like to invite you to the tearoom across the street.'

Louisa hesitated.

He looked crestfallen. 'Of course, I've monopolised you for too long.'

'No, don't be daft. It's just . . . oh, ignore me.' She took his arm. 'I'd love to take tea wi' thee.'

She could pretend they were an ordinary courting couple for a little while longer.

25

Two weeks had passed since Ginny had crept out of her brother-in-law's house in search of the man whose head now rested on the pillow next to hers. She gazed at Joe's sleeping profile and stroked his chest in slow, circular motions, moving her hand gradually lower. She switched her gaze to the thin gold wedding band she wore, the ring that Peter had pushed onto her finger when she was carrying Isaac in her belly. Legally, she was still Mrs Hinchcliffe but Joe had advised her to get accustomed to calling herself Mrs Crookes and to flash the wedding band at the landlord when he came to collect the rent. They risked eviction, otherwise, for living in sin. So now she was, to all intents and purposes and excepting the actual marriage papers, Ginny Crookes.

Mrs Ginny Crookes. She whispered it aloud. Joe had told her they would formalise their union as soon as all the inquiry nonsense was over, with Louisa and Seth as witnesses.

She played her fingers over the line of hair that ran from his belly to his groin.

Joe growled deep in his throat. 'Keep doin' that an' I can't be 'eld accountable for what might 'appen.'

She smiled. 'I thought you were asleep.'

Joe opened his eyes and frowned at her. 'What's the time?'

'Must be dinner time. I'm hungry. Are you?'

'Hungry for thee, love. Allus hungry for thee.'

He gathered her hair in his fist and pulled her towards him — 'Gi' us a kiss' — then sighed in exasperation when Seth's knuckles drummed on the closed door.

'Are tha pair comin' or what?'

Ginny sighed and pushed herself upright. 'Alright,' she called. 'We're just getting ready.' She tapped Joe's chest. 'Come on then.'

He groaned. 'Already tha's the naggin' wife.'

Joe had persuaded Seth to give up his bed by explaining that he and Ginny couldn't very well be expected to sleep on the settee every night. He'd promised Seth they'd have their own place before long, once the inquiry was done and dusted — 'The inquiry tha's somehow escaped, brother.' Ginny was starting to get a little bit tired of Joe's constant refrain — everything, it seemed, even finding a job, must wait until the inquiry was over and Joe had received his certificate of exoneration.

Half an hour later, they knocked on Louisa's door and she emerged carrying a wicker basket. Seth took it from her and the four of them strolled through the town, leaving the busy streets behind as they crossed the canal towards Clay Wood. Joe cast a longing glance back at the White Lion as they passed the alehouse.

'Bit early,' said Seth.

'We can 'av an ale on the way back,' said Louisa. 'Av brought some pop but in this heat we'll soon be thirsty agen.'

Ginny was walking ahead, arm in arm with Joe. She glanced back. 'Don't you two make a lovely pair.' She laughed when Louisa raised her eyes to the smoke-stained sky above. When Ginny had suggested a Saturday afternoon picnic, Louisa had, for some reason, wanted to invite that supercilious clerk, Daniel Housley. 'No,' said Ginny, 'it would be better if it was just we four. Our merry little band. I don't think he'd want to come, anyway, not with my brother-in-law pouring poison in his ear about Joe.' Even saying this much riled her, but perhaps Louisa saw that and to avoid an argument had simply agreed that Ginny was right.

Louisa's face had rounded out with her pregnancy and her dimples were even deeper when she smiled. Despite her scandalous status, she seemed the happiest Ginny had ever seen her. Ginny was glad for her, and equally glad she wasn't in Louisa's position. When she got pregnant again, she would be Mrs Ginny Crookes. Officially.

'Is it Seth's?' she'd asked Louisa, mock-innocently. A tiny part of her wondered if it could be Joe's. She had never entirely believed that Joe and Louisa had not slept together.

Louisa had laughed. 'That's one thing I can be definite about.'

'So?'

'No.' Louisa had sighed. 'It's not Seth's.'

'It's a girl,' Ginny had said. 'I can feel it. It's a skill I have.'

'If tha says so.'

Now, the path they were on steepened and Ginny could see a pinnacle reaching into the sky a short distance from a stand of trees.

'What's that?' she said.

'Cholera monument,' said Louisa. She sounded slightly out of breath. 'We can sit an' 'av our picnic there. It's a good spot.'

When they reached the monument, Ginny's gaze

was level with the tops of the town's church spires and chimney stacks. Isaac would love it here. He would say he was a bird, high above the ground, and run about flapping his arms for wings. Her breath caught in her throat, and she wondered whether the Hinchcliffe factory was visible from here. If she had a telescope she might see Isaac playing in Harriet's garden with Shandy the dog. She had visited twice since leaving, with Louisa for support; both occasions had been painful. She'd told Isaac she would send for him as soon as she found a lovely house for them to live in, and wouldn't that be grand? She had collected her few possessions, Harriet insisting she keep the clothes she had donated. Peter's folks had been informed, by Silas, of her engagement to a man from the town. To her astonishment, their answering letter contained two five-pound notes. Joe had been less impressed. 'Least they can do.' He'd held out his hand, palm up, and gestured with his fingers. 'Give 'em 'ere then, Mrs Crookes.'

A man was sitting at the foot of the monument, smoking a pipe. He hailed Seth.

''ow do.'

Seth nodded to him as they walked by. 'Ey up, Mikey. How's thee?'

''ow do,' said Joe.

The man's eyes passed over Joe and back to Seth. 'Am recruitin' again if tha's lookin'.'

'Joe's after a job,' said Ginny. Joe glared at her. 'Well, you are!'

'I've got nowt for 'im,' said the man flatly, still looking at Seth.

'I weren't askin',' said Joe, but Ginny could see the hurt in his eyes. He strode off, to where Louisa had found a spot for them to sit, spitting his parting words over his shoulder. 'Tha lot can 'av thee chinwag. Am getting' me dinner.

* * *

On the way home, Joe stalked ahead of the others, having rejected Ginny's attempt to take his arm, and when they reached the White Lion he slipped inside the alehouse without looking back at them.

'Looks like we're gettin' that ale then,' said Louisa.

Ginny threw her a grateful look.

The lounge was dingy and almost bare of furniture. The four of them congregated around the only table in the place, a beer barrel stood on end. Men stood in clusters and the air was heavy with tobacco fumes from the clay pipes hanging from the mouths of most of them. A woman Ginny guessed must be the landlady stood at the end of the counter, watching a maidservant serve ale to the customers.

'Who's payin'?' said Joe. He was looking at Seth.

'Am not actually made o' money, tha knows,' said Seth, but he went to the counter.

Louisa called after him. 'I'll take a cheese an' onion breadcake if there's one goin'.'

'Aren't you full?' said Ginny.

Louisa just patted her stomach.

Alerted by the sound of a female voice, the landlady turned her disapproving glance on the two women. A brindle greyhound sat by her side, eyeing the room magisterially. Ginny returned the landlady's glare until the woman dropped her eyes.

'We're paying customers, aren't we?' she said.

'Don't start,' said Joe. 'Am not in the best o' moods.'

Seth returned with the drinks. 'She's gettin' thee a snack when she can,' he said to Louisa. 'Busy in 'ere. Wages burnin' a hole in lots o' pockets.'

Joe grunted.

Seth sipped his beer. 'We'll be reight, Joe. Don't worry theesen.'

'Am not worried. Av got me own irons in the fire.' He put his arm around Ginny's waist, pulling her close. 'Tha'll see.'

'Am not doubtin' thee.' Seth cleared his throat. 'Looks like the gaffer's in bother. They 'ad to serve a summons on 'im to get him in front o' the inquiry, and now he's bein' recalled to gi' more evidence. He's had the stuffin' knocked out o' him, I'd say.'

Ginny stroked the hand that Joe had clasped around her waist. 'Joe's just waiting for that certificate, aren't you, Joe?' He glowered into his tankard of beer. 'And then we can forget about the whole lot of it.'

She turned to Louisa. 'I hope you and Seth will witness our marriage. You will, won't you?' She leaned close to whisper in Louisa's ear. 'And if you and Seth get together we'll be real sisters and Isaac will have a cousin to play with and to love.'

Louisa laughed. 'Tha doesn't give up, does tha?'

Ginny suddenly felt herself turned loose by Joe, and stumbled into Louisa. 'Oh!'

The table rocked as Joe threw Seth against it. 'Tha's a smug git!'

Seth swung his arm, clumsily, caught off guard with an almost comical look of surprise on his face. But his fist connected square on Joe's jaw. Joe stumbled into a group of men who pushed him back at Seth. The room filled with jeers and catcalls and a space cleared around the brothers. Joe punched Seth in the stomach and Seth staggered back, winded. Joe kicked out but slipped and landed on his back on the sawdust floor with a thud. Ginny cried out when the greyhound leapt towards them and stood over Joe, showing its teeth. The landlady clobbered Seth behind the ear and, with a ferocious strength Ginny would not have thought her capable of, lifted Joe from the ground by the collar of his shirt.

'Gerrout on it!' she said. 'And tha pair o' tarts an' all. Go on. Get out.'

Smarting from the insult but unwilling to tackle the landlady, Ginny ran outside, Louisa, Seth and Joe on her heels.

Joe sat on the edge of the pavement and Seth leaned against a nearby lamp-post, examining his nails. Ginny bent to try to inspect Joe's face but he brushed her off. 'Tha like a gnat in me ear.'

'What were all that about?' said Louisa. She sat on a low wall, her face turned towards the warmth of the sun. The interior of the alehouse had been so dim, Ginny had forgotten what a beautiful summer's day it was.

'He started it,' said Seth. 'Nearly got me crown jewels an' all.'

'Tha dun't use 'em, anyway,' said Joe. 'No loss.' He wheezed with laughter. Seth joined in.

'Come 'ere,' said Joe and Ginny reluctantly sat down beside him. 'Nowt to worry about, love. Brother stuff.'

'He lost 'is temper because I said no to another loan,' said Seth. 'Reckon Joe owes me 'is own weight in sovereigns by now.'

'Joe, is that why tha went for 'im?' said Louisa. 'Tha needs to curb thee temper. Somebody could've got hurt.'

Joe got up and offered Ginny his hand. 'Aye, well, I don't 'av 'is way wi' words.'

Ginny took his hand and got to her feet. She brushed her skirt down, Louisa stood up from the wall and they set off for the walk home. 'Never a dull moment with you, Joe. Hang on.'

The others stopped and turned to her. 'What?' said Seth.

Ginny laughed. 'Who's going back inside to get the picnic basket?'

26

Louisa looked around the kitchen table. She had the full attention of the others, whose serious faces looked faintly demonic in the lamplight. Even Shandy, sitting by Silas's side, was watching her, the dog's head tilting from left to right and back again. The only sound in the room was the ticking of the clock on the mantelpiece. Harriet had cleared away the plates and returned to sit opposite Louisa, breathing out slowly and resting both hands flat on the oak surface. She had nodded for Louisa to begin.

Louisa's gaze passed over Daniel to settle on Silas. 'Ha,' she said.

Silas whipped his head around to Harriet. 'Ha ha.'

Harriet's lip twitched but that was all. She turned to Daniel. 'Ha ha ha.'

Daniel pressed his lips together and looked into Louisa's eyes. She widened them slightly while keeping her face straight. He burst out laughing. 'I can't do it!'

'Dan loses again,' said Silas.

The clerk held up his hands. 'My stomach hurts. I'll sit the next one out.'

Louisa was aware of Daniel's merry eyes on her during the next round of the game.

The three of them managed six 'ha's before Harriet dissolved into giggles, pressing her shoulder against Silas, who put his arm around her, laughing. Daniel gave Louisa a broad smile. This was the most relaxed she had ever seen him. He'd taken off his necktie and unfastened the top button of his shirt, and his hair was tousled.

'Shall we go an' get comfy in the front room?' said Silas. He patted Harriet's arm. 'You an' all. Go an' sit down and I'll mash us a pot of tea.'

'I've not got long before Albert comes for me,' said Louisa.

'Time for a cup of tea, I hope?' said Daniel. He looked away and fiddled with his collar, shy again.

'Aye,' said Louisa. She tucked her arm in his. 'Kind sir, let us stroll to the parlour where we may rest our . . . backsides? . . . on the chaise.'

They were still laughing when they entered the front room to find Isaac curled up on the settee, fast asleep. The dog licked his face.

'Stop it, Shandy,' said Louisa. She picked up Isaac as gently as she could. He stirred in her arms but didn't wake. 'He's fast on. I'll put 'im back to bed.'

'Do you want me to carry him up?' said Daniel.

'I can manage 'im. He's light as a feather.'

Harriet came in while Louisa was tucking the bed-sheet under Isaac's chin.

'He hates missing out, doesn't he? Always wants to know what's happening.'

'Aye.' Louisa straightened. 'Poor lamb.'

Harriet opened her mouth to speak but then seemed to think better of it. Louisa knew it wasn't Isaac and his absent mother she was thinking about.

'I know I shall 'av to tell Dan,' said Louisa, 'sooner or later. Am just enjoyin' his company, for now.'

'He might be more sympathetic than you think,' said Harriet. 'He's fallen in love with you.'

Louisa patted her stomach. 'This'll cure 'im o' that.'

She had tried for a light-hearted tone but sounded only sad about it. Harriet squeezed her hand. 'Not everybody's as forgivin' as thee, Harriet. Let's go an' see why it's so quiet. Think they're hidin' from us?'

This was another one of Silas's favourite games, waiting for one or two people to leave the room then instructing everyone else to hide themselves away.

'Oh, I hope not,' said Harriet. 'Silas is always in the place I expect him the least and frightens me half to death.'

But when they got downstairs, the two men had their heads together over the *Sheffield Telegraph* newspaper.

'Just talkin' shop,' said Silas, folding up the newspaper and putting it down on the settee beside him.

Harriet picked it up and sat down next to him. 'You're reading about the inquiry, aren't you? I saw the headline earlier. All these union men are being painted as devils, especially the leader. I imagine that's not what he was expecting.'

Louisa sat in one of the fireside armchairs, facing Daniel. She busied herself pouring tea into cups and passing them around, trying to think of a different topic she could use to change the subject and finding her mind had gone completely blank.

'The notorious William Broadhead,' said Daniel.

'Tell thee what, though,' said Silas. 'He's puttin' us on the map. Got to give him that. Our trade unions are the talk o' the country, talk o' the world, even. Scoundrels.'

Harriet separated the pages of the newspaper and began to roll them into tubes and knot them into balls. 'The owner of this,' she said, waving a ball at Silas, 'is the servant of the masters, not the workers.'

'It's not the masters blowin' up and shootin' all over town,' said Silas.

'They might not be using violence but they do enough damage you won't read about,' said Harriet. 'What about the puddlers, only this last winter, who had their wages cut in half? Who's going to fight for their rights if not the unions?'

Louisa tutted, keen to change the subject. 'I don't know where Albert's got to.'

'Is there a taphouse nearby?' said Daniel. They both laughed.

'Tha's on thee high horse again,' said Silas to Harriet.

There was a moment of silence, then Harriet said: 'Why don't you try telling the man leading his wife and children to the workhouse that it's all his own fault?'

Louisa saw she had tears in her eyes.

'Alright, that's me told,' said Silas. He tried to hug Harriet but she shook him off. He looked to Louisa for support. 'How can tha defend 'em, though? An' our Ginny's got hersen mixed up wi' one o' em, hasn't she, and now she's gadding about town like a . . . like a . . .'

Louisa pursed her lips. She glanced at Daniel who was helping Harriet ball up the newspaper pages, stacking them neatly next to the grate.

Silas sighed. 'Am sorry, Lou. Am sick of it. All I will say is this lot acts in the shadows an' thugs are attracted to dark places. Thugs like that Joe.'

'Well,' said Harriet, in the brisk tone Louisa recognised meant the debate was over. 'It will all come out in the wash. There's a free pardon to everybody who makes a full confession. We might learn the identities of those who murdered that poor man in Change Alley.'

Louisa jerked and put her hands to her throat. She shuddered, horribly aware of the concerned look Daniel gave her.

'Is everything . . .'

'Tha knows that shudder when somebody walks over tha grave . . .' She leapt to her feet and opened the curtain, pressing her forehead to the pane so they could not see her face. 'Am fed up waitin' on that man.'

'I offered Ginny's bed to you,' said Harriet. 'Why not stay?'

Louisa clung to the curtain, staring into the dark yard. There'd be no velvet curtains in prison, no games of Ha Ha, only the prospect of the hangman's noose. She knew there'd be no pardon for the killers of a night watchman.

She breathed out, trying to slow her heartbeat, and cleared her throat when she could trust herself to speak. Keeping her back to the room, she said: 'I thought Change Alley weren't part o' the inquiry?'

She heard the quiver in her own voice and prayed the others hadn't.

'What I heard,' said Harriet, 'was that the police are no closer to solving the case but if it can somehow be drawn into the inquiry there might be somebody who would come forward, with information, perhaps, or even an outright confession. They can send those who refuse to answer questions to prison. The whole set up is most extraordinary.'

'I thought the inquiry were nearly over,' said Silas.

Louisa's breath had misted the glass so the light that appeared in the distance was blurred. She rubbed the pane. It was a carriage lamp on the road, coming closer.

'Al's 'ere,' she said quietly. 'I'd best get movin'.'

She didn't remember saying goodbye to Daniel or to Harriet or Silas, and the journey home was a blur. She let herself into her cottage, pausing on the threshold. Then she stepped back into the street, closed the door, relocked it and walked the few paces to Seth's, where she hammered on the door.

'Hold thee horses,' said a voice from within, then Seth was there, frowning at her. 'Lou. What's up? Tha looks like tha's seen a ghost.'

Seth shouted upstairs to summon Joe down. Louisa sat on Seth's settee, on the blanket that was thrown over it. Joe pounded downstairs with Ginny following more cautiously, wrapped in a sheet, her shoulders bare and hair mussed.

''ey up, Lou,' said Joe. He peered at her. 'What's the matter wi' thee?'

Ginny sat beside her. 'What's wrong, Louisa?'

She shook her head, sickened by the false concern on all their faces. They'd betrayed her. Joe — or Seth, come to that — had already agreed to confess to Change Alley and not told her about it. They'd have to give her name, too, or it wouldn't be a full confession. She closed her eyes. Her name in the headlines, her baby wrenched from her arms for its own good, her life, over.

'Louisa!' Ginny shook her shoulder. 'You're scaring me.'

She told them, haltingly, watching Joe for his reaction. He appeared genuinely mystified.

'But the gaffer told me it wun't be included,' he said, when Louisa had finished.

'What did 'e say, exactly?' said Seth.

'I can't recall. Summat about them 'aving enough

on, an' it were a bit late, weren't it?' Joe looked at Louisa. 'A bit late in't day to add it in, like? I did ask him, 'cause I remember wonderin' if we could get away wi' murder.'

Louisa shivered and closed her eyes, but the red-tinged blackness behind her eyelids was the colour of the watchman's blood-soaked cloak, and she opened them again, a sob wrenching her gut. Ginny touched her knee, hesitantly.

'I'm sorry, Lou,' she whispered. 'It should've been me. I was weak. I should have gone.'

'Aren't tha glad now tha din't?' said Joe.

'Shut up, Joe. Lou has been a good friend to me . . .'

'Stop thee quarrellin',' said Louisa, 'an' tell me straight. I need to know — Joe, Seth — will thee admit to it to save tha skin, if it comes to it?'

The brothers exchanged glances.

'No, a'course not,' said Seth. 'We've seen what's 'appened to them that's admitted lesser deeds than ours. They're pariahs now. If folk found out we'd killed a watchman . . .'

Louisa nodded. 'That'll 'av to be good enough.'

Joe was biting his knuckle.

'Joe?' she said.

'I know what tha sayin',' he said, 'but if we can get away wi' it entire, by confessin', how is it different to owt else? How is it different to Linley?'

'It's different,' said Seth. 'The whole police force'll be gunnin' for thee, Joe. For us. Linley were against the union an' had it comin'. That other poor bloke were just in the wrong place at the wrong time.'

'Who's to say?' said Joe.

She fought a rising panic. 'Joe, am beggin' thee.'

'You shouldn't have to beg!' said Ginny. 'Joe, how

can you think of . . . ?'

He cut her off. 'Shurrup. It's nowt to do wi' thee. Tha chickened out o' it.' He ignored Ginny's pout of displeasure. 'Here's what I'll do. Summat got said in the White Lion about the gaffer bein' recalled to gi' more evidence.'

'I 'eard that too,' said Seth. 'It's on account of him not 'aving given up enough names for the rattenings.'

'So,' said Joe, 'I'll try an' 'av a quiet word wi' him, while he's got his legal mates around 'im. See what the lie of the land is.'

'When?' said Louisa.

'It's on Friday,' said Seth. 'They're gettin' near the end now.'

Louisa dropped her head. Her job, the baby, her determination to make amends, and Daniel. A flimsy life she had created, as small and easy to tear apart as a shred of baking paper. 'The end o' it can't come soon enough for me.'

27

Joe pulled his hat low over his brow and leaned against the wall of the narrow corridor outside the council chamber, examining the toes of his boots. Seth had offered to go in his place but Joe declined. He'd planted the bomb and lit the fuse. He had the most to lose. If there was to be a chance to confess, he'd take it and damn the rest of them. He had another reason for wanting to be there but Seth didn't need to know that.

He heard the gaffer before he saw him marching his way.

'Now I'm accused of having a false sense of honour,' William Broadhead was saying to the clerk hurrying to keep up with him, 'when I'm merely trying to protect loyal men of the union. Well, I can't do aught but give everything up, along with all the rest.'

As the gaffer entered the chamber, Joe spun on his heel and slipped through the door behind him. 'I'm wi' 'im,' he told the clerk when that man lifted an enquiring eyebrow. William Broadhead was fussing with papers at the witness table and snapped his fingers for the clerk's attention. He paid no attention to Joe whatsoever.

'Gaffer.'

Broadhead looked up at him. 'What,' he said flatly.

Joe leaned in close and the gaffer inclined his head towards him. 'Joe, I thought we were finished?'

'Just listen.' Joe took a deep breath and glanced

around the room, and back at the gaffer, who looked impatient. 'Remember I mentioned that last job to thee, the one in . . .'

'I know the one. And I know where this is going.'

'So, if I ask to be recalled . . .'

'No, Joe. The gentlemen of the inquiry won't hear about that case.'

'But why . . . ?'

'Leave it.' The gaffer straightened and nodded at someone in the room. He looked back at Joe. 'It's not going to happen just so you can save your scrawny neck. It's sorted. You can thank your brother, in part, for that.'

He turned away and started a conversation with the clerk. Joe was confused. How could Seth have been involved? Seth had never had any dealings with the gaffer.

He walked away from the desk, taking up a position against the back wall and glancing around. The room was quieter than the last time he'd been in it, giving his evidence, and he didn't recognise any of the faces around him. He breathed a little more easily. Forget about Change Alley. Pretend Louisa had never raised it. Focus on the next thing, now, and that was he had to see — to hear — Seth's name finally given. They'd had another fight about it and Seth had accused him of becoming obsessed.

'Am sorry I've not been called,' Seth had said, once they'd both calmed down. 'Am grateful to thee for not namin' me when tha were questioned.'

''ow would that have looked? Dobbin' in me own flesh an' blood?'

The judge was droning on. Joe could tell how riled William Broadhead was from the set of his shoulders.

The gaffer would not be issued with his certificate if he did not give up *everything*, if he *withheld* names, if he refused to be *explicit, clear and candid*. The gaffer was being patronised, spoken to as if he was a dribbling infant, and Joe wished he could see the expression on his face but didn't want to attract attention to himself by moving across the room for a better view. He could hear him well enough when he named Dennis Clark as the man he'd paid to blow up Joseph Helliwell. More names followed. George Peace. Elijah Smith. Phineas Dean.

Joe stifled a gasp when Wheatman's name came up, followed swiftly by his own. *Was any person concerned in this intimidation besides Crookes?* The gaffer shook his head. 'I do not know. I do not remember.'

Joe's face burned. He clenched his fists.

I warn you again. It is very easy to implicate Crookes as others and as he himself did. But he was not alone. Are you attempting to screen another person?

'I do not know of any other person.'

Seth would get away with it while he, Joe, was forced to skulk about pretending not to be offended by the dirty looks thrown his way by all and sundry. It wasn't fair.

Now the judge was referring the gaffer to letters he had written to the newspaper, where he had expressed his abhorrence at the Linley shooting and reinforced that stance when the poor man died of his wound six months later.

William Broadhead raised his chin. The whole room was hanging on his reply. 'I know that I shall be held up to the execration of the whole world.'

I know how tha feels, mate. Joe shook his head, resigned to the fact that Seth would remain blameless, and left the chamber.

Outside, he patted his pocket to check the knife was safely on his person. It was a habit now, almost as bad as an involuntary twitch. He couldn't help himself. On the street corner, he hesitated, unwilling to return to Seth's place, especially with Ginny gone to visit her boy. What he really wanted was a jar of ale but he'd overheard his name being mentioned the last time he'd been in the Blue Pig. He no longer walked into inns alone, but didn't want to drink with Seth, not until he'd calmed himself down. He decided he'd go to the money lender in Fargate and change into coin the notes Ginny had been sent by her family. He'd been promising to do it for days. She'd asked for fare to catch the omnibus that morning and he'd sent her along to Louisa's. If she wasn't in to lend a few pennies — she seemed to be permanently at Greaves' stables these days — then Ginny would just have to walk. 'The exercise'll do thee good,' he'd said. 'Tha startin' to look a bit chunky, love.' Ginny had slapped his arm. 'I could be pregnant, Joe. Have you thought about that at all?'

That had rattled him. He turned off the high street onto Fargate, hopping into the road to avoid walking under a scaffold. Colourful shop awnings stretched ahead and the pavement was crowded with pedestrians. Joe scowled. He walked in the gutter, quickly, towards Barker Pool.

'Sorry, mate,' he mumbled when he turned a corner and came up against a tall and burly man. The man scowled, moving forward to knock into Joe. 'I said am sorry, din't I . . .'

Now there was a man behind him too, and Joe was sandwiched between them. 'Oy! What's goin' on?'

He knew all too well. Finally, what he feared most was happening. The rough justice of retribution. They might kill him. Adrenaline coursed through his body. He'd stick them with his knife. He reached for his jacket pocket but before he could take out the knife his arms were pulled back, pinned behind him and the two men had forced him into a ginnel. Joe looked around wildly. The narrow passageway was deserted. He was marched halfway down it, his heart hammering. 'Tha can't do this! Tha's got the wrong man!' Neither thug had spoken and neither responded to him now.

He was slammed against the brick wall, the air whooshing from his lungs. The men were on either side of him now, punching with short, hard jabs, into his ribs, his stomach, and then pounding his head, blows that dizzied him. He fell to his hands and knees and tried to crawl away but got no further than lifting one hand when a searing pain between his legs floored him. He bit back a scream. He was sprawled in the muck, choking on some stinking slime. The sour smell of vomit and pungent smell of shit. Lying in it, its taste in his mouth, his stomach heaved but he was too afraid to move a muscle. He squeezed his eyes closed, listening to the harsh breathing of the men who stood over him. A brief respite. But what next? His gut contracted with fear. A knife? A gun? The lethal stamp of a boot to crack his skull? Heavier breathing now, close to his ear. Gobs of spittle flung on his cheek. Then there were hands in the pockets of his jacket and rummaging in his trousers. His boots were roughly hauled off. Then nothing. He remained limp, eyes closed. Play dead or soon be dead. His legs were kicked, not hard, and his feet stamped on. They were playing with him. He moaned, a small sound for all the shame and fury that filled him.

'Tha's a marked man,' one of them said, conversationally.

Then they were walking away, their laugher echoing down the passage.

* * *

He'd cleaned himself up as best he could ahead of Ginny returning. Seth had given him beer but Joe's hands were shaking too hard to get the cup to his lips. Eventually, he'd asked Seth to leave him be.

He'd gone to bed and that was where Ginny found him.

She sat on the side of the bed and touched his puffy eyes and swollen mouth with her fingers, tears on her cheeks. 'I should have gone with you.'

'Then tha'd be in this state, an' all.'

'They wouldn't attack a woman!'

'How does tha know? Anyhow, I need to talk to thee, about that farm tha's come off.'

Ginny frowned. 'What about it?'

'We should go there, me an' thee an' Isaac. All that land he'll inherit once the old 'uns are gone.'

'But Silas will inherit first, and he'll sell it to fund his ever-expanding empire.' Her smile was bitter. 'Don't talk soft, Joe. We're stayin' in town.'

He hadn't the energy to argue with her, and his heart wasn't in it either. He knew he wouldn't get along with farming, he was a town boy. But this town had turned against him.

'Alright, love. I 'av got another idea in mind.'

Ginny lowered herself down beside him and cradled

him in her arms. 'What's that?'

Joe winced. 'Be careful, love, am as battered as owt.'

'What's going on inside that head of yours, Joe?' He yawned, triggering bolts of pain all over his head.

Those bastards. If he ever found them he would kill them. 'Joe?' He closed his eyes. 'Can tha leave me be, Gin? Tha's just goin' to 'av to trust me.'

28

Louisa closed the ledger and sat back, her hands resting on her belly. The kicks from within were no longer butterfly strokes but more like the insistent jabs of a cat's paw. She smiled to herself. Isaac had been given one of a litter of kittens that would have been drowned in the river if Silas hadn't got to them first. The collie's reaction had been droll. Shandy hadn't known whether the tiny creature was a snack or a pup to protect. She was now the kitten's mattress and plaything.

Louisa yawned and gazed out of the window at the pearly light of the dying day. At the stables below the office of Greaves & Sons, horses clopped to and fro, adding to her sense of drowsiness. 'Bedtime,' she said, looking at her belly. 'For thee, an' all, please.' Her condition was all too visible when she was seated but, standing, her skirts and the longer blouse she had made continued to disguise the bump. She looked plump, rather than pregnant. Daniel had told her she bloomed like a rose in summer. She was putting off telling him the reason for her bonniness. Dan was kind, but he was also proper, a stickler for rules. He had taken her on that promised promenade through the park, told her all about himself, how he was an only child given a good education by his parents, who doted on him, how he was determined to make his mother proud, and had promised to marry a beautiful girl who would give her lots of grandchildren. He had laughed and squeezed Louisa's arm when he said this, and she had tried to return his warm smile.

If circumstances were different . . . she batted the idea away. It wasn't possible and she should accept her lot now. It wasn't a bad lot, after all.

She faced only a short walk home so she decided she would check in with Jemima Greaves before Jemima retired for the night. The older woman was in her kitchen, drinking tea.

'I can mash some more,' she said when Louisa knocked and entered.

'No, it's late an' am off. Thanks, though.'

'All good?'

'Aye.' Louisa paused. 'Takin's are down again.'

'Ah, that's nowt to worry about. Rich folk walk about more when the sun's shining an' the nights are light, so we lose those shorter journeys for a bit. Come September and we struggle to keep up wi' demand right through to May.'

Louisa would be mother to a six-month-old by then. She pondered this unfathomable fact on the walk home. She took a slightly more circuitous route so she would not have to cross the foot of Change Alley but the watchman was always in her thoughts. Look, she wanted to tell him. See, I've a proper job now, and am off the booze for good. I'm a different person to that one that carried a pipe bomb in her sleeve. Seth and Joe will find a straight path too. She flexed her shoulders, sloughing off the busy day even if she could never shake off the burden of guilt she carried. But it didn't do to dwell.

The shadows had lengthened into night by the time she reached her door. A man was leaning against it. Louisa put her hand to her heart.

'Tha startled me.'

Seth took off his cap. 'Sorry, Lou. I were about to give up an' go back.'

'What's up?' She unlocked the door and Seth followed her inside. 'Has that pair o' lovebirds chucked thee out?'

'I pay the rent, so they'd be soft arses to try it,' said Seth.

Louisa laughed, then paused when she saw the shadow on Seth's face. 'What's up?'

He told her what had happened to Joe, standing in the middle of the dark room, his eyes glittering in the dark. Eventually, Louisa lit a lamp.

'Sorry,' said Seth, 'there were no need. I know tha'll be wanting to get to thee bed. I just want to ask thee if tha'll come to the town hall wi' me in the mornin'. Am feelin' a bit wary meesen about bein' out an' about alone.'

'Aye, I can do,' said Louisa. 'What for?'

'To pick up Joe's certificate for 'im. Inquiry's over.'

'In't that a good thing?'

'Aye, but he's reight shook up. It's been four days now. Me an' Ginny, we can't persuade 'im to leave the house.'

* * *

The next morning, Louisa answered the door to Seth's knock. It was half past ten and he was bang on time. Those wanting their certificates had been asked to report to the council chamber from eleven onwards. Louisa was working for Greaves from midday to eleven at night so the timing of their errand suited her. She decided she'd ask Ginny to accompany her to the market tomorrow morning. She needed buttons and wool, not to mention a good natter.

''ow's Joe today?' she said.

'Still in a nark. I just 'ope they gi' him the paper,' said Seth. 'Maybe he won't be so fed up wi' me. His face is a mess, an' all.'

'Poor Joe.'

'Aye, I suppose. Poor's the reight word. He needs to get himsen some work.'

'What about thee?'

'I've a job lined up at a wool-shear forger's. Tryin' to get summat in the factory for Joe an' all, even if it's just sweepin' up.'

'Good luck wi' that.'

'Somebody'll gi' him work.'

'I meant Joe. I can't see 'im wi' a broom in 'is hand, somehow.'

Louisa gazed with interest on the goings-on inside the town hall. Men in clerks' uniforms, gentlemen in toppers and several men in working clothes were milling about. The working men were probably here for their certificates too. She wondered what they had done, what acts they had committed that were being wiped clean from the record, whether any of them would be disappointed and arrested for their crimes before they could leave the building, manhandled into one of the cells beneath the ground. She shivered. No wonder Joe had wanted to stay away.

She had never been inside the council chamber before, the seat of power for the men that ran the town. Proceedings were already underway, the judge explaining to the men before him that he was anxious to carry out the spirit of the act of parliament and grant indemnity to every man who had confessed, provided it had been a full and frank confession.

Louisa supposed he would be the judge of that.

'What do we do?' she said.

'Just wait, I think,' said Seth. He walked to the back of the room and Louisa followed. 'I'm guessin' 'is name'll be called.'

An extravagantly coiffed man — Seth told Louisa this was the lawyer representing the trades — was appealing against the judge's decision to deny the granting of a certificate to the scissor union secretary, Joseph Thompson. It had been deemed he hadn't made a full disclosure. Louisa guessed he was the white-faced man now arguing with his perplexed representative. It wasn't a given, then, as Seth supposed. Then her attention was caught by mention of Joe's name.

The judge was looking around the chamber. 'Does not any person appear to ask for a certificate for Crookes?'

Louisa nudged Seth and he stammered a response. 'I'm 'is brother and can collect on 'is behalf.'

'Very well.' The paper was waved in the air and Seth went forward to take it. 'This is a list of offences. It is not the certificate.' The man finally relinquished it. 'Mr Crookes must read this, and confirm it is complete, and then he may attend here and go to Mr Barker over there,' — he gestured towards a clerk barely visible behind the forest of men standing around his desk — 'and receive a proper certificate signed by us. That will be his protection hereafter.' He dismissed Seth with a wave of the hand.

Seth cleared his throat. 'Beggin' your pardon, sir, I can vouch for Joe an' assure thee that this is all correct. Can I not get it signed for 'im reight now?'

The judge pursed his lips and glanced at the man

sitting on his left, who shrugged. 'Yes, alright. I see no reason why we can't expedite this matter. You may go and wait your turn.'

Half an hour later, the certificate was signed. Outside, Seth stopped on the pavement to examine the inky flourish that gave Joe his freedom. 'Well, that were a relief. For a minute, I thought we'd be sent packin,' he said, passing his hand over his face. 'Joe's free an' clear. It's over, the lot o' it. An' he's taken his lumps for Linley, or whatever it were he got attacked for, so let's 'ope that's an end to that.'

'Din't they say? The ones that attacked him, din't they say owt?'

The sleeping snake in Louisa's mind stirred itself. *Change Alley*. What if Joe had been beaten up because of that? There'd been no more visits from the police-detective but that didn't mean the investigation had been closed. What she did know for certain was that the police were no nearer catching the culprits. Perhaps others knew this too, and knew who had been involved, and had acted.

'Nah, they said nowt, just robbed 'im,' said Seth, 'so maybe that's all it were, a robbery. Nowt personal against Joe. Anyhow, like I say, it's over an' done wi'. Come on, let's go an' cheer up that narky sod.'

When they turned the corner into Barker Pool, Louisa could see from one end of the terrace that Seth's front door stood wide open at the other. She drew in her breath and put her hand on Seth's arm, stopping him.

'What?'

'Did tha leave thee door hangin' open this mornin'?'

Seth trotted towards his cottage. 'Wait outside,' he said, ducking through the door.

Louisa looked up and down the street, at the houses that stood implacably in the mid-morning quiet. There was not a soul abroad, nobody strolling or hurrying along, no faces at windows or people nattering on their doorstep, no animals making their noise, not even any children squatting on the pavement. The gutter down the middle of the road was as dry and dusty as a grinder's lungs. She could hear all the usual town noise from the surrounding streets but there was a stillness to the air here that made her feel cold, despite the warmth of the day, and alone in the world.

She tapped on the window next to the open door. 'Seth?' There was no response. Louisa blew out her cheeks — *sod this for a lark* — and stepped over the threshold.

* * *

Seth was perched on the edge of a chair, staring at his clasped hands. He didn't look up when Louisa entered. She glanced around the room and at the ceiling, as if she would be able to see through it to Ginny and Joe in the bedroom, where they seemed to spend most of their time. But the silence had that peculiar quality that told her nobody else was in the house. She was certain of it without even looking. She glared at Seth with an anger born of fear.

'Tha'd better tell me what's goin' on.'

He ignored her.

'Seth!' She clamped her hand on his shoulder and shook him.

'Aye.' He seemed to come to himself and smiled apologetically at her. 'Sorry, love. I were just tryin' to get me head round it. It's nowt for thee to worry theesen about.'

'Head round what?'

He pointed at the boxy clock on the wall. ''e's taken the lot. Well, I mean to say, what were left.'

'Left o' what?' Louisa looked at the face of the clock as if it could give her the answer. It was quarter to twelve, nearly dinner time. Her stomach rumbled. There were toasted pikelets in the house; she'd eat one on her way to work. 'I've got to get off, Seth. What's 'appened?'

'I knew,' he said, 'soon as I saw that open door. He allus were a careless bugger. They're gone, the pair of 'em, an' I reckon we shan't see 'em again.'

Louisa's stomach fell. 'No, tha's not makin' sense. She'd never leave Isaac, not in a million years. An' she'd tell me, if they were plannin' owt. I know she would.'

'Aye, well. They've gone an' the reason I know it is because me savin's 'ave disappeared.'

'No.'

Louisa ran upstairs and into the bedroom. The bed was mussed up, a sheet trailing onto the floor like an abandoned bridal veil. She yanked open drawers and the wardrobe door. There were a few men's bits she assumed must be Seth's because there was no sign a woman had ever been in the room. Seth was right.

She walked slowly downstairs. He was sitting where she'd left him.

'But where would they go? An' why now, when Joe's got 'is certificate, that he asked you to fetch . . . ?' She trailed into silence.

'They got me out o' the way, thinkin' it'd take a while. Must've left reight after we did.'

'Am goin' to Greaves an' I'll get a cab to Harriet's. Ginny'll 'av gone there. She won't 'av gone off wi' Joe. I can't hardly believe it.'

Louisa clamped her lips together, afraid she was about to begin bawling like a baby. Joe might have stolen Seth's savings but she felt Ginny's betrayal as a knife in her heart. After all Louisa had done for her. And not a word said. It couldn't be true. It wasn't.

She stood over Seth. 'Am goin'. Does tha want to come?'

'I don't see the point, love. They've gone, wi' all me coin. Could be halfway to . . . I don't know, to anywhere. How'd we find 'em now?'

'Alright, well, I'll see thi later.' Louisa stopped on the threshold. 'How much did he take?'

Seth ducked his head again, and clutched his hands together as if he was praying. 'I reckon I 'ad about a hundred sovereign left.' He looked up at Louisa, the rawness in his eyes making her flinch. 'I 'ad more'n three hundred but I spent most o' it.' He hesitated. 'I spent it on payin' me way out o' being named, an' bribing the bobbies. That's the reason I never got called to gi' evidence. Over two hundred sovereign it cost me, an' Joe'll 'av that knowledge now.'

29

As soon as the front door had banged closed behind Seth, Joe leapt out of bed like a jack out of a box. Ginny propped herself on her elbows and watched him stagger about trying to get into his britches. The bruises on his body were dark patches in the gloomy light and his hair was sticking up on end.

'You'd do better if you slowed down a bit,' she said. 'Open the nets? I want to look at you.'

She'd been lying curled up against his back, thinking about her recent trip to see Isaac, and Joe had given every impression of being fast asleep. She'd been thinking her little boy looked more like Peter every day. At first, she had felt relief when Isaac was friendly towards her, wanting to show off the kitten he'd been given. He had cuddled up to her and demanded she pet the animal and coo and fuss over it. But over the course of the visit, Ginny had become increasingly out of sorts and couldn't put her finger on why that should be, until the moment the cat bit Isaac's arm with its tiny pointed teeth. It was Harriet he'd run crying to for consolation.

She watched Joe lace up his boots. 'Joe, why aren't you talking to me? Are you going with Seth after all? Joe!'

Finally, he turned to her. 'Come on.' His voice was rough and urgent. 'Get theesen dressed.'

'Why do I need to come?'

For a heart-sickening moment, she believed Joe was

throwing her out. He'd had enough of her. Another girl had caught his eye and it was Ginny's doing, because she'd become complacent. Tears sprang to her eyes. 'Joe, tell me what's going on!'

'We're leavin',' he said. 'Right now. Don't get hysterical. Just do as I tell thee. I'll explain it all on't way.'

He didn't wait for her reply but dropped to his knees and felt under the wardrobe, pulling out a burlap sack and throwing it onto the bed.

'All tha stuff. In 'ere or tha'll not see it again. Quick as tha likes.'

He waited by the door, arms folded, tapping his foot. Ginny dressed as quickly as she could and stuffed her possessions into the sack alongside his few garments. Fastening her boots, she tried again to ask what was happening, and he cut her off.

'Just get a move on, will tha.'

She could refuse, she could plant herself down on the bed and demand he talk to her, but she had a feeling Joe would simply leave her sitting there and disappear, and she would never see him again. Then Silas would send her packing, back to the farm. Better to hold her tongue for now. She followed Joe downstairs.

In Seth's front room she watched him stretch up to take something down from the flat surface on the top of the wall clock. In one quick motion, he threw whatever it was he'd retrieved to her and she caught it in her hands with a gasp. It was a small fabric bag, dyed green and tied with a yellow silk string.

Ginny looked at Joe, open-mouthed. He nodded briskly and she worked at the knot with fingers made clumsy from fright. A puddle of gold and silver and copper coins sat inside the bag.

‘Joe.’ She spoke in a whisper. ‘We can’t. It’s not right.’

‘Who’s to say what’s right an’ what’s not? Look at me.’ He gestured to his purpled eyes and swollen lips. ‘I’m gettin’ out o’ this town an’ I want thee wi’ me.’

He took the bag from her and weighed it in his hand, and a frown creased his brow. Then he took his coat from the hook and stuffed the bag into an inside pocket.

‘Reight, come on. We’re goin’ to Victoria.’

⋆ ⋆ ⋆

They hurried down Fargate and the high street, Ginny convinced that every eye she met glared back with a look of pure condemnation. Past the market and down Snig Hill, they took a circuitous route to reach Lady’s Bridge that meant they would not have to pass by the town hall and risk bumping into Seth and Louisa. She glanced at Joe, at his hunched shoulders, the stubble on his cheeks above the upturned collar of his coat, the scowl on his face. Gone was the swagger, the bluster and cockiness of the Joe she knew. He looked like the hunted man he was.

Perhaps she had thrown her lot in with the wrong man. Perhaps the timid clerk might have saved her. Ginny could bet that the clerk would soon stop mooning after Louisa when he learned she was carrying a bastard, father unknown. Ginny couldn’t understand what Louisa saw in him anyway, especially compared to Joe, or even Seth. What would they say about Ginny when they discovered her gone? She stumbled and would have ended up in the road under the wheels of a passing carriage if Joe hadn’t reached out to steady her. She would write a letter, once they had reached whichever mystery destination Joe was leading her towards, and explain herself. Runaway lovers. It sounded romantic. She could almost believe it herself.

Crossing Lady's Bridge, she looked down into the swirling water of the Don, only now fully contemplating her departure from the town she had been so determined to remain in. If she went to Harriet and Silas now, explained that she had broken off her engagement to Joe . . . but there was the possibility she was carrying his child, and then she'd be no better off than Louisa. Silas would send her back to the farm in disgrace. She had no choice but to follow the path she'd chosen and see where it led her.

She'd dropped behind Joe slightly and now hurried to catch up with him. 'Joe, where are we going?'

'The station, I told thee.'

'You know what I mean.'

He stopped and took her by the shoulders. 'Ginny, are tha committed to me? If it's the boy tha worried about, we'll send for 'im like we were goin' to. It's just the same. Might take a bit longer, is all. Alright? Alright, Gin?'

When she nodded, he took her by the hand, pulling her along. 'Reight. We're nearly there.' He laughed, a little wildly, pumping her hand up and down. 'I told thee I'd tek thee on an adventure.'

On the station platform, Joe led her to the back of a queue of people at one of two arched ticket windows. There was a uniformed train guard at the other window, assisting a tall gentleman who was with a boy about Isaac's age. The boy was sitting cross-legged on top of the man's trunk, his chin in his hand. He looked bored. Isaac would be running about getting under people's feet, although Harriet did seem to exert a calming influence on him. Harriet had talked about putting him in a dame school, initially, then a proper school paid for by Silas. He'd get the proper education Ginny had not had.

The gentleman finished his business at the ticket window and told the boy to jump down from the trunk. He took his hand and they walked away down the platform, the train guard and a second uniformed man following with the trunk. Ginny had the absurd feeling she should not lose sight of the boy. She was seized by terror at the thought she might never see Isaac again.

'Joe, we have to go and fetch Isaac.'

He shook his head. 'Don't be soft.'

'I'll go. I'll run and get him.'

Joe didn't bother responding. Ginny shook his arm. 'You could've told me what you were planning. I could've fetched him.'

'There were no time for that.'

He moved forward and Ginny stepped up beside him.

'You know I wouldn't have told.'

'Do I?' He looked at her from the corner of his eye. 'Thee and Louisa are thick as thieves wi' each other. I couldn't risk it.' He peered towards the front of the queue. 'C'mon. C'mon.'

Ginny pointed. 'There's nobody at that other window. Let's go there.'

'That's for first-class passengers. We're third,' Joe said, his voice clipped. 'We might 'av been travellin' in first but av got a feelin' there's not as much coin in that bag as I were expectin'.'

'It's not an auspicious start to this adventure then, is it?'

He ignored her. Ginny entertained a brief fantasy where she returned to the Hinchcliffe household to discover Daniel Housley had rejected Louisa and needed a shoulder to cry on, a feminine shoulder Ginny would be pleased to provide. She would throw herself on his mercy, explain that Joe had corrupted her, had kidnapped her. She had been too weak to deny the scoundrel. She and Daniel would marry quickly so that any child she might be carrying could be credited to the clerk. Mrs Ginny Housley.

'Are tha comin' or what?'

Joe stood a couple of feet away, waving train tickets in his hand. Ginny smiled, sourly. 'Sorry, I were miles away.'

'Tha soon will be.' He held out his hand and she took it, reluctantly. 'Don't be mardy, love. I'll tell thee all about it once we get movin'.'

The cheerless carriage she followed Joe onto provided roomy accommodation for a dozen people but there were probably double that number already onboard. Joe and Ginny squeezed onto the end of an un-cushioned bench. They rested their feet on Joe's burlap sack. The carriage was lit by a single oil lamp hanging from the middle of the ceiling. Ginny tensed her body as the train began to move. After a few moments, the woman sitting thigh to shoulder against her began to snore gustily, her head dropping towards Ginny's shoulder. Each time it did, Ginny jerked her shoulder to dislodge the woman, off whom came the stench of rotten fish.

She hissed at Joe. 'How long are we on this train?'

'Not long.' He seemed unperturbed and had closed

his eyes as if he would nod off too. 'Headin' north a few miles. Then we get on another to go west, reight to the coast.'

A snore rattled in Ginny's ear. Her patience expired, she elbowed her companion in the ribs and the woman awoke with a screech. 'Joe, you tell me right now or when we get off I'm going back, even if I have to walk all the way.'

He took her hand. 'Gin, we're goin' to make a fresh start where nob'dy knows us.'

'*Where?*'

Instead of answering, he took out the bag of coins. 'Hold out thee 'ands. No, not out there. Don't let anybody see.' He tipped the coins into her palms and counted them back into the bag. When he'd finished he pursed his lips and put the bag back in his coat pocket.

'Well?' said Ginny.

'It's less than I thought.' He dipped his chin and studied the ground. 'Aye. Much less. Our Seth must've split 'is savings into different places. We should've searched the 'ouse. Ah well, no use . . .'

'Joe!'

'Hold thee horses.' He was frowning mightily. 'Av just thought o' summat. Am thinkin' I've discovered why Seth never 'ad to admit to owt, why he never got hauled up before that judge. He must've spent more'n two hundred sovereign . . .'

Ginny took in a sharp breath, her destination momentarily forgotten. 'He paid them off,' she said, 'the others. What a scoundrel.'

'Aye, even the gaffer, and nowt ever got said to me. They were laughin' at me all along.' Joe looked sorrowful. 'Seth never did the same for me, though, did

’e? I got put through the wringer, an’ worse. I ’ope tha feels less guilty now about takin’ ’is money. Serves him reight, the little . . .’

Ginny put her fingers against his lips. ‘Alright, love. Like you said, we won’t be seeing Seth again.’ She didn’t care about Joe’s brother. Isaac was her main, her only, concern. ‘Now then, you’ve got a plan of your own. What is it?’

Joe’s face brightened.

‘Aye, so we’re aimin’ to get to Liverpool but we don’t stop there.’ He leaned over so he was whispering in her ear. ‘I seen this advertisement. Excellent accommodation on an American ship. They leave every ten days an’ we’ll be on the next ’un. Steerage, o’ course, but needs must, eh? As Lou likes to say. Needs must. What does tha say?’

Ginny tried to quell her rising panic. ‘Do we have enough money?’

‘Aye, we do.’ But he looked uncertain. ‘Anyhow, we go to the docks. Tha applies direct to the captain on board, or there’s an office tha calls into. We can ask when we get there.’ He kissed her ear, gently. ‘Tha knows I can’t stay in town to be a punchbag for them that’s aggrieved wi’ me. Gi’ me a smile, love.’

She did, and it became a rictus fixed on her face. She’d been right all along. She’d never see her son again.

30

They were going on an expedition — Louisa, Daniel, Harriet and Silas, and Isaac — to Clay Cross, where Hutchinson & Tayleure's travelling circus had pitched up on a field alongside the Queen's Head hotel. It was a fortnight since Ginny had disappeared, and the boy had not yet been told the reason for his mother's absence, which Louisa thought was asking for trouble later on down the line, but held her tongue.

What Isaac had been told was that Ginny was busy finding work, and then, by an increasingly desperate Harriet, that she was setting up house for him to live in. Harriet had told Louisa that he had responded to the latter by demanding he be allowed to stay at the Hinchcliffe's house with Shandy and Kitty the cat. Perhaps, Harriet had told him, that might be possible, and she gave the generic parental refrain. We'll see. Louisa knew her friend still held out hope that Ginny would return, chastened. Some hope, she thought grimly.

There had been no letter. 'They could be anywhere,' Louisa had told Jemima Greaves. 'Anywhere in or out o' the country or the continent by now. They could be down the road in Blonk Street for all we know.'

Jemima had made clear her own position in two words. *Good riddance*. She had also warned Louisa that she was showing now. By her own reckoning, she was seven months gone. When she had last undressed for bed, she had examined her profile in the dressing table mirror, stroking her hands over the taut drum of her belly. She'd need to find a midwife soon and prepare for the birth. Jemima would help her with that daunting prospect, but could offer no assistance with the other task she faced, except to nag.

'When are tha plannin' on tellin' that boy that's so interested in thee?'

Louisa had yawned and rocked in her chair by Jemima's fireside. 'If I were a rich lady,' she had replied, 'I'd be well settled into me confinement by now, eatin' chocolates while a maid puts me slippers on me feet and a cook makes me owt I fancy for me dinner.'

Jemima had cackled and tapped her on the knee. 'Aye, well. No rest for the wicked, eh?'

The outing had come about because Silas wanted to celebrate winning his biggest order yet for saws. 'We'll break into America next!' he'd declared. Daniel told Louisa the total value of goods sent from Sheffield to America in the first six months of the year was well over a million pounds. A million pounds. She couldn't comprehend it. Silas decided Isaac needed cheering up and bought the circus tickets and paid for seats on the omnibus. Extra services were laid on to get people from the town down to Clay Cross, a hamlet near Chesterfield. Isaac wanted to sit on Louisa's lap for the journey but Daniel Housley had frowned and lifted the boy onto his knee. 'You look tired,' he said to Louisa.

'Thanks a bunch.'

'No, no, I only mean that . . .'

She touched his arm — 'I know. Am joshin' wi' thee.' — and wondered whether he had guessed, had seen her belly creep over her thighs when she sat, but could not broach the subject. If he did know, she took comfort from the fact he continued to be as solicitous as ever towards her.

When the bus rocked and she was jolted forward, Daniel cupped her arm to prevent her from falling. 'Ta, love,' she said. He kept his hand on her arm for a few moments and his light touch occupied her mind for the rest of the journey.

The din of the crowd, which had been partly drowned out by the rain drumming on the roof of the omnibus, intensified as Louisa alighted. Daniel carried Isaac off the bus, made sure the boy was holding the hands of Harriet and Silas, then turned back to help Louisa down. They stepped carefully, arm in arm, over the soaked planks and reeds that had been scattered on the muddy trail leading to the circus tent. Once inside, Daniel took off his coat and folded it inside out to make a cushion for the bench, insisting Louisa sit on it.

'Tha's too good to me, Dan,' she said, gazing around. She'd expected the interior to be cavernous, but the canvas ceiling billowed down to head height around the edges of the tent and the space was crammed with hundreds of people sitting on benches around a ring full of apparatus she couldn't identify. She was sitting by one of two tall wooden structures that supported a tightrope. What looked like swing seats dangled from the apex of the ceiling, high above. Despite the height of the tent, the effect was claustrophic.

She dismissed the sense of foreboding that rose in her chest and squeezed Dan's arm. 'I think I'm more excited than this lad here.' Isaac was hopping up and down on the bench between Harriet and Silas. 'I'm glad o' tha company.'

'If it were possible, I would spend all my time with

you,' he said, and blushed. 'I'm sure you must have guessed already, Louisa, but I have something to ask. It seems I can never seem to find the right . . .'

At that moment, a trumpeting of horns heralded the arrival of three male acrobats on horseback who galloped around the perimeter of the ring throwing sweets into an audience that roared its approval. Silas snatched a piece of toffee out of the air and handed it to Isaac who crowed with delight. Louisa clapped along, her mind racing. She had known this moment was coming and was woefully unprepared for it. How could she answer Daniel without first explaining her situation? The last thing she wanted was for him to experience the embarrassment of being forced to withdraw what she was certain would be a marriage proposal. If she accepted, there would be the humiliation of having the engagement broken off by him. If she rejected his proposal, he would withdraw from her and that would be equally heart breaking.

If only they could continue on for a short while, just the way they were.

Isaac appeared in front of her and patted her hands with sticky fingers. 'Look, Aunt Louisa! They're flying!'

She raised tear-filled eyes to the trapeze artists working their magic high above their heads, and was soon hypnotised by their graceful swoops and dives. Then a clown appeared, balancing on a wheel on the high wire, and the crowd screamed in delight. She watched Dan, never having seen him laugh so unselfconsciously before.

He caught her eye. 'You're staring at me.'

'Aye,' said Louisa, and held his gaze until they were both laughing, and he clasped her hand and the acrobatics around them went unnoticed.

'It's still silin' down!' said Silas as they emerged from the tent and hurried towards the faint lights of the buses waiting on the edge of the field.

In the blackness, Louisa's boot sank into the sucking mud. 'Oh!' She leaned against Daniel to free herself, enjoying the weight of his body pressing against her.

'Over here, my dear,' he said, guiding her towards a less churned-up section. 'This bit's better.'

'Thank . . .' She gasped when her feet slipped from under her, reaching for Daniel but finding only air in her fists. She fell backwards, landing heavily and biting her tongue. She moaned in dismay; now she would have to make the return journey coated in mud. Her back hurt and she tasted the metallic tang of blood in her mouth. Then a cold fear filled her gut and she pressed her wet hands against her belly, forgetting all about her undignified state, spread-eagled in the mud. Her clothes were already soaked by the rain and clung to her skin. She was aware of Daniel standing over her, offering his hand, but both of hers were busy, flattened against the mound of her belly, pressing, rubbing, feeling for signs of life. And finally, she was rewarded with the churn and flutter of movement. *Sorry, babby. Kick me all the way to kingdom come if tha wants*.

'Are you able to rise?' said Daniel. His voice was faint. Louisa looked up, unable to see the features of his face in the dark. Water pattered from his hat onto the ground and his shoulders had a defeated look about them. He had seen her skirts plastered to the unmistakable swell of her belly and now he would turn away from her, leave her in the mud. It was no more than she deserved.

Instead, he squatted so she could put her arms around his neck and with a grunt pulled her back to her feet.

Their faces were close, almost touching, and for a thrilling moment she thought he would kiss her. She could feel his breath on her mouth and parted her lips. It would be all right, after all. He loved her too much to abandon her.

Then he turned his face away and she dropped her arms from around his neck and took a step back. 'Dan, I . . .' She didn't know how to go on.

When he spoke, it was in the polite tones of a stranger. 'Can you walk?'

She swiped whiplash-wet strands of hair from her face and tried to laugh. 'Look at the state o' me. Am as clumsy as them clowns.'

Daniel Housley made a non-committal sound and took her by the elbow, and she allowed him to lead her on, catching up with the stragglers. Silas waved to them from the footplate of one of the buses and Daniel steered her in that direction. He didn't reply to Louisa's observation that surely there couldn't be any moisture left in the sky, there was so much on the two of them. He only spoke when they reached Silas, and it wasn't to Louisa.

She could no longer hide from the truth of it. The charade was over.

'I'm afraid she's had a fall.'

'Oh dear, love,' said Silas. 'What a state tha's in.'

Daniel handed her up gently. She wondered whether that would be the last time she'd feel the touch of his fingers around hers. From the safety of the deck, she looked down at him standing in the rain but he wouldn't meet her gaze.

Silas hooked his thumb at Isaac. 'Up tha gets.' He lowered Louisa into the seat Isaac vacated as if she was a precious piece of porcelain. It made her want to cry. 'Let's get thee sat down.'

Harriet made some feeble attempts to wipe the dirt from her clothes, her eyes dropping to Louisa's belly then darting away, throwing an anxious glance at Daniel and turning her mouth down at Silas. If Daniel hadn't already guessed her condition, Harriet's pantomime would convince him. Pressed between Harriet and Daniel, Louisa lowered her chin and briefly closed her eyes. Her hands lay curled in her lap and she prayed he would take one, squeeze her hand, let her know without speaking that he wished to marry her still.

All the way home, Daniel made a song and dance about dandling Isaac on his knee, asking the boy what he had enjoyed most about the circus, offering to teach him his numbers, all the while keeping his face carefully averted so he would not have to look at Louisa. She had deceived him. The truth was a remorseless stone in her heart.

When the bus rattled into the high street to disgorge some of the passengers, Louisa stood too.

'I thought you were staying with us tonight?' said Harriet.

Louisa glanced at Daniel. He was staring out of the window.

'I've changed me mind,' she said.

'Are tha gettin' off 'ere?' said Silas. 'I'll walk thee 'ome.'

'No!' She shook her head. 'Sorry, love, but no thanks. It's a minute's walk.'

'Are you sure you're alright?' said Harriet.

'Aye, aye. Oh.' She breathed in sharply. A stabbing pain in her side must be how it felt to have a knife go in.

Harriet looked alarmed.

'It's nowt,' said Louisa. 'Hurt pride, no more.' The pain had moved around to the small of her back and she rubbed it with both hands, arching her back. No reason to hide now, except, she thought, catching the eye of a middle-aged woman who pleated her lips in distaste and whispered in the ear of the man sitting next to her, the usual. Women weren't supposed to flaunt their fecundity. 'Best get movin'.'

Harriet's kind smile almost undid her. 'Let's go for a picnic on Sunday. We'll call for you.'

'Aye, alright.' She made her voice chipper. Had the fall done some damage, after all? All she wanted to do was close her cottage door behind her, get out of her wringing wet clothes, slide under the covers and turn her face to the wall. 'That'd be lovely.'

She took a few steps, screwed up her courage and turned back to look at Daniel. He was now staring at the floor of the carriage.

Louisa lifted her chin. 'Ta ra, then.'

He looked up, and met her gaze. His face was a ruin. Louisa turned and stumbled away, reaching for the rail at the top of the carriage steps, trying and failing to close her ears to the single word he uttered.

'Goodbye.'

31

The smell of smoke from the office fireplace couldn't entirely mask the ripe odour of manure rising from the stables below. Louisa looked down on the shining courtyard cobbles through the small sash window she'd opened a crack to relieve the stuffiness of the room. She twisted the narrow gold band she wore on the third finger of her left hand.

A cold rain was falling. Harriet said this time of year, when autumn's riotous colours began their fade to grey, made her melancholy but Louisa was glad of it. She'd rather sit wrapped up in front of a blazing fire than sweat in the clammy heat when the rank smells of the town were at their worst.

The room was stuffy because she'd just bidden farewell to the family that had crowded into it, there to put a down payment on a hearse. A visit from the head of the household would have sufficed but she saw how the father's hands shook, how the mother leaned against his arm when he put his signature to the bill and how the two boys, not much older than Isaac, watched their parents with round eyes. Their little sister had died from smallpox. A one-horse carriage would carry her to the graveyard. Louisa always booked the same animal for children's funerals, a gentle giant of a chestnut brown mare with white fetlocks.

Jemima Greaves had told her the child would be glad to be transported by such a lovely animal in its white stockings.

Smallpox. In this day and age.

She turned from the window and leaned over the bulk of her belly to tidy up her desk. She could not put off going to the place she refused to think of as home any longer. She'd brought herself up to date with the advance hackney cab bookings as well as met with the grieving family. All the drivers were out plying for trade or, in Albert Rowbotham's case, searching for the nearest taproom. The cab business had duly picked up as the weather cooled, as Jemima had predicted. She had taken on two new drivers, given Albert a final, final no-coming-back-from-the-next-misdeed warning, and promoted Louisa to manager of her business. This had given Louisa the opportunity to ask for an increase in wages, with winter approaching and a baby to keep warm, and Jemima told her she would consider a pay rise before the end of the year, provided business continued to boom. She gave her the use of a book-keeper, a semi-retired man that Louisa privately decided had amorous designs on Jemima Greaves. He would take over the general running of the business when the baby came and for up to a month afterwards. On Louisa's return to work, Jemima advised her that, for a few pennies from Louisa's pocket, her ten-year-old girl would look after the infant. She would fetch Louisa when the baby needed to be fed.

Louisa had been saving a percentage of her wages so that she could survive a month without pay but the fear she would end up destitute as well as a disgraced mother was a constant needle, a worry that made her yearn for the gin bottle. Whenever she was tempted, she remembered the face of the night watchman, his look of surprise at his own ending, and she resisted the craving. Her life had changed for the better since the start of the year, although she'd always carry that desperate girl deep within her bruised heart. She was a survivor, and managing for herself, but that didn't mean she wasn't afraid of what was still to come.

Now, she put on her black wool cloak and bonnet, deciding she would walk to the place she had agreed to meet Harriet and Silas via Barker Pool, for old times' sake.

'Si thee tomorra,' she called to the stable boy who was sluicing out the yard. He raised his hand in acknowledgement. Louisa stepped carefully around the muck.

It had stopped raining but she felt the cold in her fingers, the chill penetrating her mittens. Still, she paused on the uneven ground where her rickety terrace had stood, wondering if she was stepping on the ghost of her own cottage, or Seth's place, perhaps in the room where the clock had hung on the wall, the hiding place where Seth had inadequately concealed what had remained of his savings. She covered the small patch of ground in a few strides and wondered how a row of cottages ever fit on it. According to Harriet, who had read it in the paper, a music hall was to be constructed where she stood. It would be named for Albert, the Queen's consort. The Albert Hall. It sounded grand.

Ginny had been fascinated by the names given to the streets and buildings of the town, and Louisa had been amused by her enthusiasm for discovering how Portobello Street got its name. Ginny had twigged the meaning behind the streets and squares named Devonshire, Furnival, Percival and Norfolk — these were the dukes that had carved up the lands between them; she understood how Collier, Exchange and Tenter streets got their names from the trades; there were the saints, of course, while Castle Street and Fargate and West Bar dated back to the days when a medieval castle stood in the centre of town, that later became a prison for Mary Queen of Scots. But what about Portobello? It was so much more exotic-sounding. Louisa smiled at the memory. The girl had been like a dog with a bone. Harriet had told her she believed it had to do with an eighteenth-century war with Spain, a battle in the town of Portobello, won by England. Silas had shaken his head. 'Nah, it's named after the mushroom, love.'

Ginny had wanted a street named for her, for some achievement she was bound to accomplish. Louisa recalled Harriet asking whether her name was an abbreviation of Imogen or Genevieve.

'It's just Ginny,' she'd replied, lifting her chin.

Just Ginny.

Louisa had finally received a letter.

It was shortly before she moved out of her cottage in Barker Pool so it was only by the skin of her teeth that she learned Ginny was still at large somewhere in the world. She had felt a rush of affection for her erstwhile friend. She missed her, it was as simple as that.

The letter was postmarked *Waterford* but Louisa had no idea where that was. It was a brief note, containing a gift that she shook from the envelope and held up to the light, contemplating it, before slipping it on her finger and reading the note.

Composed on behalf of Mrs Peter Hinchcliffe: I have come to the post office where a kind gentleman is helping me write to you. Joe told me to pawn this but it is all I have left. I wish to give all I have left to you, it is my way of saying sorry. It will be of practical benefit too, I am sure. Kiss Isaac for me.

* * *

After leaving Barker Pool, Louisa ducked into the Sycamore Street mart where she found Harriet and Silas standing side by side, arguing with each other's reflections in the looking glass built into the top of a rosewood chiffonier.

'But we came here to purchase a dining table,' said Harriet.

Silas blew his wife a kiss through the mirror. 'It's lovely, though. Not as radiant as thee, love, but a fine piece o' work.'

'Are you comparing me to a lump of wood?'

'I wun't dare . . . here's Lou!' He stepped back and gestured to the chiffonier. 'What does tha think on it?'

Louisa pretended to give it some thought. She shrugged. 'Be quite difficult to eat off, won't it?'

'Thank you,' said Harriet. 'We can't waste money on fripperies, especially now.' She walked amongst the pieces of furniture that surrounded them, mahogany sideboards, maroon upholstered easy chairs, pianofortes, walnut-wood occasional tables. Louisa inhaled the combined scents of polish and leather. It was the smell of money.

'Here,' said Harriet. She patted the surface of a table. 'Spanish mahogany telescope table. Not too big. Perfect condition. It'll fit nicely in the dining room.'

'Tha sounds like the auctioneer,' said Silas.

Harriet began ticking items off her fingers. 'We need a towel rail and new kitchen pots. A panshon, too, and a set of knives.'

Silas grinned at Louisa. 'Made o' finest Sheffield steel. Does tha need owt, love, to furnish thee dwellin'?'

Louisa shook her head. She'd managed to keep her friends away from Hawley Croft, and rejected as kindly as possible their offer of a room in the townhouse they had purchased in Wellington Street. There were three bedrooms, as well as an attic and, in the sloping yard at the back of the house, a raised soil bed for Harriet to cultivate her vegetables. Harriet told Louisa she missed having a stream run along the bottom of the garden but their home in Neepsend had gone the same way as Louisa's humble cottage. Silas had decided to expand his existing factory site, rather than move to new premises, and had demolished the house to make way for a new wheel. He explained the place was too big, too noisy and crowded, for them to live on site. 'Buildin' your empire!' Louisa teased.

She was pleased for her friends, who had found a modern build at a reasonable rent, considering it came with new-fangled items such as a separate bath room, a water closet and a copper water boiler with a brass tap installed in the kitchen. The construction of the town's sewerage and drainage system to allow for indoor water closets had begun only eighteen months earlier, Silas liked to tell guests as they tucked into one of Harriet's chocolate cakes, so they counted themselves very lucky to have one.

Now she had another life to consider, she might have to think about swallowing her pride and accepting their generosity. In any event, Harriet had insisted that she give birth in the bedroom that had Louisa's name on it, and she had grudgingly — while secretly feeling relief — agreed to go and stay with the Hinchcliffes and accept the services of a midwife, paid for by Harriet.

Harriet ran her hand along the back of an easy chair upholstered in maroon leather. It was one of a set to be sold together. 'I like this but we can't afford it.'

'Let me test it out for thee.' Louisa sank into the chair. 'Ah, that's better.'

Harriet frowned. 'It can't be long now, surely. Why don't you come to us tonight, to be on the safe side? Let me look after you.'

'My mother had nob'dy watchin' over her an' were outside shearin' sheep the day after I arrived,' Silas said.

'Silas!'

Louisa laughed. 'I'd quit there, Silas, if I were thee.'

'What?' He mock-cowered away from Harriet's glare. 'What 'av I said?'

'Silas,' Louisa held out her hand. 'Help us up an' I'll go an' find a field to squat in.'

Silas hugged her to him when she was back on her feet. 'I can't get me arms around thee.'

She left them arguing over a pianoforte.

32

The streets were busy with early evening traffic when Louisa exited the mart, her eyes immediately watering from the gusty wind that funnelled through the centre of town. The air was thick with the familiar scent of smoke and the street lamps flickered like candles placed in the way of a draught, a contrast to the steady golden glow coming from the windows of the houses and shops she hurried past.

It was full night by the time she reached her lodgings in Hawley Croft, off Campo Lane. The tall blackened-brick Georgian buildings, every window divided into a dozen dirty panes, gave her a sense of foreboding that sent a shudder down her spine. She shivered as she opened the front door of one of these properties and entered the dark and narrow hallway. Her landlady had the ground floor and made her living from renting rooms by the night in the three storeys above, and providing meals and a laundry service for those like Louisa who paid monthly in advance for a long-term let and didn't question the landlady's assertion that she ran a respectable house, and most certainly not a brothel.

It was all Louisa could afford. She had sold off her few sticks of furniture when her Barker Pool landlord had advised her to leave within the week or be buried under rubble, and used the money to put down the advance.

Now, the next payment was coming due and Louisa

had managed to scrape together enough money but she had a suspicion the landlady would ask her to vacate her room. Mrs Nightingale wouldn't want a screaming baby in this house, and had already expressed her doubts about Louisa's ability to keep up with the rent. 'I'm not a charity for abandoned mothers an' babbies,' she'd warned.

Louisa moved aside on the staircase to allow a besuited gentleman and a woman, wearing a velvet dressing gown too loosely tied for decency, to descend. 'Ey up, Lou,' said the woman cheerfully. The man ducked his head and kept walking. The woman blew him a kiss. 'Bye, love.' She looked Louisa up and down critically. 'Not long before tha goes pop, eh?'

'Not long, no.'

'Don't thee forget what I said, Lou. Plenty to go round, love, better than sloggin' tha guts out for Jemima Greaves.'

She skipped back upstairs and Louisa followed wearily, focusing on putting one foot in front of the other. The ache in her back intensified with every step.

Safely in her room, she lit the oil lamp and sat heavily on the bed, which sank beneath her weight. She realised she was hungry and that a meal she had paid for would be waiting in the kitchen, but that meant negotiating the stairs again and waves of pain were now radiating up and down her back. She must have strained a muscle. She tried to work out how she could have done that. Bending over her office desk earlier, perhaps.

Lowering herself down, onto her side, she breathed shallowly. Almost immediately she wanted to turn onto her back but that had been an impossible position to lay in for the past month and still expect to breathe.

Her eyes focused on the fabric sampler that hung on the wall. It was the work of a child, comprising little more than row after row of differently sized letters and numbers, painstakingly stitched in red thread that looked black in the dim light, scrawled on a pale canvas.

A short rest, that's what was needed, then she'd get up and go down and eat her meal. The letters on the sampler blurred into nonsense and she shifted her gaze to the oil lamp's flame, lulled by the comforting crackle of the wick. Her eyelids drooped. A little shuteye, five minutes' peace.

* * *

Laughter woke her, coming from the room above, pounding feet, shrieks, and then, inevitably, the rhythmical sound of the headboard banging against the wall. Louisa sighed and swung her feet to the ground. She rose carefully, her shoulders bowed, feeling as fragile as the yellowed glass that enclosed the flame of the lamp. She heard a moan, followed by a guttural grunt, and then realised she was making that sound, and she was overwhelmed by terror at the same moment as a bolt of pain shot through her body. She fell heavily to her hands and knees.

A staircase, leading down. She was balanced on a tread, clinging to the banister, with no idea how she had got there. A door slammed and Mrs Nightingale peered up the stairwell, her round white face fragmenting before Louisa's eyes like the moon reflected on water. 'What's up wi' thee?'

Then she was somehow back on the bed, on her back, suffocating under the weight in her belly, trying to turn. She had to get away from the pain. She gasped. ‘What’s goin’ on? What’s ’appenin’?’

‘What does tha think?’ It was Mrs Nightingale’s voice, but Louisa couldn’t see her. Where was she? She felt a sudden chill on her legs, her belly. Then another all-consuming wave of pain. She screamed.

‘Can tha hear that? That’s the neighbours bangin’ on the wall. Tha needs to tone it down, love.’

The woman’s cold hands were on her belly. Louisa bucked and heaved.

‘Calm down, tha’ll be reight.’

She whispered through cracked lips. ‘Fetch a midwife.’

‘Does tha ’av the coin to pay for it?’

‘She’ll get ’er money . . . from me friend.’

‘Aye, that’s what they all say.’

‘I can’t do this on me own!’ Another wave of pain took hold of her, and this time she was overcome by an irresistible urge to push.

‘Tha can an’ tha will.’ The woman’s voice was steady and calm and went on and on. ‘An’ tha’s not on thee own. I’ve delivered a few babbies in me time. Shush now. Tha wastin’ energy makin’ that racket. Here we are. Babby’s crownin’. Hoist theesen up and shove it out, love. Won’t take long now, won’t be long. Soon be over.’

She couldn’t do it. She was going to die after all, and leave a motherless bastard to fend for itself. The noose she had so feared couldn’t compare to this torture. She was being battered to death, ripped apart and stamped on by the hooves of horses. Her body went limp, and she realised the pain had disappeared.

A thin squeal shook the world.

Mrs Nightingale’s voice was soft. ‘Why don’t thou

open thee eyes?'

She did, and gazed in awe at the tiny, fierce life the woman placed in her arms. Mrs Nightingale covered Louisa's shoulders with a blanket and tucked a sheet around mother and baby.

'What will tha name her?' She chuckled, and Louisa laughed too, for pure joy. 'Not to sway thee, but Elsie is a good name.'

Louisa shook her head. 'She's already named. She's Alice. Alice Millicent Leigh.'

33

Louisa let herself into the house on Wellington Street and followed her nose to the kitchen, where Sarah Hodgetts, newly employed by Harriet as a live-out general servant and cook, was in the act of turning a tin containing a joint of pork in the open-fronted oven beside the blazing fire-box. The rings on the hot plate were occupied by bubbling pans of vegetables and potatoes. Shandy lay under the kitchen table, patiently awaiting the scraps she knew would be coming her way, eventually. Isaac lay alongside her, his stockinged feet sticking out.

'Loo Loo!'

'I nearly tripped over thee,' said Louisa. 'Havin' tha tea down there wi' the dog, then?'

'Don't encourage him,' said Sarah. She fanned her face with a folded newspaper. 'Is it cold out? Am not relishin' me walk home.'

Louisa unwrapped her shawl and lifted Alice out, balancing the baby on one arm while she spread the shawl on the table. 'Brass monkeys. Summat smells good.'

'Pork an' all the trimmings.'

Louisa lay the baby on the shawl and gently stroked her soft round cheek with one finger. Alice had been wrapped snug against her mother's body, and slept on, only beginning to stir when Louisa removed her wool cap and mittens. As well as presenting Louisa with a gift of swaddling flannels before the birth, Harriet had crocheted and knitted an entire wardrobe for the baby, as Louisa had discovered two weeks earlier when she took her new-born to meet her Aunt Harriet and Uncle Silas and Cousin Isaac.

'Isaac, stop kicking me ankle. Come an' see who's 'ere.'

'Av seen her before,' he mumbled from under the table.

Louisa smiled. She could happily do nothing but gaze at Alice all day long. She bent to kiss her head, which was fuzzy with a light dusting of hair, inhaling her sweet scent. In this house, she could pretend to be a lady of leisure, with nothing to do but feed and rock her daughter. The reality was that in a week's time she'd be back at work and Alice would be in the care of Jemima Greaves' sullen daughter. Louisa pushed the thought away but that only left room for consideration of another problem she faced. She couldn't contemplate remaining in Mrs Nightingale's house, not with this innocent mite, but she was struggling to find respectable accommodation for a mother and baby. Even when she flashed the wedding ring and spoke of widowhood, landlords and landladies were suspicious. Some knew of her previous circumstances and weren't prepared to have her under their roof, and told her as much.

The baby began wriggling vigorously.

Isaac came out from under the table. 'It sounds like a sparrow.'

'I think she's wantin' a feed.'

Sarah peered over Louisa's shoulder. 'Tha'll want to swaddle her up. They don't like their arms an' legs wavin' about like that.'

'Come 'ere, love.'

'Tha shouldn't be constantly pickin' them up, neither.'

Louisa cradled Alice in her arms. The baby caught her scent and, her eyes still closed, opened her mouth and twisted her head, rooting for milk.

* * *

After they'd eaten the dinner Sarah had cooked, Silas and Harriet invited her to stay the night. They had a spare bedroom and had supplied a crib and blankets for the baby. Filled with good food, and drowsy, Louisa accepted. Harriet seized her opportunity. 'Lou, please come and live with us. We have plenty of space, and . . .'

'I can't afford thee,' said Louisa. 'I've all on payin' the rent in the place I'm in.'

'But tha's livin' in a hovel!' Silas had exclaimed. Harriet had shaken her head to silence him.

'Louisa,' she said, 'we can work out a rent later on, when you're back at Jemima's and earning again. Just agree to stay for a few days only, and then we'll see.'

Louisa had fought back tears. 'I can manage for meesen. I shan't be beholden, not to nob'dy.'

'Of course not.' Harriet had looked at Silas, at a loss.

'Tell thee what,' he said, 'let's leave it at just this one night tonight, and we'll see how we go.'

When the baby cried to be fed in the night, Louisa barely registered the small valise that sat on the rug in the middle of the room, stepping over it to lift Alice from the crib, anxious about waking the household. Later still, rising to attend to Alice again, she wondered where the bag had come from and what was in it, but was too exhausted to look. When the clock on the wall told her it was time to go down for breakfast, Louisa lit a lamp and her gaze fell immediately on the bag. She left Alice grizzling in her crib and opened the valise. It contained her meagre possessions and all of Alice's knitted baby clothes.

Silas was sitting at the kitchen table, spreading dripping liberally onto a slice of bread, when Louisa entered the room. He grinned at her.

'Good morn . . .'

'How did tha know where I were stayin'?'

'Sit down, Lou. Make theesen an' Alice comfy.'

She continued to stand over him, one hand on her hip. Alice snuffled into her chest.

'She's hungry,' said Silas.

'Don't thee tell me what Alice is or isn't. Tell me what tha did.'

'All right.' He made his face serious but she could see the laughter in his eyes.

'It's not funny, Silas.'

He held up his hands. 'Listen, then. I'd 'eard where tha was livin' from one o' the men who knows tha landlady. She were braggin' about deliverin' a baby an' I put two an' two together. Clever, eh?'

She was sure Mrs Nightingale would have had more to say than that. An unwed mother, no coin for a midwife, giving birth to a bastard child with no father in sight. Silas was being kind.

'Tha's too clever by 'alf.' She sighed and sat down opposite him. 'It weren't a good place to be. I should be thankin' thee.'

'Nah, am sorry I went behind thee back.'

Harriet came into the room, wringing her hands. 'Louisa, I'm sorry. I was just so worried about you.

Please don't be cross.'

Silas jerked his thumb at Harriet. 'See? It were all the wife's fault. I only do as I'm told.'

Harriet put her hand on Louisa's shoulder and bent to kiss the baby. 'Darling Alice.' She straightened. 'Why don't you go and feed her in the parlour? I'll bring you a cup of tea and some breakfast.'

Louisa wanted to sob with relief. Instead, she laughed. 'I could get used to this. But, you pair, listen to me now. I'll be payin' thee back for the room.' They nodded earnestly. 'An' it's only 'til I find a place o' me own.'

She waited for them to agree before leaving the room. In the parlour, she sank into the same leather upholstered chair she'd rested in at the auction house. Harriet had bought the pair.

34

Isaac prodded the baby's belly through the layers of cotton and flannel, and untucked one of her feet from the blanket. He tickled her toes. Louisa caught the shifty look he gave her but ignored him. Finally, he pulled at the gauzy hairs growing on the top of the baby's head. He was breathing heavily, a congested noise like water coming to the boil. Louisa tried to move away from the dry heat radiating off the boy's head but she was trapped amongst the cushions on the settee, Alice attached to her breast, and Isaac had decided to curl up against her, his snotty nose close to her cheek. He coughed and Louisa flinched away from him.

'Give over. She's not a toy for thee to prod an' poke. Go an' blow thee nose.'

He snuggled closer. 'I want to play wi' it.'

Louisa sighed and gently disengaged the baby from her breast. Alice had stopped feeding and fallen asleep on her. Louisa adjusted her clothes and put the baby against her shoulder to burp her. 'That cough's no better, is it? Tha'd be better off in bed, I reckon.'

'When will it play wi' me though?'

'When she's bigger.'

'When will that be?'

'When tha's learned all thee letters and all thee numbers.'

She ducked her chin to kiss Alice on her plump little cheek, hiding from Isaac the tears that sprang to her eyes as she was reminded of the last time she had seen Daniel, the memory as painfully fresh as if the trip to the circus had occurred the day before. Daniel had told Isaac he'd teach him his numbers, and Louisa knew he had been focusing on the boy because he could not bear to look at her, but she wondered if he'd kept his promise. He still lived in the clerk's cottage at the Neepsend yard, still worked for Silas, but his name never came up in conversation, and she would not ask after his health in a month of Sundays.

'All the alphabet?'

'Backwards, an' all.'

Isaac wailed. 'That'll be never then!' He rolled off the settee, landing on top of Shandy and burying his face in the ruff of the collie's neck. He looked up at Louisa, spots of high colour on his cheeks. 'Borin' babby. It's borin'.'

'She's borin', stop callin' her it,' said Louisa. The boy didn't look well at all. He coughed, a rattle in his chest.

'Where's your mother? Go an' find 'er and ask 'er to give thee some cough stuff.'

Isaac had begun referring to Harriet as his mother and Silas as his father when Alice was born and none of them had the heart to correct him. To all intents and purposes, Harriet and Silas were his parents. Sarah Hodgetts had assumed so, from the moment she met the Hinchcliffe family, and as far as Louisa knew, nobody had put her straight. She supposed it helped matters, sharing a surname.

She tucked Alice into the wooden crib Silas had made to fit snugly into the alcove on the left side of the fireplace — Harriet's books and magazines and newspapers were in an untidy stack in the alcove on the right — and absently patted Shandy, who had taken up station beneath the crib. She'd been at the Wellington Street house for a fortnight now, and was back at work, where she would occasionally hear the baby wail from Jemima's house while her daughter watched Alice, running to fetch Louisa when she needed feeding. If the baby cried and the girl didn't come, Louisa paced her little office, her breasts leaking milk through her stays and blouse.

Sometimes, Louisa wondered what Ginny would make of her set up, of this house and all of them living cosily together in it. She twisted the wedding ring around and around. Ginny had been right; it did help to wear the band when she took the baby to work or to market. A respectable wife and mother. The pretence seemed to suit even those who knew the truth. *It smooths the way, Jemima Greaves had told her. We don't want customers feelin' awkward, do we?*

Louisa smiled ruefully. God forbid Jemima Greaves should lose business.

'Penny for them?'

Harriet came into the room, winding a scarf around her neck. Her nose was red and pinched.

'They're not worth half a farthing,' said Louisa. 'Tha looks perished already.'

'I need to fetch a tincture for Isaac. His cough's getting worse by the hour.'

'I'll go. I need the exercise.' Louisa looked into the crib. The baby slept peacefully. 'If tha can keep an eye on this one, as well as tha poorly boy? She should sleep on for a bit.'

Harriet's features softened into a smile. 'I would love to.'

When Louisa let herself into Barber's chemist shop,

Milly beamed from behind the counter. She was tying string around a parcel for a stooped customer whose twisted shoulders belied the youthful face he turned towards Louisa.

'Good day to you, sir,' said Milly.

Louisa had told herself that this time she wouldn't glance towards the curtain that concealed the room that contained the chaise longue she'd laid herself down on, but she did anyway. Was there a desperate girl in the room behind the shop even now being helped by Milly's mother? Louisa had never regretted her decision and would not judge those who made a different one.

'The folks are on a day trip to Cleethorpes so I'm holding the fort,' said Milly, as if she had read Louisa's mind. 'It's lovely to see you again.'

'Thee an' all.'

'So, what can I do for you?'

The bell above the door tinkled and two ladies came in. 'Be with you in a minute,' Milly told them. She turned a friendly, enquiring gaze on Louisa.

'I need cough stuff,' said Louisa, suddenly shy, 'an' I wanted to ask thee summat.'

'Fire away.' Milly came out from behind the counter to examine a display of glass bottles. She picked one out. 'This syrup soothes the throat. Is that what you need?'

Louisa shrugged. 'Aye.'

'And what did you want to ask me?'

She hesitated. 'Me friend's lad, they're puttin' on a little celebration for when he turns five an' I wondered if tha'd like to come, 'av some cake wi' us?'

'I would! I'd love to. Wait.' She rummaged in a drawer and produced pen and paper. 'Write down your address?'

While Milly served the other customers, Louisa carefully printed the address in Wellington Street, the time of the celebration and the date, two weeks hence in mid-November. They would be celebrating the fifth birthday of an abandoned little boy. It had been Harriet's idea to give him a party; he had been unusually fractious since Alice was born, and he deserved, thought Harriet, to be paid a bit of special attention. Sarah Hodgetts would bake the cake and Isaac, a winter baby, would get a snow sledge for a present.

Back outside, Louisa lifted her scarf to cover her mouth. It was a dry day, but cold and her chest was tight. She should have asked Milly if she sold anything that might ease her lungs, now she had the means to pay for medicines. Silas was refusing to accept rent for her room. 'Tha's leavin' soon anyhow,' he'd said, with a wink. She was able, for the first time in her life, to put some of her wages aside. She could spare a few shillings for a tincture that might allow her to breathe more easily. She made a mental note to seek Milly's advice at Isaac's party.

Louisa stepped quickly across a busy junction and gave a wide berth to a group of men who were approaching the entrance of the Blue Pig. The alehouse had been Joe's favourite haunt in the short period of time between his falling out with the gaffer and getting beaten up on the street. She wondered whether he was still with Ginny. There would be fireworks between that pair, she could guarantee it.

'Lou! Louisa!'

She recognised his voice immediately. A man separated himself from the group and trotted towards her.

'Ey up, Seth.' She smiled. 'It's grand to see thee. What's tha been up to? Where's tha livin' now? Has tha 'eard from Joe?'

'Steady on!' He laughed, and she could smell stale beer coming off him in waves. 'Time for a drink? We're celebratin' a win on the dogs.'

'I need to get back . . .' she trailed off.

'Ah, yeah, 'ow is the babby?'

'She's doin' well. Keepin' me on me toes.'

Seth rubbed his hands together. 'Cold enough to freeze hell over, in't it? Just come in for one, eh? A quick catch-up, just me and thee.'

'I can't, Seth.'

'Go on, for old times' sake.'

She hesitated and Seth's face brightened. 'Alright, then. Just one, mind.'

Seth steered her to a small table in the corner of the alehouse and went to re-join the group of men. He pointed at her and said something that made them all laugh, before going to the counter. A couple of the men leered at her, nudging each other. Louisa dropped her eyes and sighed with relief when Seth returned with a tankard of beer and a glass half-full of orange liquid.

She accepted the glass from him. 'Ta. What did tha tell 'em about me?'

'Who? Oh, that lot.' He gulped his drink down. 'Ah, needed that. Told 'em I'd got lucky.' He winked at her. 'Another?'

'I've not started this 'un.' She frowned and took a tentative sip from the glass but already knew from the familiar smell what the contents were. Gin and orange. The alcohol burned in her throat. 'So, has tha 'eard owt from Joe?'

'Nope. Thee?'

'No, I've not 'eard from him.' It wasn't a lie. 'So, what's tha up to these days?'

'This an' that. Keepin' me head above watta, just about. Din't help that he stole all me savin's.'

Louisa nodded sympathetically. Seth looked like he'd lost weight, and he'd not been a big man to start with. The skin on his face was rough and reddened. 'Where's tha livin'?'

'Funny enough, am rentin' a room above the Royal George in Carver Street. Did tha hear what 'appened to William Broadhead?'

'No, what?' She took another sip from her glass then put it down on the table and glanced towards the door. She wasn't really interested in what had happened to the orchestrator of the outrages. A shadow bloomed in her mind, the dark blot of a night watchman's cape spread on the pavement. She shuddered, and reached for the glass of gin. She would drink it down and then she could leave without appearing rude.

'Magistrates took his licence off 'im. There's a new landlord in there now. Garland is 'is name. The gaffer were furious.'

'Oh aye?' She shuddered and pushed the glass away.

'Tha drinkin' that?'

Louisa shook her head and Seth took up the glass and drained the liquid before continuing his story.

'Said he'd been a licensed victualler for twenty year, wi' never a conviction, fine or complaint made against 'im. So the Mayor's response to that is to say things 'av come to light that might show he's not a fit nor proper person to 'old a licence.'

'Ah, reight.'

'Aye, he kicks off about it an' all, but the next minute

he's resigned as secretary o' the saw-makers' union.' Seth gulped his beer. 'I think nob'dy expected the full story to come out o' that inquiry.'

Louisa shivered. 'It never did though, did it? Not the full story.'

'Put that behind thee. I 'av.' Seth's leg jiggled under the table. 'It's grand to see thee, Lou, 'av another one wi' me.'

She pitied him, although all she wanted to do was leave. 'I wish I could. Maybe another time, eh?'

'Am in 'ere most Fridays.'

'Aye, alright.' She had already decided she wouldn't set foot in the Blue Pig ever again. That chapter in her life had closed, and she was glad of it.

'Am waitin' on Joe walkin' through that door.' Seth shook his head. 'Am a silly bugger.' He drained his tankard.

'Might be best off wi'out Joe around,' said Louisa, but Seth wasn't listening to her. He was gazing pensively at the door.

When Louisa stood, clutching the bag containing the cough syrup, one of the men who had been leering at her let out a long, slow whistle. Another called out. 'What's tha got in there, love? A bottle I can 'elp thee drink?'

Seth took her elbow. 'I'll see thi out. This lot are gettin' the worse for wear.'

On the street, she hugged him, quickly but tightly. 'Take care o' theesen.'

'Wait.' He pulled her against the wet brick wall of the alehouse. 'I know tha's got a few bob now . . .' His back to the street, he fished in his pocket and brought out a balled-up handkerchief, opening it carefully to reveal a delicate gold watch. 'Av come into possession o' this. It's worth four pound but I'll sell it thee for two.' His eyes searched her face, feverishly. The look of desperation in them was heart-breaking. 'I've got a fair few of 'em. Got gents watches, an' all, worth six pound but I'll cut that by 'alf for a mate.'

Louisa didn't bother to hide her dismay. 'Stolen watches? Oh, Seth. I thought tha were goin' straight.'

His face hardened and he folded the handkerchief over the watch and stuffed it back into his pocket. 'Aye, well. Needs must, eh? Weren't that tha favourite expression, back before tha got so hoity toity?'

'Seth . . .'

He shook her hand from his arm, lifted the collar of his coat and walked off without another word. Louisa watched him for a few moments then turned and set off for home.

35

The baby's screwed-up face was dark pink, its eyes tight shut and its mouth opening and closing like the blue-and-silver fish Isaac had captured in a jam-jar from the pond on the common. He'd got into trouble for that — not for stealing a fish, but for going to the pond by himself, and without telling a grown-up. They didn't understand he knew how to keep himself safe. He'd laid flat on his belly in the reeds so only his arm was over the water, sweeping the jam-jar backwards and forwards until he'd got his prize.

Before it died, the fish had opened and closed its mouth a lot but it had been silent and there was noise coming out of the baby's mouth. A lot of noise. He reached into the crib and put his hand over Alice's mouth and nose in an attempt to stifle the wails that were hurting his ears, wondering when an adult would come and save him from this terrible creature. He had tried curling his index finger, as he'd seen Aunt Louisa do, and putting his knuckle in Alice's mouth. The baby had clamped her hard gums around it, making him squeal in surprise, and sucked so powerfully he thought his whole hand would be going in, but then had jerked her head away, and screamed even more loudly.

At least, with his hand over her face, her cries were muffled. Isaac pressed down a little harder. He was getting bored. He'd been asked to stay in the front room, watching his noisy cousin, while the grown-ups did some secret grown-up stuff in the kitchen. It wasn't fair. It was supposed to be his day.

'Shurrup,' he said, putting his other hand on Alice's belly. The baby squirmed. 'I said, shurrup!'

'What's goin' on!'

Isaac jumped back in fright, colliding with Aunt Louisa who must have crept up behind him. She reached over his head into the crib and lifted Alice out.

'What were tha doin' wi' thee hand over her face?'

'She was hurting my ears.'

'I'll do more than hurt thee ears if I see thee doin' that again.'

He seemed always to be in trouble with Aunt Louisa. He glowered at her as she lowered herself onto the settee and opened her blouse to feed the baby. He winced to see those jaws clamp around her breast but Aunt Louisa seemed untroubled by it. It had shut Alice up, that was the only good thing about it. He wished his aunt would look at him like the way she looked at Alice. Isaac patted her knee.

'Am sorry.'

She sighed, the special tired sigh that grown-ups did all the time, and smiled at him. 'I know. Tha just needs to be careful wi' her while she's so tiny. So, tha's five today, eh? Gettin' to be a big man.'

Isaac puffed out his chest, thrilled by her words, his mood as instantly lifted as if Father had done his favourite trick of turning him upside down before plonking him on his shoulders. He considered he was getting a bit old for that now.

'An' today's the party,' Aunt Louisa said. 'We've got Jemima comin', an' my friend Milly, an' Mrs Hodgetts has baked thee a special cake for it.'

Isaac allowed himself a secret smile. He'd already nibbled some of the icing from the edge of the cake that sat on a low shelf in the pantry. They should have put it higher if they didn't want him to have a taste of it. *You've a sweet tooth, like your mother*, Aunt Louisa had once told him.

He felt sad again and the middle of his chest hurt just like his knees had when he'd fallen off the garden wall. Aunt Louisa had not told him whether his mother, his real mother, was coming to eat cake on his birthday. They all thought he had forgotten all about his real mother but he never would. He called Harriet 'Mother' and Silas 'Father' because he was afraid they would leave too, and so would Aunt Louisa and Mrs Hodgetts and he'd be in this big house all by himself. Or, worse, they'd run off and he'd be left with Alice.

He had to be as good as gold so his family wouldn't disappear but he was always getting told off. Yesterday, it had been for bringing a load of sticks and branches into the dining room and spreading them on the shiny table top. He'd started to arrange them into a shape that he thought looked like a boat but Father had swept them up and thrown them out before Isaac could explain what he was trying to build. A few days before that, he'd put a frog in the kitchen sink and Mrs Hodgetts said he had nearly given her a heart attack, as if that was what he'd meant to do. He didn't know what had happened to the frog because Mrs Hodgetts had pulled his britches down and smacked him on his bare bottom and then he'd been sent *straight upstairs to bed and no supper for thee*.

'Go an' see what's on the kitchen table,' Aunt Louisa said, startling him out of his thoughts. 'It's summat for thee, for tha birthday.'

He ran from the room, pounded down the hall and into the kitchen.

'Whoah there!'

Father picked him up and tossed him in the air.

'Don't!' He wriggled like a worm to free himself. 'Am five now, not a babby anymore!'

Mother and Mrs Hodgetts were standing in front of the table, blocking his view of it. 'Aunt Louisa says I've got something for my birthday.'

'Does she?' said Mother, smiling fondly at him.

'Tha's a lucky lad,' said Mrs Hodgetts. 'We never had owt like this when I were little.'

Isaac ignored this. He couldn't believe Mrs Hodgetts had ever been a child. Then they moved aside and his eyes widened to see the entire table covered by a mound hidden from view under sheets of newspaper. Whatever it was, it was big. He ripped the newspaper away. It was a wooden sledge, painted red. He yelled in delight.

'Summat for when it snows,' said Father.

Isaac jumped up and down. 'I know what it is! It's a sledge!'

'What do you say?' said Mother.

'Thank you!' He hugged her, burying his face in her stomach. She was getting fat, Mother was. He'd better eat her share of the cake. He was about to tell her this when the big silver doorknocker that he couldn't yet reach sounded, a sharp bang followed by three more hesitant taps.

'I'll go,' said Mrs Hodgetts.

'It must be your friend, Milly,' Mother said to Aunt Louisa, who was carrying Alice into the kitchen. Isaac hoped there would be enough cake to go around. They were all looking in the wrong direction, not at the cake that sat on the dresser, but at the door Mrs Hodgetts had closed behind her. He hopped up and down impatiently.

'Shall we shout boo at Aunt Louisa's friend?' he said.

Mother laughed. 'I'm not sure that would be an appropriate welcome.'

But when the door opened and Mrs Hodgetts led a man into the room nobody said anything at all. Grown-ups could be very strange.

'Are you coming to my birthday, Mr Housley?' said Isaac.

'Ah, is this the gentleman who's teachin' you your numbers?' said Mrs Hodgetts.

'Aye,' said Silas. 'This is Dan. He's our wages clerk.'

When Mr Housley spoke, his voice stumbled like Isaac did sometimes when he was running too fast for his legs to keep up with him. 'Isaac's had a letter, and I know it's his birthday today so it must have to do with that.' Isaac saw the worried look he gave Mother. 'I would have left it but this lady insisted I come in.'

'An' I'm glad I did now,' said Mrs Hodgetts, 'if tha's come all the way from the other side o' the Don.'

Mr Housley held out an envelope to Isaac, who didn't know whether he should take it. 'This came to the yard, addressed to you, Isaac.'

'Give it 'ere,' said Silas. He peered at the postscript, shaking his head. He muttered something Isaac didn't hear.

He wondered why Mr Housley was staring at Aunt Louisa. He moved to stand in front of her, feeling somehow that she needed to be protected.

'Louisa, it is . . . wonderful to see you. I was not expecting . . . I did not know that . . .' he trailed off.

Isaac looked round and up at her, and tugged her skirt. At this rate, he'd never get his cake.

Aunt Louisa's mouth was working, opening and closing a bit like the baby's did when it was hungry. Right now, it was sleeping peacefully in her arms, which was a relief. There was only so much cake to go around.

Finally, she spoke.

'It's Miss Leigh to thee.'

36

She wanted to run away, to leave them in the kitchen and retreat to her bedroom where she could drop her burning face into her hands and weep, but Milly arrived, apologising for her tardiness, presenting Isaac with a football, everyone laughing at the chastising she received from Harriet for spending too much on him, and Louisa painted on a rictus smile and sat in a kitchen chair while all this went on around her, holding Alice against her body like a shield.

She wouldn't acknowledge him, she would remain aloof. But even with her gaze averted she felt his presence with every cell in her body. It was like closing her eyes to the glare of the sun. It would burn her just the same. They ate cake, drank tea and watched Silas trying to pull Isaac around the room on his sledge. When the boy went near the football, Mrs Hodgetts snatched it away. 'For outside only,' she said.

After more cake and another pot of tea, Milly said it was time for her to go, and that Louisa should not get up to see her out. 'We'll meet soon,' she said, squeezing Louisa's hand and stroking the baby's head. Louisa guessed she had picked up on her mood and probably thought Daniel Housley was Alice's father. She smiled bitterly to herself.

After Milly had gone, Daniel cleared his throat. 'Now that I am here,' he coughed, 'and have the, um, pleasure of your company, I wonder if I might have a word in private, Miss Leigh?'

Just glancing his way was almost more than she could bear. She shook her head.

Isaac looked around the room. 'Where's my letter?'

'Shall I read it to you?' Harriet said brightly.

Silas handed it over. He'd read the contents during Isaac's brief foray into the garden with Milly and his new football, and told the others it contained no startling revelations. Harriet took out the thin sheet of paper. 'It's from your mother, Isaac. Isn't that lovely? Oh, what's this?' Harriet shook from the envelope a half-circle of silver metal and handed it to Isaac. 'A gift for you, Isaac.' Louisa was reminded of the gift she had received in her missive from Ginny. She twisted the wedding band around her finger, then hid her hand in the folds of Alice's gown. She wondered whether he had seen the ring, whether Silas had told him all about the sham. Her stomach squirmed, but then a feeling close to rage rose within her. She was doing her best and would not be judged by the likes of Daniel Housley.

Isaac put the fragment on the palm of his hand and touched it, then gave Harriet a puzzled look.

'It's broke.'

'Let's find out why, shall we? Listen.'

My lovely boy, my little man.

Harriet pursed her lips before continuing.

I can hardly believe that you are now five years old. Here is a special coin. It is special because it is cut in half. I have the other half and when I return we will put the two together, and each be whole again.

Silas made an exasperated sound.

It is a silver dollar.

Isaac lifted his hand to his face to peer more closely at the coin. He curled his fingers over it when Mrs Hodgetts tried to get a closer look.

With all my love, your mother. If Isaac has been sent to Peter's . . .

Harriet stopped reading abruptly.

'The last part is for me,' she said.

'Short an' sweet,' said Silas. 'Just like tha mother.'

'Are you alright?' Harriet asked Isaac.

'Yeah.' He shrugged. 'Can I 'ave a bit more cake?'

Alice began to wail and Louisa finally found the strength to get to her feet. Daniel Housley leapt up too and opened the door for her. She slipped through it, finally raising her eyes to his. He looked as wounded about the eyes as the last time she had seen him, as though no time had passed at all. Louisa's eyes filled with tears as she nodded her thanks and walked away.

In the front parlour, she settled herself on the settee and unbuttoned her blouse.

'Let's get thee fed,' she said, 'an' forget all about 'im. It's me an' thee, love, an' there's nowt wrong wi' that.'

There was a gentle knock on the door. Surely, he would not . . . but it was Harriet who poked her head into the room then entered quietly to sit beside Louisa.

'Look at those eyelashes,' said Harriet, 'and those perfect little ears.'

Louisa smiled. 'Aye, she'll do.'

'Can I say something?'

'I can't stop thee.'

'I don't think it was an accident, Dan turning up today. He knew you'd be here, on Isaac's birthday. He held onto that letter for a few days, according to Silas.'

Louisa kept her eyes on Alice. The baby was sucking hungrily. She'd have a good sleep afterwards and Louisa could make her excuses and go upstairs for a nap. 'What's that matter? He made himsen clear a while back that he wants nowt to do wi' me, wi' us.'

Harriet glanced at the door. 'I probably shouldn't say, but he asks after you all the time. He wants to apologise . . .'

'He dun't need to.'

'. . . and he says he acted too hastily. He was surprised, that was all.'

'Aye, well, I've experienced a few surprises in me time. That man wants to grow up.'

'I think he has, in the past few months. Grown up, I mean. Will you talk to him?'

'Has he asked, or is this thee, Harriet, pokin' tha nose in?' Louisa sighed. 'Sorry. Am out o' sorts.' The pull on her breast had stopped. 'An' now look, this one's fell asleep on me, as usual. I'll be feedin' her all night long.'

Harriet wouldn't be deflected. 'Your paths are bound to cross again. Why not clear the air now?'

'Me own mother never nagged me like tha does.'

Harriet gave her a satisfied smile and held out her arms for Alice. Louisa handed her over, re-adjusted her clothes then gestured for the baby's return. If she was going to talk to Daniel Housley she wanted Alice Millicent Leigh in her arms.

* * *

Louisa Leigh stood on the doorstep and watched Daniel Housley walk away down the tree-lined street.

Harriet had left her waiting for Dan in the front parlour. Now she was decided, it had been easier to face him. He was only a man, no different to the rest.

He'd stood in the middle of the room, framed by the dim light of the window, and clasped and unclasped his hands. Louisa raised her eyebrows enquiringly and waited for a few heartbeats before exasperation got the better of her.

'What's tha come 'ere to say, then? Tha's neither use nor ornament standin' there on the carpet.'

'I know I've been weak.' He opened his hands in a gesture of surrender. 'I have missed you, Louisa. I've come to admit that I made a mistake. It was the shock of it, I suppose.'

'Ah, I see. An' now tha's changed thee mind?'

'That sounds a little . . . well, yes, I have but I'm not trying to . . .' He shook his head.

She waited.

'I wonder if I might call on you, one day soon?'

'On me an' Alice?'

'Of course, you and Alice.'

Her child's name on his lips. She remembered the look on his face when he had discovered she was carrying a child.

'Please don't shake your head. Louisa, please think on it. I know that I have shocked you. I am sorry for it. Please don't be as hasty as I was.'

'But that's the thing, Dan. Tha was. Tha was hasty, as tha puts it,' she said, 'an' how can I ever put me trust in thee again?'

He looked at her helplessly.

'Tha'd better be on thee way,' she said, rising to her feet and turning away to put Alice in her crib, tucking a blanket around her. 'I'll see thi out.'

He followed her into the hall, stumbling over words he was attempting too quickly. 'Louisa, do you remember when we played the Ha Ha game? I think that was the happiest night of my entire life.'

'But I was hidin' the truth from thee then, just the same.'

'It doesn't matter. I don't care about that.' His voice rose in desperation. 'Louisa, if I have to defy my mother, my church, I will do it.'

'That's big o' thee.' Louisa opened the door and stood aside so that he could pass through.

He paused on the doorstep, and touched her hand tentatively. 'Please think about permitting me to call on you.'

She told herself the cold evening air had lifted the hairs on the back of her neck, and made her lips tingle. She realised that she and Daniel had never so much as kissed each other. There had been that moment in the rain, outside the circus tent, when she'd thought their lips would meet. That had been the same moment he rejected her. He would resent her, resent Alice and be cruel to her.

But Dan didn't have a cruel bone in his body. He loved her.

He had let her down and she couldn't get past it.

Louisa sighed. She couldn't think straight, either, with him standing in front of her waiting for an answer.

She kept her voice light. 'See thi, Dan.'

'Please, Louisa.' He stepped down onto the tree-lined pavement. 'Don't say goodbye now.'

'Right now, love, I can't think of owt else to say to thee.' She hesitated. 'I were a fool . . .'

'No, Louisa . . .'

'I were foolin' meesen and thee an' all, an' I'm sorry for that.' She put her fingers to her lips to hide their tremble. 'An' there's nowt more to be said, Dan.'

He opened his mouth to speak then closed it when Louisa shook her head. He looked down, then turned on his heel and walked away.

Louisa wondered whether he would look back before he turned the corner at the end of the street. He didn't. She raised her gaze to the darkening sky and followed the progress of a flock of birds swooping and wheeling, perhaps heading for warmer climes. From inside the house, a thin wail rose. Everything that was important to her was between these four walls. Still, she lingered for a few moments longer on the doorstep before stepping back and gently closing the door.

For a moment, as she gathered herself in the dimly lit hallway, there was silence, then Alice's cries redoubled, and Louisa wondered at the piercing sound such tiny lungs could make. She could hear voices now — Silas asking Harriet whether they'd be shut in the kitchen forever, and Isaac yelling for his football back. Her family. She hurried in to Alice. There was so much to do. And work tomorrow; she hoped she'd get a few hours' sleep first.

What was it Jemima had said? No rest for the wicked.

Author's Note

Sheffield is credited as the birthplace of trade unionism, and it was a blood-soaked period of history. The bombings, shootings and vandalism that were dubbed the Outrages — many carried out on the orders of the infamous William Broadhead — had much to do with unions finally becoming recognised as legal entities. Joseph Crookes is a fictional character, an amalgamation of some of Broadhead's henchmen. The Change Alley Outrage is fictitious, too. One of the earliest streets in the centre of town, Change Alley no longer exists. The area is now home to the rather more prosaic-sounding Arundel Gate transport interchange. But there is an echo in history; Change Alley was a staging post for travellers. It was also the location of the grandly appointed King's Head Hotel, where Charles Dickens stayed on two occasions in 1858 while on a reading tour of England.

Acknowledgements

Emma Clark-Lam, Sara Cox, Sarah Daniels, Asha Hicks, Carly Reagon — I'm so lucky to have you; the same sentiment to my wonderful family and friends. A few to single out — Diane Mills for research assistance, Tom Clague for helping me navigate the socials, Janet Cooke and Jess Cooke for early reading, and to Jackie Bridson, who hung around in the UK for days just to attend my first book launch. To my agent Kate Nash and my editor Emily Bedford, and the teams behind them. And to Alan, always.